Begin Again

by

NICOLE PYLAND

Begin Again

Tahoe Series Book #4

Chris Florence's circumstances had never been ideal, but they'd gotten worse after a car accident took the lives of her parents and left her with a kid brother to support. She'd always wondered if she was raising Wesley the way they'd want him to be raised while she juggled waiting tables at a pizza place in South Lake Tahoe with parenting a now teenage brother. She had friends, but their lives were so different from her own, Chris had always felt like she was on the outside looking in.

Paxton Williams only planned to visit her sister, Adler, in South Lake. She was supposed to stay for a few days, check in on her big sister, and return to Seattle. Instead, Paxton finds an old rundown hotel, meets Christina Florence, and her life suddenly has a purpose. She could return to Seattle and remain the owner of her real estate business, or she could take a chance and turn a rundown hotel into the best place to stay in Tahoe and take a chance on the woman that doesn't let her get away with anything.

With the arrival of Paxton, Chris's life turns upside down. It's Chris's decision, though. All those changes, all those feelings could cause Chris pain or could possibly give her the life she'd always dreamed up for herself and her family.

To contact the author or for any additional information visit: **https://nicolepyland.com**

BY THE AUTHOR

Stand-alone books:

- The Fire
- The Moments
- The Disappeared

Chicago Series:

- Introduction – Fresh Start
- Book #1 – The Best Lines
- Book #2 – Just Tell Her
- Book #3 – Love Walked into The Lantern
- Series Finale – What Happened After

San Francisco Series:

- Book #1 – Checking the Right Box
- Book #2 – Macon's Heart
- Book #3 – This Above All
- Series Finale – What Happened After

Tahoe Series:

- Book #1 – Keep Tahoe Blue
- Book #2 – Time of Day

- Book #3 – The Perfect View
- Book #4 – Begin Again
- Series Finale – What Happened After

Celebrities Series:

- Book #1 – No After You
- Book #2 – All the Love Songs

CONTENTS

CHAPTER 1

CHRISTINA FLORENCE WAS exhausted. She'd pulled double shifts at Donoto's for the past two weeks. Since a normal shift was between four to six hours, she'd worked at minimum twelve hours a day. On Fridays and Saturdays, though, she'd worked fourteen to sixteen. Those were the busiest nights at the best pizza place in South Lake Tahoe. She'd been working at Donoto's for years now. She was the most tenured waitress in the place by five years easy. She also bartended when they needed extra hands. She used the gig to make herself some extra and much-needed tips. Money had been tight for a very long time. At this rate, despite being thirty-one years old, she wasn't sure money would ever be loose. That wasn't the expression, but that was how it felt to Chris.

"Excuse me?" A woman at one of her six tables called her over.

"What can I get you?" Chris asked her, sliding the empty brown tray under her arm.

"I asked for no sausage on this pizza, and there's sausage," she replied.

"You asked for no sausage?"

"I did. I specifically said *no sausage*," the woman said.

"I'm sorry. I'll have them make you another one. I'll get it out as soon as it's ready," Chris replied and reached for the pizza on its stand.

"What are you going to do with this one?" the man across from the woman asked.

"Take it back to the kitchen to get you a new one," Chris answered.

"Right. But are you just going to throw it away? If so, I'll just keep it," he said.

"Should I still go ahead and put in the other order, though?"

"Yes," he said with a glare. "This is free, though, right? I mean, you messed up the order."

"Right." Chris choked back her words. "I'll ring up the new one. Would you like a box for this one?"

"No, I'll eat it now," he said.

She smiled, nodded, turned, and walked back to the kitchen. The woman had not asked for no sausage. She had, in fact, only asked for the meat lover's pizza. She'd made no alterations to the order whatsoever. The man across from her hadn't ordered anything at all. It wasn't uncommon for people to split a pizza between the two of them, but the woman had ordered a small one. The man was built like a damn house. They'd planned this. As she typed in the order for the extra pizza she'd then have to comp, she seethed, because she hated people getting away with free food like this. She also knew this kind of table would tip fifteen percent if she were lucky. She could only hope for a day where she would no longer have to wait on tourists in her tiny lakeside town.

***

"Hey, Chris?"

"What's up?" Chris asked as she flopped down onto their secondhand sofa.

"I need that check for the trip," her brother, Wesley, replied.

"Oh, right," she sighed out. "My checkbook is on the counter. Can you grab it for me?"

Wesley walked over to the counter, grabbed the checkbook, and brought it back to Chris. He then sat on the sofa next to her and turned her way.

"How was work?"

"Long. How was school?" she replied while reaching for the pen on the coffee table in front of her.

"Fine."

"Fine? That's all I get?" She started filling out the check for Wesley's school-sponsored trip to the local university where he'd fall in love with the place. He'd want to attend. She'd have to figure out how to pay for it. She wasn't exactly looking forward to that part but didn't want to stop him from experiencing the trip with his friends. "Nothing happened today that's worth talking about?"

"You said your day was long. I said mine was fine. Why do you get to give me a one-word answer, but I can't give you one?"

"Because I'm in charge," she answered, tore the check out of the book, and passed it to him. "I hope they wait until Friday to try to cash that."

"The trip isn't until Friday. I doubt they'd do anything with this until we get back," he replied, tucking the check into his pocket. "Are you sure we can afford this? It's a weekend away. It's three hundred dollars, and because I'm there, I won't be able to work at the bookstore for my normal shifts. It's too much, Chris."

"Wes, you're a junior in high school."

"Exactly. I can do this whole thing as a senior. I was just being greedy, wanting to do it now. I can save up for it myself by next year," he said.

"Wes, it's fine. We're okay. I shouldn't have said that Friday thing. I just haven't been to the bank to deposit my tips. I'll go tomorrow."

That wasn't totally wrong. She hadn't deposited her tips; that was true. She also knew their bank account had exactly enough money to afford their bills. They rarely had any left over to use for frivolous things like cable or fast food. Most of the time, it didn't bother either of them. There were some moments, though, she'd see a look in her kid brother's eyes that caused her pain. She knew he wasn't ashamed of them. He was, most likely, embarrassed and concerned. He was seventeen. His parents were gone. They had been for eleven years. She was the closest thing to a parent he had. Chris didn't consider herself to be a particularly good one. She did do the best she could, though.

"I have some homework I still need to finish." He stood, ran his hand through his sandy blonde hair, and gave her a two-fingered peace sign before he walked off.

He looked so much like their father when he did that. Sometimes, watching him grow up was actually hard for Chris. It only reminded her of their dead parents and how she was all he had left in the world. There were good times, though. She focused on those whenever she could. Wes was a bright, athletic, respectful teenage boy. He worked on the weekends, did his homework, didn't cause any trouble at school, and helped around the house. He'd always seemed to understand the sacrifice she'd made when she was twenty years old. She'd left college for Wes. When she couldn't find good enough work in their own hometown, she'd moved them to South Lake Tahoe and took the job at Donoto's. It paid enough to support both of them and not much more, but they got by.

It was well after midnight when she finally retired to her bedroom. She'd paid a few bills, checked the classifieds online for the possibility of a second job, and then did the dishes. She fell asleep around one in the morning, woke up at seven to send Wes off to school, then showered and dressed to head back to the restaurant that sometimes felt more like home than the two-bedroom rental they lived in.

***

"Chris, hey," Morgan Burns greeted from her booth.

"Hey. Is it just you and Adler tonight or are James and Riley joining?" Chris asked, sitting on the other side of the booth from her friends.

"We only sit on the same side of the booth when other people are joining. We're not *that* couple," Morgan replied, looking over at her girlfriend of just over a year, Adler Williams.

"You say that, but I see it literally every night," Chris replied.

"I draw the line somewhere," Adler said with a wink. "I do like sitting next to her, though."

"James and Riles are on their way. You on a break any time soon? You could join us, too," Morgan suggested.

James was Kinsley James, and *Riles* was Riley Sanders. Kinsley and Riley had been engaged for a few months now. Their wedding date hadn't yet been set, but Chris had seen her friends, including Reese and Kellan, the married couple of the group, more and more around Donoto's. Whenever she waited on them, she'd hear snippets of conversation revolving around the upcoming wedding. Chris liked her friends, but she'd always felt like an outsider looking in. She wasn't even sure she could call them friends. They'd all been customers that had turned into regulars. She'd spent some time with them outside of the restaurant, but not all that much. They didn't invite her places often. She didn't take offense to it. She knew she couldn't go, anyway. It either cost too much, whatever they were doing, or she'd be working.

"I just took my break, unfortunately."

"Bummer," Morgan said. "Hey, a bunch of us are getting together at our place this weekend. Do you want to swing by? It's an all-day kind of thing. We're going to barbecue and have some drinks. We're celebrating Addie making the official move to Tahoe."

"I'm working." She shrugged.

"It starts at, like, two. What time do you have to be here?" Adler asked.

"Not until four," Chris replied. "I guess I could stop by for an hour or something. Do you want me to bring anything?"

She prayed they'd say no.

"No, we're good. Reese and Kellan are in charge of chips and stuff. James and Riley are bringing the booze. We've got the meat and the location covered," Morgan said.

"Okay. I'll try to stop by," she replied and stood. "Drinks?"

"The usual for me," Adler said.

"Me too," Morgan added. "And probably the same for Kinsley and Riley. If not, I'll just drink them." She turned to Adler and smiled when Adler rolled her eyes at her.

"Congrats, by the way. The move, I mean."

"Thanks," Adler said. "It took forever to finally get it all worked out."

"She was moving for months," Morgan said.

"That's an exaggeration. We were working pretty hard there for a while. We opened another store in between me deciding to move here and today, remember?" she asked Morgan.

"Yes, but you told me how much you loved me, how much you loved working with me, and then took forever to actually get all your crap here."

"I had to sell my place and get movers, Morgan." Adler laughed.

Chris walked off, recognizing that as her cue to leave. It was always interesting to her as a waitress. Sometimes, people would have a conversation as if she wasn't even standing at their table waiting for them to order or tell her to go. Her friends were normally good about the fact that she was at work and would have to wait on them, but sometimes, they did the same thing. She didn't fault them for it. They were very nice women who had their own lives that existed outside of Donoto's Family Italian Restaurant. She grabbed the beers from behind the bar herself. When she dropped them off at the table, she noticed Adler's phone on the table. It wasn't ringing, but it was vibrating with a call. On the screen was a picture of a woman and the name, Paxton.

CHAPTER 2

"YES, I'LL BE THERE. My flight is at four," Paxton told her sister over the phone. "Where are you, anyway?"

"Out, with Morgan. Kinsley and Riley are on their way. You'll meet them this weekend, too."

"Right. The engaged couple."

"Yes, Pax. They got engaged a few months ago. Reese and Kellan are married. They'll be there. Remy is Reese's twin sister. She'll be there with her boyfriend, Ryan. I think a few others will be there, too. It's an all-day thing, so people will come in and out, I'm sure."

"I don't know if I'm going to be up for all that entertaining, big sis. I'm super busy these days. I'm tired a lot. Plus, I was looking forward to having some sister time with you."

"You're young, Paxton. You can't be that tired," Adler replied.

"I'm thirty-three; that's not all that young. And I'm the hottest real estate agent in our hometown – that makes me pretty busy; our hometown that you ditched for greener pastures and hot sex with your live-in girlfriend, by the way."

"You're right. It is greener here most of the time, and it is hot, Pax. It's really, really hot. Like, when she–"

"Okay!" Paxton yelled through the phone to get her sister to stop talking.

Adler laughed wildly and said, "I wasn't actually going to finish that sentence."

"Thank God."

"Pax, I can't wait for you to see this place. I think you're really going to like it."

"I don't have the hot live-in girlfriend, remember?" Paxton said. "And I'll see you in a few days, sis. I have to go now. I've got to put in an offer before the clock strikes midnight or my clients will lose out on their dream home, and they'll have you to blame."

"I'll see you in a few days, Pax," Adler replied through laughter. "Thanks, Chris."

"Who's Chris?" Paxton asked.

"Our waitress," Adler said. "And a friend," she added seemingly hastily. "She's a friend, too."

"Oh, okay. I'll see you soon," Paxton replied and disconnected the call. She put in another hour of work on her laptop before she finally climbed into her bed. For some reason, after she pulled the covers up to her neck, she said, "Chris."

***

Paxton had been a realtor since she graduated from college at twenty-two, pursued her license, earned it, and started in a large, nationwide realtor office. She liked that enough but knew she wanted to break out on her own one day. It took many years and a lot of hard work, but by the time she was twenty-eight, she was at a small, boutique agency. She became a partner there by thirty. Now, at thirty-three, she owned her own business. She had the overhead from her office space. She had employees on the payroll. She had a thriving business with high-powered clients. Things were going well. There were just three problems for Paxton.

Her first problem was simple: she was overworked. She needed to hire more office staff and, likely, agents, too. Her heart also wasn't in it as much as it used to be. Paxton still liked selling homes. She liked making the people that bought and sold them happy, which was typically the case. And she didn't even particularly mind that some clients could be difficult. She just wasn't sure she was up for the grind. She worked every single day, even when she was off the clock, so to speak. Saturdays and Sundays were big open house days. Clients were off work and wanted to be taken on tours of the houses on their lists. Other clients wanted to meet after hours on weekdays, since they had jobs, too. It meant that she was never actually off the clock. She was always tired as a result.

Her second problem was that she missed her big sister terribly. They'd always lived in Seattle. They'd been best friends even when they were kids, when people generally hated their siblings. When Paxton had come out as a teenager, Adler had been so supportive of her. Little did they know that Adler would later find her – not so straight, as it turned out – self, loving a woman named Morgan Burns, who lived and loved Lake Tahoe. Now that Adler was there permanently, Paxton's life in Seattle didn't seem all that great to her.

Adding to all this was, of course, the fact that she was still single. Her straight older sister had managed to find and fall in love with a beautiful woman, but Paxton, who had always known she was gay, had zero luck in that department. Her third problem, though, was perhaps the one she needed to fix the most. With Adler gone now, and most of her friends married or seeing someone seriously, Paxton was kind of on her own.

When she made her way outside the airport, Adler was standing there, waving wildly at her. Paxton rolled her eyes. They'd seen each other only a month prior. Paxton had to admit to herself, though, that she missed her sister. Did that make her co-dependent? She didn't care if it did. She loved her sister. She missed having her stop by her apartment at night or on the weekends. She missed stopping by Adler's very nice apartment that she'd had to sell for her when she left the city.

"Hey, big sis."

"Hey, little sis. I missed you." Adler reached for her and hugged her hard.

"Missed you, too," Paxton replied, hugging her back just as hard. "I can't believe I've never been to Tahoe."

"I know. It's crazy; right? It's not all that far away from Seattle, and it's beautiful here. We should have visited long before I met Morgan." Adler smiled at the sound of herself saying Morgan's name.

"God, when's the wedding?" Paxton replied sarcastically.

"I don't know. One day." Adler shrugged and took Paxton's roller bag.

"Really?"

"Is that surprising? I moved here to move in with her," Adler asked as they walked. "We've been together for over a year now."

"I know. It's just weird to think of you married."

"Why?" Adler laughed.

"Because you never really seemed interested in it before," Paxton replied as Adler placed her roller into the trunk.

"I wasn't until Morgan. I mean, we haven't talked about those steps like we're about to take them or anything, but we both want the same things whenever they happen."

"I think that's great," Paxton replied, sitting in the passenger's seat of Adler's car. "Are those hiking boots behind your seat?"

"Morgan's are behind your seat. We keep them in the car in case we get the urge to go hiking or something," Adler said.

Paxton shook her head and replied, "How are you even still my sister?"

"It's fun. I didn't use to like it, obviously, but that's how Morgan and I met. It's like our thing now. It's also easy since we work at an outdoors store. We have extra hiking boots in her car and at home, too."

Paxton rolled her eyes at her changed sister. Then, she watched as Adler pulled out into traffic and they began the drive back to Adler and Morgan's house. The ride wasn't a long one. The view was pretty standard from what she could see at first. Then, Adler pulled them onto a different road that was lined with thick, tall trees. She couldn't see the lake from the road, but she could somehow sense that it was present.

They pulled into the driveway. Adler turned off the car. When they got out, Adler walked to the front door, leaving Paxton to retrieve her luggage. She was a guest in their home, but she was also the little sister. Adler gave her the quick tour of the whole house she and Morgan now shared. Technically, Morgan owned the place, but it was their home. She dropped her bag in the guest room and made her way back downstairs, where Adler had opened a bottle of red and poured out two glasses.

"Morgan just texted. She's still at the store. I was thinking, we could do something simple tonight for dinner, since I'm too lazy to cook, Morgan will probably be too tired, and I don't trust you with cooking," Adler said before sipping her wine.

"One time, I almost burned the down the kitchen," Paxton replied with a wink.

"What do you want? Want to order a pizza?" Adler asked.

"From that pizza place you guys go to all the time?"

"Donoto's? We do usually go there instead of getting it delivered. That's mainly because their delivery isn't always fast. Happens in a town like this, apparently. Plus, Chris is there."

"Chris again?"

"She's a friend of Morgan's. Everyone's, I guess. I've

only ever seen her at the restaurant, but she's very nice."

"Does she, like, own the place or something?"

"No, she just works there, but she's been there forever. We're regulars. How about that? *I'm* a regular somewhere now." Adler lifted her eyebrows.

"You really have changed, huh?" Paxton took a sip of her drink. "I think it's good. You needed a change. You seem happier."

"Now, I just have to work on you," Adler said.

"What do you mean?"

"Come on, Pax. I know you. Something's up."

"Nothing's up."

"Liar."

"I'm not lying, Adler."

"Fine. Whatever you say," Adler replied. "But you're lying."

"When is your girlfriend getting home, so I have a *sane* person to talk to?" Paxton fired back.

CHAPTER 3

CHRIS REALLY ONLY HAD an hour. She needed to have time to run home and change into her uniform before the start of her shift at four. She knew these people had all seen her in her uniform before. Some of them had *only* seen her in uniform. There was still no way she was showing up to a backyard barbeque in her black and red checked shirt, black pants, black apron, and black non-slip shoes. She was also not going to change for work at Morgan's, and management frowned on them changing at the restaurant for some reason she'd never attempted to dive into further.

She was planning to ring the doorbell but heard chatter out back and decided to take a chance. She headed around the side of the house, wondering just how it was people around her age were able to afford a place like this when she was barely scraping by. She wasn't envious. She'd worked hard for what she and Wes had; in the same way that these women had worked hard for what they had. She admired Morgan and Adler for how much and how hard they worked. She just wondered how life managed to throw so many curveballs her way when everyone else seemed to get those fastballs right down the middle.

"Chris, glad you could make it," Morgan said the moment Chris rounded the corner into the backyard.

"Thanks for the invite. I brought this." She held up a six-pack of beer. It was domestic and on sale. "I didn't know what else to bring."

"This is great. You didn't have to bring anything," Morgan replied, taking the beer, and placing it onto a folding table they'd set out back. "We're still picking out our patio furniture. This will do for today, though." She motioned toward the table. "You know pretty much everyone, I think. We invited a few people from work, obviously, but I think you know the rest."

"Right," Chris said, feeling completely out of place among friends.

"Addie's over there." Morgan pointed at her girlfriend, who was talking to Riley.

"I'll go say hello."

"Great. I'm going inside to grab the burgers. We'll get cooking soon, but there are snacks and stuff. Make yourself at home."

Morgan ran off into her house. Chris looked around. She knew most of the people as Morgan had said, but she didn't know exactly how to approach them. Everyone she knew was talking to someone else. She didn't want to interrupt their conversations, but she also didn't want to stand around looking like the loser kid at a high school dance. She'd been that kid. It wasn't fun the first time.

Chris checked her phone. She had exactly fifty-four minutes before she had to leave. She approached one of the tables where chips, dip, veggies, and other snacks had been laid out. She stacked a few things on a paper plate with blue and green flowers around the edges; their throwaway dishes were nicer than her real ones. She grabbed a bottle of water and sat in a folding lawn chair off to the side of the rest of the group. There were probably about twenty or so people there. She knew about half of them. She decided she'd sit and eat. If someone wanted to talk to her, they'd come over. If they didn't, no big deal. She'd have some good food and head off to work.

"Anyone sitting here?"

"No," Chris replied, looking up from her plate at a woman she hadn't met before.

"Cool. Thanks."

The woman grabbed the other folding chair, carried it across the yard, and placed it next to two other women.

"What the fuck?" Chris muttered under her breath.

"Hey, Chris." Adler approached, blocking her view of the woman who'd just been completely rude to her for no reason. "How are you?"

"I'm okay," Chris replied. She shook her head a little, trying to get the woman's strange move out of her mind. "Who's that?" She nodded toward the woman.

"Oh, that's Pax. That's my sister," Adler said with a smile.

"Pax?"

"Paxton. Our parents picked weird names. I was named after Irene Adler, and Paxton was named after a city in Massachusetts. My parents got stuck there once during a snowstorm. Guess what they did to pass the time." She lifted an eyebrow at Chris. "I got a little sister out of the deal. She's in town for the week."

"Oh, I just didn't recognize her. She looks like you a little, I guess, though."

"Same hair. Light brown runs in the family. But she has green eyes. I got the gray ones. She got the better nose, though, I think. I'm okay with it." She turned to see Morgan coming out of the house, carrying a plate of uncooked hamburgers. "I should go help Morgan. Do you want me to introduce you around to any of the people you don't know?"

"No, I'm okay. You take care of your guests," Chris said.

"You are our guest, Chris," Adler reminded. "Kinsley and Riley are over there. Reese and Kellan went inside for a few minutes."

"Okay. Thanks."

Adler left her in her chair off to the side of the rest of the people. She and Morgan stood at the grill, taking turns flipping the burgers and talking to their guests. Kellan and

Reese made their way outside a few minutes later, came over and chatted with Chris before they moved along to talk to their friend Stacy and her husband. Riley and Kinsley stopped by, too. They pulled up chairs, talked with her for a few minutes, and then left to go inside the house. Chris stayed sitting in the chair, holding her plate of half-eaten food, and stealing glances at the rude girl she couldn't call rude because she was the hostess's sister. Then, she stood up, tossed out her trash, waved goodbye to a few people, and got in her car.

The party had been a mistake. She'd spent so little time with these people outside of the restaurant. Today only proved to her that she wasn't meant for this crowd. She was better off in her checkered uniform shirt with her nametag. She fit in at Donoto's. She fit in with her kid brother. That was enough for her. She'd make it enough.

***

By eight, Chris was tired. It would be a long night, since it was a typical busy Saturday in the tourist-friendly and family-friendly restaurant. She'd be there until at least midnight, and she wasn't even closing tonight. She grabbed the check off the table and saw the twenty percent tip. That was helpful. It had been a party of eight. They'd ordered two appetizer platters, four pizzas, three rounds of drinks, and four shared desserts. This was the kind of tip that helped her make rent. They'd been a fun table, too. Exhausting, but fun. Now that the party had left, she helped Max, the busboy, move the two four-top tables apart. Just as she finished putting the chairs back in place, she noticed Paxton enter the restaurant. She appeared to be alone and was giving the hostess her name or, perhaps, asking where to place a to-go order. Chris couldn't tell due to the chattering guests and loud overhead music. She made her way to one of her other tables to refill a Diet Coke. When she returned, Paxton was sitting at one of her empty tables, with a menu in hand. This was just what Chris needed. She took a deep breath, made her way over to the table, and looked down.

"Welcome to Donoto's. My name is Chris. I'll be taking care of you tonight."

Paxton looked up at her and replied, "I know you." She squinted at her. "How do—"

"I was at Adler and Morgan's today. You borrowed a chair."

"Oh, right." Paxton leaned back in the dark wood chair. "You're Chris. Adler mentioned you worked here."

"I do." She shrugged. "Are you waiting on Morgan and Adler?"

"No, I'm here by myself," she said.

"Oh." She tapped her pen to her tiny notebook. "Can I get you something to drink?"

"Just water with lemon. Can I get it with no ice, though?"

"No problem." Chris walked off, grabbed the water with no ice, put the lemon wedge on the edge of the glass, headed back to the table, and placed it in front of Paxton. "Do you need a few more minutes?"

"What's the best pizza here? My sister and Morgan won't stop raving about this place."

"Depends on what you're into, I guess."

"Pizza?" Paxton shrugged, and – God help her – Chris thought it was adorable when Paxton combined it with a scrunched-up nose.

"I meant: are you a vegetarian or anything?"

"No, I pretty much eat anything." Paxton's eyes got big. "That sounded bad."

"Why?" Chris asked.

"No reason."

"No reason?"

"Just the lesbian in me thinking a comment about me eating anything being inappropriate for this conversation," Paxton replied with smile. "Sorry. My jokes are so lame, I have to explain them."

Okay. She wasn't all that bad then. She was kind of funny. She was definitely cute. She was also a lesbian.

"We're known for our deep-dish pizzas here, but we have all the other crusts, too."

"Can I get the special that's on here, with the thin crust?"

"What size?"

"It's just me; small will do."

"I'll put the order in." Chris turned and walked off.

Why was this weird? She'd waited on Morgan and her friends countless times. It hadn't ever felt *this* weird. Paxton was just sitting alone at the table, doing something on her phone. Chris normally walked over to the table and sat down when people she knew came in. She'd join in on the conversation if she could. Sometimes, she'd just use it as a chance to take a load off her feet for a few minutes. With this stranger, though, she couldn't bring herself to sit down at her table.

"Thanks," Paxton said when Chris brought over her pizza.

"Sure. Can I get you anything else?"

"I'm good for now. I might need dessert later, though. I'm killing time."

"Killing time? Aren't you here to visit Adler?" Chris asked.

"I am. But Adler is currently *visiting* Morgan very loudly in their bedroom, which shares a wall with the room I'm staying in."

"Oh," Chris replied with wide eyes.

Paxton laughed and replied, "I know. It's gross. It started with giggling. I thought someone must have said something funny. Then, I heard a couple of moans and got out of there. I tried hanging out in the living room, but just knowing my sister was upstairs getting laid was enough to make me leave the house. I borrowed her car and came here."

"That sucks."

"Yes, it does." Paxton looked down at the pizza. "This looks great. Thanks."

"Oh, sure."

That was the end of the conversation. Paxton said her food looked good, dove into the pizza, and looked back down at her phone, which appeared to be constantly buzzing. She was done talking to Chris.

Chris walked off to the kitchen, where she grabbed another order for a different table. The next time she looked over at the table, Paxton was gone. Did she dine and ditch? Chris hadn't even brought her check.

"Hey, where did table fourteen go?" she asked her manager.

"Oh, she grabbed me and asked for her check. Said she had to go." He passed Chris the check with some cash. "She said for you to keep the change."

When the guy walked back toward the kitchen, Chris looked at the check, which had come to under twenty dollars. Paxton had left a fifty. While Chris normally loved big tips, she didn't like them coming from a woman who had few moments of polite conversation mixed with a rude and dismissive attitude.

How was Adler Williams even related to this woman?

CHAPTER 4

"I CANNOT BELIEVE you two got it on last night. I was in the other room," Paxton said to Adler while she poured milk into her cereal.

"Sorry." Adler sat down at the kitchen table. "She was – I don't know – in the mood. And I like when she's in the mood. I am powerless to resist her. I tried to keep it quiet."

"You failed." Paxton sat down next to her sister. "I went to that pizza place just to get out of here."

"I know. Morgan told me before she left this morning to go hiking with Reese."

"She's hiking without you? I thought that was your thing."

"It was, technically, their thing before it became our thing."

"And it doesn't bother you that your girlfriend is out with her ex-girlfriend?"

"Reese is married, Pax. Besides, Morgan loves me. She and Reese are friends."

"I know, but still. I think it would've bothered me a little," Paxton said.

"That's because you have never been able to remain friends with an ex. You've tried and have been unsuccessful, little sister."

"Not really a priority in my life right now." She took a bite.

"What *is* a priority?" Adler asked, sipping coffee while looking comfortable in her flannel pajamas, with a foot up on the chair and her coffee cup resting on her knee.

"Work, I guess. I actually closed a deal last night. I got

the email that an offer was accepted. I rushed back here to grab my computer. It's a nice commission. I might actually go on a vacation with that money," she replied.

"And women? Are you dating, or at least trying to date?"

"I date when I meet someone and I'm interested in them, but I haven't met anyone in a while."

"Didn't you used to tell me I worked too much to meet someone?" Adler asked.

"Yes, and I stand by that," Paxton argued. "You were always working. But it was more about the fact that you were still trying to date guys you clearly weren't in love with. It was like you felt like you should have someone, so you dated."

"I guess." Adler shrugged. "It didn't feel like that at the time."

"I'm sure it didn't." Paxton took another bite of her cereal. "What are you up to today?"

"Hanging out with you."

"I was thinking we could go for a drive around the lake. It's not an all-day thing, right?"

"No, it's not that long, and it's a great way to see everything."

"We can make it an all-day thing and stop to check places out along the way. Then, I'll know what I want to go back to later."

"Morgan or no Morgan? Do you want some alone time with your big sis, or should I invite her? She is a walking textbook about all things Tahoe."

"She can come along. I love Morgan." Paxton pushed her now soggy cereal away. "She's great for you."

"I know." Adler couldn't help but smile. "I'm glad you're here, though, Pax. How about she joins us today when she gets back from her hike with Reese? Tomorrow, though, it's just you and me. I took a couple of days off this week. I might have to check on a few things, but I want to make sure we have time together."

"Sounds like a plan. I should go shower then." She stood from the table. "I'm looking forward to getting a tour from an insider today. Maybe it'll turn out that I really like Tahoe, after all."

***

Morgan was a great tour guide. She did use to do it professionally, so it made sense that she would be good at it. They drove for about forty-five minutes before they stopped for a late lunch and ate by the water. Paxton had caught glimpses of the lake from the plane before she'd landed and a few between houses and trees. But sitting out on a patio, overlooking the lake and the mountains while they ate, was the first time she was really able to take in all its beauty. She had been a fan of the outdoors for most of her life, unlike her older sister. She'd hiked a little and had gone camping a handful of times over the years, but it had always been in the Pacific Northwest area. She'd never seen water this blue outside of a vacation to Fiji she'd taken with an ex-girlfriend a few years ago. It had been their last vacation together. Well, it had also been their only vacation together.

On the way back toward South Lake, a building caught Paxton's eye. It looked old and definitely hadn't been kept up. It was a hotel or maybe a bed and breakfast. It wasn't overly large. It looked more like a house than a traditional business. It was called *"The Pine Tree Guest House"* as indicated by the sign in the front yard, likely, made of the wood. The place was surrounded by its namesake. It was old, to be sure, but it also looked comforting. It looked like something Paxton wanted to know more about because there was a *"for sale"* sign in the yard, too.

She didn't typically work in commercial real estate, but she did dabble here and there when a client called for the work. When they arrived back at Morgan and Adler's, they ate dinner together before Paxton went to the guest room and pulled up the listing. The hotel had been built in 1924. It had ten guest rooms. At first, it was a bed and breakfast, but the most recent owners had turned it into a more traditional hotel over the past twenty years. The hotel had a restaurant, a small gym with out-of-date equipment and not even much of that, and a nice backyard that did have a lake view. As Paxton stared at the picture of the property that would need a lot of work, she wondered why she was even so curious about it. It was a battered hotel that had one shutter hanging loose on a top floor window, needed several coats of paint, and, likely, a lot of interior work to bring it into the modern age. Still, though, she couldn't look away. She checked out the information that only realtors could see and discovered that it was family-owned and operated, but the operations ceased the previous winter when the patriarch of the family passed away. The owners were ready and willing to sell. Paxton decided that she'd give their agent a call the next day. Then, she noticed the name of the agent.

***

"You're interested in the Pine place?" Kinsley asked her the following day.

"I saw your name on the listing," Paxton said. "Figured, I'd just stop by to talk about it."

"I've been trying to offload that thing for months. Are you interested in buying or flipping?"

"I don't know. Honestly, I saw the place while we were driving yesterday, and it just kind of spoke to me," Paxton replied. "I saw the asking price, and I can swing it. Let's keep that between us agents, though." She winked at Kinsley. "Adler's here now. I guess I just miss my sister. I'm also looking for my next challenge at the same time."

"Any idea what you'd do with the place? It's pretty massive for a house. And it's not exactly modern."

"You're a great agent, aren't you?" Paxton asked through laughter.

She sat in front of Kinsley's desk in the woman's office with a coffee in hand. Kinsley was looking at her like she was a crazy person, which only made Paxton laugh because Paxton was the same with her own clients. If a house or property wasn't for them, she didn't hesitate to tell them. She liked commissions. She enjoyed making money. But she didn't want to sell something to someone who would end up regretting it if she could prevent it in the first place.

"I want the sale if you're really interested."

"I'm interested in checking out the property," Paxton said. "I can't guarantee anything other than that."

"I have a showing this afternoon, but I can do tomorrow morning."

"I'll borrow Adler's car," Paxton said.

"Bring her along."

"I don't want her to know what I'm doing just yet."

"Why not?"

"Because if nothing comes from it, then it wasn't worth bringing up, anyway. I just don't want her to think I'm moving here or something when I have no idea why I'm even interested in looking at an old, abandoned hotel."

"I see."

"It took her a long time to actually move here. I'm part of that reason. She's always been there for me. I think she worried about leaving me there on my own, which is ridiculous because I'm a grown woman. I have my own place. I run my own business. She's just the big sister."

"She talks about you all the time, too," Kinsley replied.

"She's my best friend. I'm her best friend, too. So, her moving away has been kind of hard for both of us. Don't get me wrong... I'm so happy for her and Morgan. I just know that if I mention wanting to check out property here, she'll latch onto it, and I'm not ready for that yet."

"We'll start with a showing tomorrow and go from there then," Kinsley offered.

"Thanks. I appreciate it," Paxton said and stood. She placed the coffee cup on the desk and reached for Kinsley's hand. "I have no idea what's got me so interested."

"It's a charming place, really. It's got a lot of work ahead of it; that's why it hasn't sold yet. But it's got the history angle, and the view is one of the best I've seen."

"Tomorrow morning. I can't wait to check it out," Paxton replied.

***

Paxton decided to grab herself a late lunch at the deli she'd spied on her way to Kinsley's. She noticed a parking spot on the street that was otherwise occupied on both sides. She also noticed the car in front of her attempting to back into it in what looked to be a fine parallel parking move. Just as she planned to drive around that car, though, the one behind the empty spot backed up to leave just enough space that Paxton was able to pull into the free spot with little difficulty. She hated being that person, but she was starving and would only be a minute.

"Are you kidding me?" The woman in the other car had actually opened her door and now stood yelling at Paxton. "You saw me. I know you saw me... Paxton?"

"Shit. Sorry, Chris. I didn't know it was you."

Paxton closed her car door and made her way toward Chris's car, which was technically blocking traffic.

"So, because you didn't know it was me, that makes it okay to just steal someone's parking spot like that? I have twenty minutes to grab food that's *not* Italian before I have to go back to work, and you have to steal my damn spot?" Chris placed her hand on the top of her car just as a horn honked behind her. "I know. I know."

Before Paxton could apologize again, though, Chris was back in her car, driving off. Paxton rolled her eyes at herself for being such an asshole. She was used to getting away with stuff like this in the city. Apparently, people in South Lake Tahoe were a little less rude about stealing spots and a little more okay with being confrontational about it.

Paxton ran inside the deli feeling like such an ass, that she bought herself the sandwich and chips she wanted along with three other sandwich and chip combo options.

***

"Hello," she said.

"Paxton?" Chris looked up from the bar.

"I am an asshole. I'm sorry. I brought you lunch." She placed the extra sandwiches she'd bought on top of the bar. "I didn't know what you liked. I got a few different things. I also got plain, barbeque, and salt and vinegar chips. I think I saw you snag some of those at the party this weekend, but I wasn't sure. I took a chance."

"Chris, why is there food from somewhere else on my bar?" a man asked as he emerged from the kitchen.

"Sorry, Marco," Chris said. "She was just leaving," she offered in Paxton's direction.

"It's my fault. I owed her lunch," Paxton said to him, feeling even worse now.

"Paxton, just go. You're making it worse."

"You're not allowed to eat food that doesn't come from this place?" Paxton asked her.

"Not when it's in front of the customers that want to buy *my* food," Marco said to Paxton.

"I'm a customer," she replied. "Or I was the other night."

"Chris, can you take care of this, please? The beer guy is here," he said.

"Sure."

"Chris, I'm sorry. I didn't mean to get you in trouble."

"I'm not in trouble. It's fine. Just go, okay?"

"I'm sorry about the parking spot and about this. I–"

"Paxton, I have to work. This is my job. Please."

"Sorry," Paxton said again, backed away, and left the restaurant.

CHAPTER 5

CHRIS WOKE the following morning to another piece of bad news. Wes's clunker of a car needed a jump. Since she didn't trust it to start again when he needed to come home, she lent him her car for the day and decided to take his to work and deal with it later. She could find someone at the restaurant to jump it if she needed. Then, she'd have to figure out if he needed a new battery, or if there was something else wrong with it that would cost even more money they didn't have.

She drove past a property she'd seen on numerous occasions. Today, though, she saw something strange in front of it. Kinsley James was standing next to someone near the sign in the front yard. She didn't have a lot of time to see the other person as she drove past, but she was certain that person was Paxton Williams. She was also certain that Kinsley was a realtor and that the property itself was for sale.

She tried to push the whole thing out of her mind at work, but her mind kept returning to the thought that Paxton might be trying to buy the old Pine place. If so, she'd be moving to South Lake, most likely. She'd at least be spending more time in town even if she was just going to flip the place. Chris didn't like the idea of Paxton hanging around any longer than was necessary to visit with her sister. She didn't like the long, light brown hair that she was pretty sure was in the single braid down Paxton's back when she drove past. She didn't like her fiery green eyes. She hated the cute three or four tiny freckles on both of Paxton's cheeks. She also didn't like the light birthmark she'd spied on Paxton's neck just above her collarbone.

"Hey, Chris," Reese greeted her.

"Hey, Reese." Chris hated to admit, but sometimes, the only thing that allowed her to tell Reese and her twin sister, Remy, apart was the fact that they had different hair color. Reese also now sported a wedding ring, so that helped, too. "Did you order carry out?"

"No, Kellan's on her way in. She's just parking the car. I have a chivalrous wife."

"Still weird saying *wife*?" Chris asked, placing a beverage napkin on the table in front of Reese and one where Kellan would sit.

"It is, yes." Reese chuckled.

"Usual for drinks?"

"That's fine. We both craved the breadsticks and wanted to share some pasta tonight."

"Menu?"

"No, I think we're going with fettuccini. Two bowls, though?"

"Of course." Chris turned to walk away but turned back. "Hey, can I ask you a question?"

"Sure."

Chris sat in what would be Kellan's chair and asked, "What's up with Paxton?"

"Paxton? Adler's sister?"

"Yeah. Have you spent much time with her?"

"She was at the party this weekend."

"I know. I saw her there, too," Chris said.

"And?"

"I don't know. She just seems really rude to me, and Adler's not that way at all."

"Rude? Really? I didn't get that from her," Reese replied, sitting forward in her chair.

"You didn't? She came up to me at the party and asked if anyone was sitting in the chair next to me. When I said no, she just took it."

"I guess that's weird, but people do that all the time, don't they?" Reese asked.

"Maybe. I don't know. It just seemed weird for a party of her sister's new friends. Then, the other day, she took my parking spot."

"She took your spot?"

"She saw me trying to back in and stole it. I was on a break and trying to get some food. Thanks to her, I didn't have time to grab what I wanted."

"Oh, that's weird. I don't really know her well, but she seemed nice at the party."

"She brought me three different sandwiches from the deli, as if that would make up for it." Chris leaned back in her chair.

"She brought you food?"

"And got me in trouble with Marco, too. This place has a strict *'no outside food'* policy. It's for the same reason we don't split checks, and you have to have your entire party here before we will seat you. It's too busy with all the tourists, and if they see us with outside food, they'll go there next time."

"But she brought you three sandwiches? I get that she got you in trouble, and stealing the parking spot wasn't exactly nice, but it seems like she was trying to make it up to you," Reese suggested.

"She came in the other night, ordered food, ate it, and then left before I could even give her the check."

"She left without paying?" Reese asked, seemingly surprised.

"No, she paid. She had my manager get the check. She left a fifty when the bill was under twenty. What exactly was she saying with that?"

"I guess she really likes your service," Reese said with a laugh. "Hey, babe," she said to Kellan, who walked up behind Chris.

"Hey, Chris." Kellan placed a hand on the back of Chris's chair. "Trying to steal my wife?"

"You know it," Chris replied with a laugh and stood. "Breadsticks and fettuccini for you two, right?"

"Chris, we can–"

"No worries. I'll be right back with your drinks," Chris interrupted Reese.

Chris grabbed the usual drinks for Reese and Kellan all the while wondering why she was even bothering to ask Reese questions about Adler's visiting sister.

***

"Wes, I'm checking your report card. You want to tell me what's up?" Chris asked from her couch a day later.

"I thought those came out tomorrow. I was going to talk to you." Wes came in from the kitchen, sat down next to her, and looked at her laptop screen. "Chemistry got the better of me this quarter."

"I can see that. Since when do you get Cs in anything?" she asked him.

"I don't know." He shrugged that typical teenage boy shrug.

"Wes, come on. This isn't your normal kind of report card. You get As and a B or two. This is *all* Bs and a C."

"I don't know, Chris." He shrugged a second time.

"You don't know? Is the stuff too hard? Do you need a tutor or something?"

"No, it's not hard. I just haven't had a lot of time to do my homework."

"Homework?" She turned to him. "You do homework all the time."

"Chris, I work at the bookstore a lot, and I have tennis practice after school now."

"Oh," she replied. "Well, I know how much tennis means to you, but the season is just starting, Wes. What happens when it really gets going? I'm worried about your grades."

"I know. I'm doing the best I can."

"I know you are." She placed her hand on his shoulder. "Let's talk to the store about cutting down your hours. Maybe twenty hours is too much when you're in school and in season."

"Chris, we need that money."

"Not if it means your grades are dropping like this," she replied.

"I'll just study more. I'll stay up later or do my homework during lunch."

"Wes, you're a teenager. I want you to be a teenager. Call the store tomorrow and ask if you can cut your hours down to fifteen. We'll start there, okay? I know you love tennis and want a scholarship. I don't want you to lose that. But something's got to give."

"Fine." He stood, grunted once, and headed off to his bedroom.

She'd work more hours at Donoto's if that was what it took, but she was seriously beginning to think about getting another job. She could be an admin somewhere, maybe, or even manage a restaurant. She wasn't convinced managers made all that much more than servers, since servers made tips and usually kept the exact amount of those tips from the US government come tax season, but managers did get benefits, which would save them money paying for their own. She spent the rest of the night searching for jobs online. She applied for a few she knew she had no chance of getting, a couple she might be able to score an interview for, and then three more serving jobs she knew she'd get if she just showed up and told them about her experience. She closed it and went off to bed, wondering if she'd ever be able to get them to a point where they wouldn't have to worry about money like this.

***

"Hey, Chris." Paxton was putting gas into her car, standing on the other side of the pump from Chris.

"Jesus, you scared me." Chris hadn't been prepared for someone to be at the gas station just on the other side of her.

"Sorry," Paxton said.

"I just didn't see you there."

"That's a different car than I saw you in the other day," Paxton said, nodding toward Wes's car.

"It's my brother's. He has mine today." She felt about three feet tall seeing Paxton's car on the other side, all shiny and new.

"This is Adler's. I'm borrowing it a lot this week." The woman looked behind her toward the gas station. "I was going to head inside and grab a snack. Do you want anything?"

"No, I'm okay." Chris capped the gas tank.

"Working today?"

"Nope."

"Okay." Paxton turned to head inside and turned back quickly. "I guess… Have a good day."

"You too," Chris replied.

"And I guess I'll see you later tonight, at Kinsley and Riley's?"

"Kinsley and Riley's?" Chris checked.

"Their dinner party? I assumed–" Paxton smacked her forehead. "I'm an idiot. I assumed you'd been invited."

"I wasn't. Thanks for letting me know that, though."

"Hey, everyone else gets a plus one because they're all coupled off. Want to be mine? I'm going solo, obviously."

"No." Chris walked around to the driver's side of the car. "Have a good night, Paxton."

"Chris, come on. I'm the worst when it comes to you, for some reason. I promise, I'm not a bad person. Come with me tonight. I'm sure they meant to invite you or that Kinsley's calling you later."

"I'm not really into dinner parties. I have plans, anyway," Chris said, opening her door.

"I'll see you around then, maybe."

Chris climbed into her car. She looked out the window to see Paxton going inside the convenience store. Then, she turned the key in the ignition, praying it would start. When it did, she thanked every deity out there and sped out of the parking lot. She needed to get away from Paxton. This woman kept popping up at the most inopportune times. And she just reminded Chris that she was indeed on the outside looking in with women she considered to be her friends. Her phone rang just as she parked at the grocery store. She pulled it out and saw Adler's name.

"Hello?"

"Hey, Chris. How are you?"

"I'm okay. You?"

"I'm good. Listen, Riley asked me to call you. She's in court today. Kinsley's showing a house, I guess. But they kind of threw together this last-minute dinner thing for tonight. It's at their place. I'm sure you're busy, but they only called me, like, twenty minutes ago. Riley asked me to ask you to come."

"To dinner?"

"It's going to be Morgan and me, obviously. Reese and Kellan will be there, along with Remy and Ryan. Pax will be there, too."

"So, all couples and your sister?" Chris asked.

"She's leaving in a couple of days. Kinsley and Riley wanted to do something nice with everyone before she goes. Can you make it?"

She'd already told Paxton that she had plans, but Adler wasn't someone Chris wanted to lie to. She'd always been nice to her.

"I might be able to make it, yes. I'll have to check."

"Sure. Okay. We're all getting there at seven."

"I'll see what I can do."

"Hope to see you, then," Adler said and hung up.

She'd lied to Paxton. If she showed up, Paxton would know that. If she didn't, she'd probably never get invited to something like this again. She had to decide what mattered most to her.

CHAPTER 6

PAXTON WASN'T SURE what to think. Chris had clearly lied to her earlier. She was currently sitting at the dinner table to Paxton's immediate right. She'd either lied about knowing about the dinner party in the first place or lied about her plans. Either way, she'd lied, and Paxton didn't really understand why. Sure, they'd gotten off to a rough start. She'd managed to bungle things every step of the way. But she didn't think that meant Chris should lie to her about attending a dinner party with their friends.

Chris had this dark brown hair that was swept back behind her ears tonight. Paxton had only ever seen it pulled up into a ponytail, which she guessed was due to Chris's work in food service. Her eyes were a magnetic blue that went so well with the color of her just barely tan from the summer skin.

"Pax?"

"Huh?" She snapped to attention to the sound of her name.

"You said you had something to tell us," Adler replied.

"Oh, I was thinking about doing that later, but okay." Paxton sat up in her chair. She glanced at Chris next to her to see that she was paying attention to her now. "Kinsley and I share a profession, as you all know."

"That's your reveal?" Adler teased.

"My reveal is that I'm buying a hotel here in South Lake Tahoe, Adler. So, thanks for ruining it," she replied but winked at her sister playfully.

"You're what?" Adler asked, leaning forward in her chair.

"There's this old bed and breakfast called *'The Pine Tree Guest House.'* It's about twenty minutes away from here. I bought it." She paused. "Well, I'm buying it."

"You're buying a bed and breakfast? Why?" Adler pressed.

"Because I saw it from the road the other day, when we were driving, and I fell in love with it. Kinsley is the agent. She took me over to the property and walked me around. I want it, Adler. It's beautiful. It's also hideous and needs a lot of work. I want to tear it apart and put it back together."

"Do you want to flip it?" Adler asked.

"I don't know. Maybe. I might not."

"Keep it? You're going to be an innkeeper?"

"I don't know yet, Adler." She leaned back in her chair. "Why do you sound irritated? I thought you'd be happy."

"I'm just confused. You're a real estate agent."

"Agents buy and flip properties all the time," Kinsley offered. "It's easier for us to do it, because we know the ins and outs of the business and what properties are up for sale."

"But you've never done that," Adler addressed Paxton.

"Not yet, no. But I'm going to start with this place. I put in an offer last night, and the seller accepted it this morning. I'm going to sign the paperwork at the end of the week. They want a fast close. I came in a little over asking, too."

"Over asking? Why would you do that?" Adler asked.

"Adler, *I'm* the real estate agent. I know what I'm doing."

"How about we congratulate Paxton on this awesome thing she's doing since it means she's staying a little longer?" Morgan suggested. "Right, Pax?"

"I'll go back home to get more of my stuff, but, yes, I'm going to come back and stay until it's up and running, or until I sell it if I decide to do that," she answered.

"Paxton, you—"

"Addie," Morgan said and placed her hand on Adler's shoulder. "Later, okay?"

"Well, this dinner party just got awkward. Sorry, guys. I didn't think my sister would be a pain in my ass about something that means I'd be staying in town longer." Paxton stood from the table. "I'm going to run to the bathroom. I'll be back."

"Pax," Adler said and stood.

Paxton left the dining room and entered Kinsley and Riley's living room, where Adler caught up with her.

"What the hell was that?" she whispered.

"Pax, I was just caught off guard. This is a big deal. You're buying a freaking hotel in South Lake."

"Where you live, Adler," Paxton countered.

"But *you* don't."

"So, you have a problem with me staying here longer, or possibly moving here if I actually like the place and want to stay?" Paxton asked.

"Pax, it has nothing to do with you being here or not," Adler said as she moved toward her. "It's just a pretty sudden decision that has a huge impact. I want to make sure you think it through."

"Adler, I have the money. I can afford to buy it and rebuild from the ground up if I want to. You know I'm good with my money."

"It's a hotel, Pax. You have never talked about buying or running a hotel in your life."

"I saw it and I knew, Adler. I don't know how to describe it... I knew it was supposed to be mine." She shrugged her left shoulder. "I had hoped you'd like the idea of me sticking around for a while."

"I do. I love that idea, Pax." She sat on the sofa, encouraging Paxton to do the same by patting the space beside her. "I just want to make sure you're doing this for the right reasons. I haven't been here all that long, but you and I have always lived in the same place. Does this have anything to do with me being here?"

"It's a plus, to be closer to my annoying sister, yes; but it's not the only reason. Adler, I'm an adult. I'm a fully-functional one, actually. I might even have more money than you at this point in my career. I'm not great at vacations. I have enough saved up to take care of my retirement and all that. I saw the property, did the whole inspection thing, and I wanted it. I know what I'm doing here, Adler. Besides, you said it yourself: something's been up with me recently." Paxton sat down next to her sister.

"And you said it was nothing."

"I'm kind of bored, honestly. I like work sometimes. I've just been doing it forever. I want to try something new. I didn't know what it was, or if I'd actually do anything about it, but when I saw *'The Pine Tree Guest House'* property, I knew I wanted it. I want to gut all the parts that need gutting myself. I'll hire people for the tough stuff, but I can do a lot of it on my own. It has a restaurant that just needs to be brought up to code. It has a patio out back that overlooks the water. I think I can turn it into a profitable hotel, eventually. It only has ten rooms. It's not too big to manage, and I can hire a consultant in hospitality to help me get going."

"It sounds like you're not just thinking of flipping," Adler commented, resting her head on her hand and her elbow on the back of the sofa.

"I don't know. I guess not. I don't know if I want to manage the place, though. I think I'd hire someone if I decide to keep it. I recognize that I have zero experience in that area, but I do have experience running my own business and with property management."

"That's true."

"And I can still be an agent until it's up and running. I can go back and forth if I need to for a while, but I'd like to just find somewhere to rent around here so I have a place to stay where my sister isn't having sex in the next room all the time." She glared at Adler.

"Hey! Morgan and I haven't had sex since the night

you told me you heard us." Adler laughed. "Well, that's not true… But you weren't there when we did it."

"All the more reason for me to stay somewhere else. You guys just moved in together. You should be able to have sex whenever and wherever you want. That's kind of one of the benefits of living with your girlfriend."

"How about this: I'll reserve judgment until you actually get going on this project of yours. I am the big sister, though, Pax. It's my job to look out for you. I've never been good at holding my tongue. You know that," Adler said.

"I do." Paxton watched as Chris entered the living room. "Hey," she greeted the woman.

"They wanted me to let you know they're taking dessert out back," Chris said, hooking her thumb toward the backyard. "Sorry for interrupting."

"You didn't," Paxton replied. "And thanks." She nodded at her and gave her a smile. "We'll be right there."

Chris didn't say anything else before leaving, but Paxton caught the woman glancing at her, and it spoke to her in the same yet different way that the hotel had spoken to her. Chris, without words, had somehow conveyed to Paxton that she had no idea what to make of her. Paxton understood, of course, because she had no idea what to make of Chris.

"She's single, you know… And gay," Adler said.

"She hates me," Paxton replied.

"What? Why?"

"I'm sure she thinks I'm an asshole. I didn't mean to be."

"What did you do?"

"Stole her parking spot, prevented her from getting food, and got her in trouble with her boss."

"Paxton!"

"Let's go outside," Paxton said through a laugh. "Maybe if I'm extra nice to her, I'll earn some points or something."

"She's an attractive woman, Pax. You're staying here

at least for a little while. Maybe you should–"

"Shut up, Adler." Paxton laughed as they made their way to the patio outside.

"Welcome back, you two," Reese said.

"All good?" Kinsley asked.

"Sort of. Adler's going to give it a rest, but I still need to figure out how I'm going to build a hotel."

Paxton sat next to Chris on a patio chaise lounge because there was nowhere else to sit. Reese and Kellan were sitting in two chairs that overlooked the trees behind the house. Riley and Kinsley were in one of the other lounges. Riley was in Kinsley's arms. It looked so sweet to Paxton. Morgan and Adler were actually standing. Adler had her arms wrapped around Morgan from behind. She winked at Paxton before she kissed Morgan's neck. She looked so happy. Morgan smiled a smile that Adler couldn't see, but it was one that told Paxton that she cared deeply for her big sister.

"Chris just told us she's looking for a second job or maybe even a new full-time job," Kellan stated.

"Oh, I'm not–"

"You are?" Paxton turned to Chris, which brought them closer together.

"I wait tables."

"The hotel has a restaurant," Paxton said without thinking. "It needs work, but I could use someone who knows food service."

"She definitely knows food service," Riley said. "They've offered her an Assistant Manager job a bunch of times. Plus, I know there are at least three other restaurants that have tried to snatch her up."

"It's just because I've been doing it for so long," Chris told Riley. "I'm probably not who you're looking for," she said to Paxton.

"Maybe Wes could help with the construction stuff," Morgan suggested.

"Wes?" Paxton asked.

"Chris's brother," Adler added for Paxton's benefit.

"He's too busy right now," Chris replied. "In fact, I should probably be leaving so I can get home and check on him."

Paxton wanted to ask why she'd have to check on her brother, but she didn't. When Chris stood, so did Paxton, for some reason. Everyone said their goodnights to Chris. As she walked into the house to head out toward her car, Paxton followed.

"Hey, Chris?"

"Yeah?" Chris turned back to her.

"If you're really considering another job, maybe we *could* talk."

"I don't think I'd want to work for you, Paxton. No offense."

"You wouldn't be working *for* me. You'd be working *with* me," Paxton replied.

"Somehow, I doubt that. Also, you don't even know me."

Paxton held up both hands defensively and replied, "You're right."

"I don't need charity, Paxton."

"Charity? I didn't—"

"Let's just be honest for a second, okay?"

"Chris, I—"

"Paxton, you don't like me. And I don't particularly like you. We're not going to work together. I don't even really fit in here. I don't know why I came; except that I felt like if I didn't, I wouldn't get an invite next time. And as much as I love my kid brother, I need some adult company every now and then. Being around a group of lesbians is a plus, but I'm not someone who wants or needs handouts."

Chris walked out the front door, leaving Paxton standing in Kinsley and Riley's living room, wondering what the hell had just happened.

CHAPTER 7

CHRIS HAD JUST MANAGED to make a fool out of herself in front of Paxton. She'd only mentioned to the group that she was considering looking for another job because they all had something to talk about and she didn't. She couldn't exactly talk about how Wes's grades were falling because he had to work to help keep them afloat. She didn't want to bring up the fact that they'd likely have to put his car in the shop. She didn't want to talk about how she'd been a waitress since she was twenty years old and had no college degree, unlike every single one of them.

"Chris?" Paxton's voice came from behind her just as she was unlocking the car.

"Come on, Paxton!"

"Look, I get that I've rubbed you the wrong way, but you're friends with my sister and her girlfriend, along with all those other women in there." Paxton pointed behind her toward the house. "I don't know anything about you, including your skillset. So, in there, yes, I was just kind of going along with the whole thing. But if what they all said in there is true, you know food service."

"I've been waiting tables most of my adult life; I should hope so."

"I don't know what I'm doing with this whole thing. Don't tell my sister that, though, okay?" Paxton laughed a little, and Chris thought her endearing in that moment as Paxton stuck her hands into the back pockets of her jeans. "I'm going back to Seattle to sort out the rest of my life. When I come back, though, I'm probably going to own a rundown hotel. So, it wouldn't be charity for you. It would be charity for me if you would consider helping out. Just think about it, okay? It would be a real job, Chris. I'd do it right." She pulled her hands out of her pocket. "Anyway, that's all I had to say. Have a good rest of your night."

***

It had been a week since Paxton returned to Seattle. Chris had worked three doubles during that time. Wes had gotten a D on his most recent chemistry exam. She'd told him he'd have to give up working at the bookstore since even working fewer hours wasn't helping his GPA. They'd had his battery replaced, which wasn't as costly as it could have been, but it was still an unexpected expense. She'd work a few more doubles and would be able to make it up, but the tips were inconsistent at best, which meant it was difficult to budget and plan ahead.

She'd had a rough few shifts at work recently. She just hadn't been focused on work. She'd been thinking about something else entirely. Well, she'd been thinking about someone else. Paxton Williams hadn't really left her mind since the last time she'd seen her looking kind of cute in the driveway of their shared friends' home. The woman had had this goofy smile on her face and appeared genuine in her offer. Chris had attempted to push those thoughts out of her mind repeatedly but couldn't seem to shake the idea of working with Paxton at her new hotel. Of course, it was a ridiculous idea.

Paxton's hotel wasn't even open yet. It wouldn't be for months, at minimum. That meant the restaurant inside it wouldn't be open for months if everything went well. Chris had never opened her own restaurant. She had no idea what needed to be done. That hadn't stopped her from doing a lot of research online and asking Marco a few stealthy questions here and there about how his family had started Donoto's along with how they'd made it so successful.

"She's really serious about this whole thing," Adler said the next night as she and Morgan sat at Donoto's in their usual booth.

"What's the problem, Addie?" Morgan asked. "I think it's awesome."

Chris had just sat down next to them, as was her custom when they stopped by and she could spare a minute.

"What do you think, Chris?" Adler asked her.

"About what?"

"Paxton buying this hotel; or bed and breakfast, I guess."

"Oh, I don't know that I have an opinion on it either way," Chris replied.

"She asked about you yesterday," Adler said.

"Who did?" Chris asked, scrunching together her eyebrows in confusion.

"Paxton. My sister." Adler laughed.

"She asked about *me*?"

"She got back in town the day before yesterday. She asked if we thought you'd consider working with her," Morgan explained.

"She did?"

"She did." Adler took a drink of her sparkling water.

Chris sat forward in the booth and replied, "She does know I'm a waitress, right?"

"That she does," Morgan answered.

Chris looked around the room and noticed two of her tables needed refills.

"I'll be back in a bit," Chris said.

But she never got around to sitting back down with them. She got busier and busier, until the restaurant closed. Then, she went home, crashed onto her bed, and fell asleep. When she woke the next morning, she was grateful she didn't have to be in until five. She was unsure how much longer she could go on like this. She knew there were bags under her eyes. She'd been surviving off of pizza, pasta, and coffee recently. She showered, dressed, and decided she'd run to the grocery store to pick up some of Wes's favorite snacks. On the drive, she passed 'The Pine Tree Guest House' and noticed something. She pulled into the drive that led to the small parking lot to the right of the building. There was only one other car there that she recognized. She wasn't exactly sure what she was doing there, but she got out of her car, walked up to the front door of the hotel, and knocked.

Paxton Williams opened the door and said, "Chris?"

"Hi," Chris replied and swallowed right after. "I was just driving by. I saw your car."

"Adler's car," Paxton corrected. "Mine is still in Seattle. I'm driving it down the next time I come back."

"Right. I guess you're back," Chris said for some reason.

"A couple of days now, yeah." Paxton held onto the doorframe with one hand. She was wearing a pair of jean shorts with a plain black t-shirt. Her hair was pulled back, and she wore no makeup. "Sorry. Come on in." She moved out of the way and motioned inside. "This is my new place. Well, sort of. I don't live here, obviously."

"Where *are* you living?" Chris asked as she entered the foyer.

"Another hotel." She smiled. "I know, right? I own a hotel, and I'm staying in another one. I'm just here to sign the paperwork and find an apartment to live in while I sort all this out." She motioned around with both hands.

"So, you own it?"

"I do. Signed this morning, actually. She's all mine now." Paxton's smile was infectious. It lit up her whole face. "I can't believe I'm a hotel owner… I don't even own a house."

"You're a realtor who doesn't own her own home?"

"I guess I never found my dream home."

"And this place… She's a she?" Chris referenced Paxton's previous comment.

"She is a she, yes." Paxton laughed. "Hey, I was asking about you the other day."

"You were?" Chris pretended she had no idea what Paxton was talking about. "Why?"

"I know you hate me, and we have this whole thing where I was a dick to you, but I was wondering if you would actually ever consider working here."

"Paxton, I–"

"I know. I was–"

"An asshole for interrupting me. How is it that you just think you know what I'm going to say or that it's okay to interrupt me when I'm trying to say it?"

"I'm sorry." Paxton held up her hands in supplication.

"This is why this wouldn't work." Chris pointed between the two of them.

"Because I interrupted you?" Paxton crossed her arms over her chest. "I apologized, Chris. God, I've actually apologized for everything I've done since we met."

"That's a lot of apologies for someone I've known for a couple of weeks, Paxton," Chris argued.

"Fine. Never mind, then, Chris." Paxton took a few steps backward to lean against what had been the front desk of the hotel. "I have a million things to worry about. I don't need this, too. I've apologized to you. You don't want to be here? Feel free to leave whenever you want."

Chris watched Paxton run her hand through her hair, rub her neck for a moment, and then look down at the floor as she walked out of the room. Chris exhaled, closed her eyes, swallowed her pride, and followed. She found Paxton on the back patio of the hotel. She also found that the back patio of the hotel overlooked the lake. She'd known that. But knowing that and actually seeing that were two very different things.

"Wow," she whispered.

Paxton turned around from where she was leaning over a railing and replied, "I thought you were leaving."

"It's beautiful back here," Chris said, unable to focus on Paxton's words. She moved to stand next to her and stared out at the water. "I live here, but, sometimes, I forget just how beautiful it is."

"It is." Paxton turned to face her. "You have a brother,

right?"

"Wes."

"How old is he?"

"Seventeen." Chris kept her eyes on the water.

"Does *he* want a job? Manual labor."

"I told you, he needs to focus on school and tennis. He works on the weekends." Chris replied.

"How much does he make?" Paxton asked with a lifted eyebrow.

Chris looked over at her. That eyebrow looked nice like that; nice and deadly at the same time.

"He's at just above minimum wage. He stocks books and helps people find them. He's not exactly performing open heart surgery."

"I pay a lot better than minimum wage, and I could use the extra hands. I plan to do a lot of this work myself; the gutting part, at least. He'd get a good workout and make good money."

"Why are you trying to employ my entire family?" Chris asked.

"Not your entire family; just you and your brother," Paxton replied with a smirk.

Chris swallowed and said, "I'll ask him. It's his decision."

"Your parents don't need to sign off on it? He's seventeen."

"No," Chris replied. She pushed back off the railing and asked, "What exactly are you hoping I would do here?"

"Help me figure out what to do with the restaurant. But you can also help knock shit down for me, too." Paxton smiled at her.

"I'd need to make more than what I make at the restaurant on a good week," she replied.

"Okay."

"You just assume you can pay me that?"

"No. I haven't actually agreed to pay you anything. I just said okay to your statement, Chris."

"I'm good at my job. I make good tips," Chris argued.

"I'm aware. Why do you think I'm arguing with you right now? I'm not. Tell me the number you need, and if I can pay you that, I will. I can't promise you anything other than that, though. I haven't decided if I'll keep the place or flip it. I don't even know if I'll keep the restaurant or not. I'm just pursuing everything right now."

"Then, I can't work with you. I need a full-time, permanent job, Paxton."

"Why don't we just start with you being a consultant, then? I'll pay you for the hours you consult for me about the restaurant. You can still keep your day job."

"Consultant?"

"Consultants make good money," Paxton replied with a smile.

Chris squinted at her and replied, "This is a bad idea."

"I'm going to give you my email address, okay? I made a professional one for this place since it's separate from my other company. You can email me your resume. If I like what I see, I'll call you. We can go through the whole interview process so it's legit. I'll think through what I need you to do. *If* there's a match here, I'll put together an offer for you. If you want it, you'll take it. If not, I'll leave you alone." Paxton stared back out over the water. "I love this place," she said it softly just as the wind blew a few strands of her hair around her face. "I don't know what it is about it, but I just wanted it the moment I saw it."

Chris stared at her for a moment before she said, "Then, you shouldn't sell it, Paxton."

"Pax."

"What?"

"You can call me Pax. Most people do," she said, turning to look at Chris.

"Okay. Pax." She nodded at her. "I have to get to the grocery store now." She walked off but turned back. "Oh, what's that email address?"

Paxton turned to face her, smirking.

CHAPTER 8

"DO YOU HAVE ANY IDEA what you're doing?" Adler asked.

"I know I don't want this wallpaper and that this wall is going to have to be replaced." Paxton smashed into it with a sledgehammer. "And now I feel all the stress leaving my body."

"I cannot believe you are tearing out walls," Adler said, stepping back.

"Miss Williams, do you want the wall in the other room torn down, too?" Wesley asked her, entering into what was left of one of the guest rooms. "The one by the bathroom, I mean."

"That one goes, too," Paxton told him.

He turned and left the room. A moment later, she heard a loud crash of sledgehammer meeting the wall.

"How's he working out?" Adler asked her.

"He's great. He's only here on the weekends. That was the agreement Chris and I had. He works four hours a day. He makes more than he did at the bookstore, working fewer hours. It was important to her." She swung the sledgehammer again.

"That was nice of you."

"It's not charity, Adler. He's a good worker. He's already finished tearing down two rooms, and it's his third day."

"And Chris?"

"What about her?" Paxton took a sip from her water bottle.

"Last I heard, you two were negotiating salary," Adler said.

"Oh." Paxton laughed. "Not really. She gave her notice at Donoto's, though. She starts on Monday. She gave them two weeks, and her boss said she could come back whenever. I'm paying her what she asked for."

"What about your employees in Seattle?" Adler asked.

"They're fine. I've given them most of my clients that I was working with. I'm going back next weekend to get the rest of my stuff and drive my car down here."

"So, you're officially moving, then, Pax?" Adler asked. "You said you still didn't know last time we talked; which was yesterday, by the way."

"I have a six-month lease on my apartment. I'm going to get as far as I can on my own with this place. Then, I'll hire people to help finish it off. We'll see how far I get, and I'll decide then if I'm going to stay permanently or go back. My place in Seattle is up for grabs as of next weekend, though. I'd have to find a new place if I decided to return."

"This is a big change... You're not worried you're making it too fast?" Adler sat on the small step stool in the middle of the empty, dusty room.

"No." Paxton swung the sledgehammer again, tearing out a large chunk of wall. "I feel like I'm right where I need to be."

"I'm happy for you, Pax. I'm happy for me, too, because it means I get to see my baby sister all the time," Adler replied.

"Well, not all the time, since you and Morgan are traveling to all your stores soon."

"It's time to make the rounds, yes," Adler replied. "But that's, like, two weeks. Then, we'll be back. I'd offer to help you get the car down here if I could, though. We could have had a fun sister road trip."

"It's only, like, thirteen hours; a couple more, with bathroom and gas stops. I'll find a hotel about halfway through and stop for the night. I'll be fine."

"Okay. Well, I guess I should go. Morgan is meeting me at home so we can pack," Adler said and stood.

"What's that feel like?" Paxton asked.

"What's what feel like?"

"Saying your girlfriend is meeting you at home," Paxton replied.

"Really good, Pax. It feels really good." She smiled.

***

"I've got all my recommendations here," Chris said, placing a folder on the front desk they'd been using as a makeshift office for the past few days.

"Thanks," Paxton replied. "I thought you were leaving, like, an hour ago."

"I was. But I got caught up in the search for new kitchen equipment and coming up with the budget. I figured I'd finish it before I left for the night," she said.

Paxton looked up and over at her, smiling as she did. They'd been working together for four days now. So far, they'd fought twice, but only over minor things. Chris had been on time each day. She'd also stayed nearly as late as Paxton. They'd agreed on a full-time job for Chris once Paxton worked out all the particulars of what she really needed. Chris had ensured her the job at Donoto's was safe should this arrangement not work out. She'd helped with some of the teardown and had already started working on plans for the restaurant once the place was open. Paxton was satisfied with her work, and that was what mattered. What didn't matter was how good Chris looked in her white t-shirt and jeans.

"So, you won't be here this weekend, right?" Chris asked her.

"No, I'm catching a flight tomorrow."

"If it's okay with you, I'll come in with Wes, then. I think there should be an adult here if he's working."

"I gave him the weekend off. Did he not tell you?" she asked.

"No, he didn't. I haven't seen him much this week,

though. He's been staying late for tennis practice and then going to the library to study until it closes. By the time he gets home, I'm usually asleep. Can I tell you how nice it is to be asleep by ten o'clock?"

Paxton laughed and replied, "Hey, what are you doing this weekend?"

"Me? Nothing. Why?"

Paxton watched as Chris must have realized that she'd just admitted to having no plans for the weekend.

"Come with me," Paxton said.

"Where?"

"Chris, come with me to Seattle," Paxton answered with a laugh. "Have you ever been?"

"To Seattle? No," Chris replied as she crossed her arms over her chest. "But I can't just go with you to Seattle this weekend."

"Why not? You just said you didn't have any plans."

"I lied." Chris shrugged.

"Come on. We can fly up together. Consider it a work trip if you want."

"Adler's busy, isn't she? You need someone to keep you from getting bored?"

"No. Well, yes. Adler is busy, technically. But I hadn't planned on asking her, anyway. I'm asking you. We can stop at a few hotels or B&Bs on the way down here and get some ideas."

"I have Wes."

"Wes is seventeen," Paxton reminded.

"Exactly, Wes is seventeen."

"He's a good kid, Chris. I've spent a lot of time with him these past few weeks. He can hang by himself for a few nights."

"A few nights?" Chris asked.

"Leave tomorrow. Spend tomorrow night at my place. I have to pack up some of my stuff to load into the car. The movers are taking care of the rest. I figured we'd leave Saturday morning. We could look up a few places to stop on the way and pick one to stop at on Saturday night. Do the same thing Sunday night. We could call it research. We'd be back on Monday."

"So, three nights?"

"Yes, Chris." She chuckled at Chris's response. "I'm driving, and the business is paying for it. All you need to do it say yes."

"I don't know, Paxton. Eight hours a day with you is already a lot," the woman replied, but Paxton knew she was only partially serious. "I don't know if I could handle three full days and nights."

"I have a second bedroom at my apartment, and we'd get two rooms at wherever we stop, Chris. Technically, it's only the three days, then." She winked at her playfully.

"How are you not a lawyer? You're pretty good at arguing," Chris said unfolding her arms. "Fine. I'll go, but only because I've never been to Seattle."

"You realize we're spending less than twenty-four hours there, right?"

"I realize that, but at least I could say I've been there. I'll go home and pack. When should I meet you?"

"I'll book your flight now. I'll pick you up at eight tomorrow morning," Paxton replied.

***

The flight to Seattle was uneventful. Chris had been reading a book the whole time. Paxton had listened to music on her phone while playing a game. Neither of them had said much since Paxton picked her up that morning. Truthfully, Paxton wasn't entirely certain why she'd invited Chris along on this little trip. It had been a spur of the moment thing. She'd said it before she'd thought it through.

They took a car from the airport to Paxton's apartment in the city. It wasn't a long drive, but still, neither of them spoke of anything of consequence. When they got to Paxton's apartment, Paxton showed Chris around, pointing out the second bedroom where she'd be sleeping. Most of Paxton's belongings were all packed up, but she'd left the bedding on both beds and the essentials out for the movers to finish up after she left.

"So, I don't have food here, obviously. I was thinking we could go out to dinner," Paxton said after Chris came out of the bathroom.

"Okay. Where do you want to go?"

"There's a great pizza place over–" Paxton stopped the moment she caught Chris's angry expression. "I'm kidding."

"You better be. I've had enough pizza for a lifetime."

Paxton thought for a moment and said, "Let me pick the place, okay? I promise, no pizza."

Chris had nodded then. Paxton knew where she'd take her. They dressed somewhat casually, though Paxton had thrown on a pair of dark gray slacks with a button-down shirt. Chris had put on a pair of jeans so dark blue, they didn't really look like jeans. She looked great in a polo shirt in a pink that was so light, it almost looked white. Paxton drove them to the restaurant after calling ahead to make sure they'd have a table. When they arrived, she valeted the car, and they headed inside.

"Paxton, this place is really nice. I can't wear jeans in here," Chris said as she tugged on Paxton's arm, trying to pull her back outside.

"We can wear whatever we want. There's no dress code. Besides, I know the chef. I sold him his house. I called ahead. We have a table in the back. Come on." Paxton pulled on Chris's arm instead and moved them to the podium. "Table for Paxton Williams?" she asked the hostess.

The woman in her early twenties checked the list in front of her and said, "Yes, of course. Welcome back, Miss Williams. Right this way."

They sat down at the table Paxton had grown accustomed to in this restaurant. It was on the seventeenth floor of a high rise and had a beautiful view of the skyline and the water just beyond. It was also a Michelin Star restaurant that served delicious French cuisine. Paxton watched as Chris looked around the restaurant, seemingly uncomfortable. She wondered if she'd made the right decision bringing her here.

"Hey, are you okay? We can go if you don't want to eat here."

"No, it's fine. I just don't usually go to these kinds of places."

"Where do you usually go?" Paxton asked as their waiter approached. He politely interrupted them to deliver the specials for the evening and ask for their drink order. "Wine?" Paxton asked her.

"I'm okay with water," Chris replied.

"Can we get the 2007 Chateau Palmer Bordeaux?" Paxton asked. The waiter nodded and left them. "It's cheaper by the bottle. I'll drink it if you really don't want any, but you should try it. It's good."

"I'm not much of a wine person," Chris replied.

"Beer, then? Martini?" Paxton asked. Chris shook her head. "Do you not drink at all?"

"I do, every now and then; but not often." She looked around the restaurant again.

"Hey, Chris?"

"Yeah?" Chris met her eyes.

"Are you okay? There are other restaurants. I don't mind picking another one."

"I'm just not this person."

"What person?"

Chris sighed and replied, "Paxton, I can't afford all this. I don't fit in here."

"Why do you keep saying that? That you don't fit in here? Why wouldn't you fit in here?"

"Paxton, I'm wearing the nicest clothes I own right now. I have a black dress somewhere in my closet, but outside of that, this is it." She motioned to herself. "I'm wearing jeans and a polo shirt to a fancy restaurant."

"That guy's wearing a polo." Paxton pointed at a man with a female companion two tables over. "And she is way too young to be his wife. Mistress, maybe."

"Or daughter," Chris replied.

"I doubt it. Let's go with mistress," Paxton replied with a smirk. "And she's wearing jeans, Chris. I think you look great." She shrugged one shoulder.

The waiter brought their wine over, along with Chris's water with lemon. He uncorked the wine and poured a small amount in Paxton's glass, which she swirled only for a moment before she took a sip. She didn't smell the wine or dawdle too much, nodding at the waiter that it was acceptable. She didn't want Chris to feel out of place any more than she already did. He filled her glass and then filled the one he'd brought for Chris, which the woman didn't touch until the waiter took their order and departed. Chris had ordered a salad. Paxton had noticed it was the cheapest thing on the menu. Paxton had ordered the steak she usually got when she came here. It had a French Bordelaise Red Wine Sauce and was served with always perfectly prepared vegetables.

Paxton raised her wine glass and said, "To us, embarking on this adventure together."

"Which adventure? The hotel, or this trip?" Chris asked.

"Both, I guess."

Chris stared at her own wine glass, nibbled on her lip, grabbed it, and they clinked them together in a toast. Paxton watched Chris take a sip of the wine hesitantly before she took a much longer drink. Paxton smiled at her then. Chris met her eyes and smiled back.

CHAPTER 9

THE WINE WAS AMAZING. Chris was certain she'd never had wine as good as the wine she'd just finished. Paxton had poured the remainder of the bottle into Chris's glass after topping off her own. Chris had just consumed the last sip after finishing a salad that was both rustic-looking and hearty. She'd never had a salad with dry-cured ham – which sounded so much better in French, walnuts, and blue cheese. It was good, though. She'd enjoyed it enough, despite the flavors being so foreign to her. Paxton had offered her a bite of her steak. Chris had declined, but she had sampled the grilled asparagus on Paxton's plate. It was also delicious. When the check came, Paxton took it immediately. She slid her card into the folio without so much as looking at Chris, and asked the waiter to take it away. When he returned, he thanked both of them. Paxton signed the receipt, pocketed her card, and they were off.

"So, I was thinking… We could go to Pike Place, which is the touristy market. You should see it once in your life, though. It's got the world's first Starbucks and the famous fish throwers, but they're done for the day. We could check them out tomorrow, though, before we leave the city."

"Okay." Chris followed Paxton out the door of the restaurant and watched her pass the ticket to the valet to retrieve her car. "What time do we need to be on the road tomorrow?"

"Whenever we want," Paxton replied, turning back to

her. "We could grab breakfast over in the market and leave after that. Tonight, though, I have something I want to show you." She smiled at Chris.

"What's that?"

"Come on." Paxton motioned toward the car as it pulled up in front of them.

They climbed in, and Paxton drove them away from the restaurant. They made a few turns here and there before Paxton pulled them into a parking garage, pulled a ticket from the machine, and parked the car. Chris assumed they were walking from there. She got out of the car. Paxton did as well and nodded to the right. Chris followed. They walked to the elevator. They took it to the ground floor and turned left onto the street. They took one more turn. Then, Paxton nodded toward the red door of an industrial building that was painted white. There was no sign that indicated this door was for any particular purpose. Nor was there a sign that said this was a place of business.

"Open it," Paxton said.

Chris did because she had no reason not to trust Paxton. Paxton followed her inside a small room that looked to be the size of a bathroom. It had one small table with an old red rotary dial phone. Chris looked around the dimly lit space and saw nothing else. She turned to Paxton, who wasn't saying anything.

"Pax? Where the hell are we?"

"Pick up the phone, dial two-zero-six. When someone picks up, tell them you need two tickets for the rainbow ride."

"What?" Chris laughed at her.

"Just do it." Paxton laughed back.

Chris picked up the phone and did what she was told. A man answered, and she felt ridiculous when she said, "I need two tickets for the rainbow ride."

"Password?" the man asked.

"He's asking for a password," Chris whispered to Paxton.

"Tell him the doctor is in," she said.

Chris said the words into the phone. The man didn't say anything back. He just hung up. Chris replaced the phone and wondered if she'd said it wrong. As she turned to Paxton, though, one of the walls in the room slid away, revealing a much larger room behind Paxton.

"What the hell?"

"Welcome to the *Midnight Oasis Speakeasy.* It's a big Seattle secret. We aren't supposed to bring tourists here, so if anyone asks, you're a Seattle native."

Paxton ushered her into a room that was just as dimly lit as the small room they'd just left. Chris watched the wall slide back into its place. She turned back around at the feel of Paxton's hand in her own. Paxton entwined their fingers to pull Chris in the direction of a wall-long dark wood bar that had deep red lighting emanating from beneath and behind it.

"What is this place?" Chris asked in a near-whisper.

People were mostly either sitting at the bar or at the tables that faced a small stage where a man was playing acoustic guitar. No one paid any attention to them save the bartender, who was a man in his mid-twenties. He wore what Chris had always seen bartenders and waiters wear in movies or TV shows about the nineteen-twenties. It was all so glamorous and kind of seedy at the same time.

"Southside," Paxton said to the bartender, who nodded at her. "Chris, want a real prohibition-style drink?"

"Sure," Chris replied, not knowing what else to say. "Whatever you're having is fine."

"Two of those, then," Paxton said to the bartender and then swiveled her stool in Chris's direction. "It's gin, mint, lime juice, and simple syrup. It got its name thanks to some gangsters on the South Side of Chicago, trying to cover up the taste of their terrible and illegal hooch."

"How did you find this place?" Chris asked as she watched the bartender muddle the fresh mint in front of their eyes.

"I sold it to the owner. One of the few commercial properties I've worked on." Paxton watched the guitarist on stage for a moment. "It's invite-only. Of course, the invitees tell people they know about it. The crowd starts to grow. They change the password every so often to keep it small and intimate. I thought you'd like to see it. I think it's cooler than the Space Needle, but if you want to check that out before we leave tomorrow, we can."

"No, this is pretty great. I've never been to a bar like this."

"They have theme nights sometimes. They did a steampunk night, which was pretty cool."

Two identical drinks were placed in front of them. To Chris, it kind of looked like a margarita with its light green shade. She liked margaritas, so she picked it up, watched Paxton take a sip of her own, and then followed suit. It was tart, with a hint of sweetness from the simple syrup. It kind of tasted like summer. She enjoyed it and took another sip. She watched Paxton watch the performer, noting how her green eyes had flecks of copper and gold in them. The woman's lips weren't full, but they were very kissable. That was how Chris would describe them. Paxton's lips were kissable. She placed her drink back down on the bar. If Paxton's lips were kissable, that meant Paxton herself was kissable. That wasn't right. Paxton annoyed her. She'd been rude to her. She was a woman of means who clearly didn't even care that the check on the bar said they owed thirty-two dollars for their drinks. Chris's eyes got wide when she noticed that. She turned back to Paxton, who was now looking back at her.

"Are you okay?" Paxton asked. "Do you need to go?"

"What? No. Why?" Chris asked back.

"I don't know. I was afraid you were feeling uncomfortable or something," Paxton replied.

"I'm okay." Chris smiled at her, picked up her drink, and took another long sip. "This is good."

Paxton smiled at her, turned, and saw the check. She

placed her card on top of it before turning to watch the performer on stage again. It was then that Chris realized that Paxton wasn't flaunting her wealth. She wasn't trying to show off. She was trying to show Chris a good time in her city. They hadn't actually talked all that much. Chris wondered if Paxton was giving Chris the headspace to get used to this new part of their relationship. They'd gone from acquaintances to a working relationship very quickly. Paxton hadn't been acting like a manager or boss, though. Honestly, Paxton had been acting more like a partner to Chris, which made no sense, because Paxton was the one in charge and with the purse strings.

They finished their drinks and watched as another performer got on stage to play the saxophone. It was a loud instrument, but in that space, despite how small it was, it felt perfect. Chris found herself looking at Paxton as the musician played a slow, bluesy song. She smiled as Paxton tucked her hair behind her ears occasionally. She ordered another round for both of them, feeling slightly tipsy already but not wanting to leave. She ordered them each a fourteen-dollar Hemingway daiquiri, which the bartender explained was rum and lime with maraschino liqueur and grapefruit. It sounded good. She slid Paxton's over to her, and was rewarded with a smile and a wink that had her thinking losing twenty-eight dollars plus tip was worth it.

After they finished their second drink, Paxton turned and whispered in her ear, "Are you ready to go?"

She wasn't, but she knew Paxton was. She nodded yes. Paxton pulled back and smiled at her again. Chris smiled back, feeling the alcohol nicely, along with the heat from her reddened cheeks. She hoped she didn't look too foolish. Maybe it was dark enough in the bar to hide it.

Paxton drove them back to her apartment, which took only fifteen minutes and wasn't enough time for Chris to get over the feeling of being drunk. She didn't want to be drunk in front of her boss, but it was more than that. She didn't want to be drunk in front of Paxton.

Paxton unlocked the door to the apartment and ushered Chris inside. Without a word, the woman went to her refrigerator and pulled out two bottles of water. She handed one to Chris before leaving the living room for the bathroom. A few moments later, Paxton emerged with ibuprofen. She passed two to Chris with a wink.

"Just in case," she said.

"Thanks," Chris replied and took the pills from her.

"I'm going to hop in the shower and get some sleep. You know where everything is, right?"

"Oh," Chris said. "Yes."

"Cool. See you tomorrow." Paxton went into her bedroom and closed the door behind her.

Chris was left in the living room wondering how she'd lost the moment she'd had in the bar. It had felt so peaceful there. Paxton's smile had lit up her whole face. Her eyes and those colorful flecks had Chris wondering what they'd look like from other angles; like, from above and below. She'd been so happy in that bar that she'd forgotten about everything else going on in her life. Now, Paxton was in the shower, having not felt the same thing, apparently. And Chris was left to sit on the end of the bed in the guest room trying to figure out exactly what was going on.

CHAPTER 10

PAXTON WOKE UP the next morning feeling tired, but excited. She'd fallen asleep around midnight, which was fine because she'd had an amazing night with Chris. After they'd gotten over the initial awkwardness of being alone together for the first time, things had gone well. Paxton was actually surprised, though, because she realized, as she stood in front of her mirror for one of the last times, that she knew very little about Chris. Wes hadn't exactly filled her in on the details of his life with his sister. She wouldn't have put him in that situation, anyway.

They'd hardly spoken to one another about anything that mattered, yet Paxton found herself happy at the thought of getting into a car with Chris and driving for hours upon hours. She had no real reason to be happy about that, but she was happy, nonetheless. She smiled at herself in the mirror more, because leaving this apartment behind was the first real step in this new part of her journey.

***

"What did you think of the fish throwing?" Paxton asked just after they'd gotten outside of the city.

"It was kind of funny. Very weird. I have no idea how they do that," Chris replied with a chuckle. "Fish are slimy, aren't they?"

"Not all fish, and not when they're frozen," Paxton replied.

"Thanks for taking me," Chris said.

"What did you think of my hometown?"

"I like Seattle. I can see myself coming back for a visit someday."

Chris leaned her head back against the headrest and closed her eyes briefly before opening them again and looking ahead at the road. Paxton turned to glance at her for a second before doing the same.

"Is South Lake your hometown?"

"You mean, was I born there?" Chris asked, turning her head to Paxton.

"Yeah. You know I'm from Seattle. Are you from South Lake, or did you move there?"

"I moved to South Lake right before I turned twenty-one. I grew up in Yerington, Nevada, which is a town no one has heard of, ever. It's probably still less than ten thousand people. There's basically nothing there," she said.

"What brought you to Tahoe?" Paxton asked, taking the turn onto the highway.

"That's a long story." Chris sighed.

"We have the next three days, Chris," Paxton replied.

"Things were going so well, Pax. Why ruin them by talking?" Chris asked, but Paxton knew it was a rhetorical question.

Paxton turned up the music, allowing that to show Chris she'd taken the hint. They drove in the car for two hours before Chris announced she needed to go to the bathroom. Paxton used the in-car GPS to help her identify if there was somewhere they could stop that was a little better than a gas station. Fortunately, there was a name she recognized from the list of small hotels and B&Bs she researched before she left. She'd found at least five worth stopping at along their drive. Chris said she could hold it for another half an hour or so. When they finally pulled up to the B&B, it was clear that Chris needed to go now. They made their way inside the small establishment, where Chris instantly went looking for a bathroom.

The front desk wasn't occupied, and in lieu of hitting the bell to let the proprietor know she was there, she decided to look around. The place was a little larger than hers. The lobby was off to the left. There was a comfy looking sofa, and floor to ceiling bookshelves were lining the back wall. Tables with a couple of old-looking yet still comfortable-looking chairs finished the room. Chris had disappeared through that room, looking for a bathroom. Paxton followed Chris's path through an open doorway into a small dining area that was smaller than her own. It only housed four tables and was empty.

"The kitchen's through there," Chris said when she emerged from what must have been the bathroom. "I saw it on my way back out. It's pretty tiny. I'm not sure they can fit more than two people in there at a time. That kind of limits what they can do food-wise here."

"Yeah?" Paxton asked.

"Plus, I haven't seen a soul since we got here. The parking lot is pretty sparse, too. I'm not sure we should model what we're doing after this place." Her eyes got big. "What *you* are doing. I meant what you're doing."

"Chris, we're in this together. I mean, literally. We're in this place together." Paxton motioned around them. "And we're trying to build something together."

Chris looked down at her hands and said, "We should get going before someone spots us and asks if we're checking in."

"Yeah, okay."

They got back in the car and hit the road. Paxton wondered what was going on with Chris because the woman was still relatively silent. They talked about the music on the radio, about the traffic, and about the weather, but that was about it for the next four hours. That was when Paxton pulled them over to stay for the night. It was a small, family-owned hotel, with fifteen guest rooms. It didn't have a restaurant, but it had outstanding reviews online. Paxton wanted to know what it was that they were doing right.

"Welcome. Checking in?" the woman behind the front desk asked Paxton.

"We don't have a reservation. I was hoping you still had something available," Paxton said.

"You're actually really lucky; we had a cancelation about an hour ago," the woman said. "I have one queen suite available."

"Only one?" Chris chimed in.

"Yes. Did you need two rooms?" the woman asked.

"Yes." Chris moved to stand beside Paxton.

Paxton tried not to take that personally and added, "You said suite, right?"

"Yes. It's a queen bedroom, but it has a pull-out sofa. Would that work for you?"

"I've been driving all day, Chris. I want to grab some dinner and get some rest. I'll sleep on the pull-out, okay?"

"Sure." Chris nodded.

They checked in and carried their bags up the single staircase to their room, since it was on the second floor. Paxton unlocked the door using an actual key, which she hadn't done in years. When they walked in, Paxton tried to put herself into the mindset of a hotel owner instead of merely a guest. The room was overly large, which was nice. There was a small living room off to the right, along with a sink and a microwave. Paxton guessed there was a mini-fridge in one of the cabinets under the sink. To the left were the bed and bathroom. The bed wasn't in a separate room. It was just sitting against the wall, with two bedside tables on either side. She'd expected a wall separating the living room from the bedroom, but they'd make do. Chris placed her bags next to the sofa and stretched. Paxton stood there, watching the woman who was wearing yoga pants and a t-shirt for the long drive. As Chris lifted her arms over her head, Paxton caught sight of the skin between the pants and the shirt. While Chris hadn't mentioned anything to her about working out, it was clear that her job waiting tables and running around for hours at a time had done her a lot of favors.

"What do you want for dinner?" Chris asked, turning

back to her.

"Oh, I don't care. Anything is fine."

"I saw a diner down the road. Want to take a walk? Might be nice getting out of the car for a while."

Paxton nodded. They freshened up a little and left the room. Paxton made notes of the wallpaper and patterned hotel carpet. She really wanted to avoid that in her place, but every hotel she'd ever stayed in had had the patterned carpet, which didn't show wear and tear as much as regular carpet. She made some other mental notes. Then, she held the door open for Chris as they made their way outside.

"You do that a lot, you know?" Chris asked.

"Do what?"

"Open doors for me," she replied.

"Is that a problem?" Paxton chuckled.

"No," Chris stated plainly.

They walked on for about half a mile without a word. The street wasn't a particularly busy one, but there were cars moving steadily past them as they made their way along the sidewalk.

"Chris?"

"Yeah?"

"Why'd you move to Tahoe?" Paxton tried again.

"Why does it matter, Pax?"

"Because we're in this together, remember? I'd like to know more about you."

Chris sighed and replied, "My parents died, okay?"

Paxton turned her head toward Chris at the same time she slid her hands into her pockets. She didn't know what to say to that or how to react. She supposed that no one really knew.

"That's why Wes lives with you?"

"They were killed when I was twenty and away at school. Wes was a kid then. He's still a kid now, but this was eleven years ago."

"And you had to go home to take care of him?"

"There wasn't anyone else. Look, when I said before

that it's a long story, I meant it. It really is a long story. It's not a particularly happy one, either. Are you sure you even want to hear it?"

"I'd like to if you want to tell me. You don't have to, though, Chris. It's up to you."

"My mom's family was in a cult in the middle of the desert, okay?" Chris stated. "My grandmother was one of thirteen wives to the leader of the cult. My mom was raised there. She was fourteen when they were about to marry her off to some man who was three times her age. She wanted to run but didn't know how or where to go. My dad's family lived in the town they used to go into for supplies. He was sixteen at the time. She told him one day that she wanted to leave. He told his parents. They helped her escape. Five years later, my mom and dad got married. I came along after that. They thought I'd be their only kid. Then, my mom got pregnant with Wes."

"That is a long story. I'm guessing you shortened it a bit, though," Paxton replied.

"Yes, it felt longer living it."

"Can I ask how they died, or should I not?"

"Carbon monoxide poisoning. They fell asleep one night and never woke up. Wes was at a sleepover that night. I was at school. I moved home right after and left school when I realized I needed to take care of him. My dad's parents had died before Wes was born, and my mom's parents were obviously not coming anywhere near my little brother. My mom had a lot of half-brothers and sisters, but they also weren't going anywhere near Wes. My dad was an only child. There was only me. I couldn't find work back home, and I knew Tahoe was a safe place to live and that I could probably find a job waiting tables or giving tours or something. We moved here, rented a tiny one-bedroom apartment at first, and then we moved where we are now. That's the story." Chris exhaled deeply. "And we're here." She pointed to the restaurant to her left. "I'm starving."

CHAPTER 11

THERE WERE PEOPLE who knew Chris's life story, but not many. Fewer knew the whole story. She'd left out the cult part to most people. It always caused them to ask more questions than she had answers for. She'd been born long after that part of her mother's life, and thankfully for her, her mother had left for her own safety. As she sat in the diner, looking across at Paxton who was looking at the table-sized jukebox that made the place feel very much retro, she wondered why Paxton hadn't asked any other questions. They sat down, they'd ordered, they'd eaten and were now waiting for their check, but Paxton hadn't said anything more to her about her story. She'd laughed as the waiter had made a joke. She'd gone to the bathroom. She'd come back to the table with a tiny container of mouthwash she'd bought in the bathroom vending machine solely because she thought the tiny container was cute and she had to have it. Chris just couldn't figure this woman out.

***

"Sorry," Paxton said when she bumped into Chris.
"Sorry," Chris said back.

Paxton was trying to get to the sofa while Chris had been trying to get to the bathroom. They passed one another awkwardly. Paxton was wearing shorts and a t-shirt with the Washington Huskies logo on the front. Chris was wearing an old t-shirt she'd gotten from Donoto's when she'd played on the softball team three years prior, and the same pair of yoga pants she'd been wearing all day. She brushed her teeth, her hair, and finished doing everything in the bathroom. Her hair was still wet from her shower, but she had no intention of drying it. She passed Paxton again on the way to the bed. Paxton had already pulled out the bed from the sofa and had the extra blanket the hotel provided lying on top of her.

"Good night, Chris."

"Night," Chris replied.

She climbed into bed, pulling the scratchy comforter up to her neck. Then, she fell asleep.

***

They spent the morning in the hotel room, packing up their things but also looking at the space and everything inside it, trying to figure out if they should include anything from this room in rooms of their own. Paxton took some pictures. Chris looked at the books and magazines provided by the hotel. Since the place didn't have its own restaurant, the owners offered delivery from the diner they'd been to the previous night as well as another local place for a small fee. Chris knew people could just order online through one of the many food delivery services for cheaper, and they likely did, which meant the hotel was out that delivery revenue. They loaded up the car soon after they grabbed coffee and pastries from the coffee place on the way out of town.

"We obviously have the added benefit of knowing Morgan. She'll hook us up with her tour guides that we can then offer from the hotel at a discount," Paxton said. "I think the restaurant is key, too. If we can keep guests inside the hotel, spending money, we make more. Pretty simple."

"You keep saying *we* a lot," Chris said.

"I told you, we're–"

"No, I don't mean you and me. I mean that it sounds like you're planning for the future, but a future you'll be involved in, Pax. Does this mean you're not selling it?" Chris asked her.

"I don't know for sure, but I'm enjoying this whole thing. I think I'd like to see how it goes in the beginning, maybe."

"That means you'll be sticking around Tahoe for a while, then," Chris replied.

"I guess so." Paxton smiled at her.

They pulled over at two more small hotels like Paxton's. They ate lunch at the first one while they questioned the proprietor about the other things the hotel offered. He was a kind old man, who volunteered a lot of details while he refilled their iced teas. The second place was a hotel that was slightly larger, with thirty guest rooms, but Paxton wanted Chris to check out the flow of the restaurant. They ate dinner there before they drove another hundred miles or so to arrive at their last stop of the night. Paxton had called the hotel earlier so as not to make the mistake she'd made the previous night. She'd made a reservation for two adjoining rooms.

For some reason, Chris was disappointed.

They checked in and went up the elevator to their rooms. This hotel was a Camden property. It had over one hundred rooms, a bar, a restaurant, and all the other more modern amenities, including an indoor pool. It was after nine when they made it inside their rooms and said goodnight. Chris called Wes to check on him. She changed into her pajamas and climbed into bed, feeling exhausted, despite not having driven a single mile today at Paxton's insistence. Around eleven, she still wasn't getting to sleep. She threw back the blanket and decided to take her restless body for a walk.

She made her way down to the lobby. Then, she turned at the front desk to walk down the narrow hall that she knew led out to the parking lot. She passed the business center, decided to check her email, since she had nothing else to do, and when she finished and stood, Chris heard a splash coming from nearby. She knew the pool was close and decided maybe she'd sit out by it for a while until she felt like going to sleep. When she made her way to the glass door leading to the pool, she noticed one woman in the water. She opened the door and sat in one of the chairs at the provided tables surrounding the pool. Chris watched the woman swim with near perfect form before she lifted her head out of the water and Chris realized who she'd been watching.

"Pax?"

"Oh, hey." Paxton made her way to the side of the pool, putting both of her arms on the side and resting her chin on her arms. "Couldn't sleep?"

"No. You?"

"This was the first place that had a pool. I thought I'd take advantage of it. I haven't gotten to swim regularly in a while."

"You have good form," Chris said and squeezed her eyes together in embarrassment. "I mean, I just saw you on that last lap back; it looked like it was good form."

"Do you swim?" Paxton asked.

"I did in high school. I wasn't bad."

"How *not* bad were you?" Paxton asked.

"I placed third at state my senior year."

"Damn, Chris. That's called being really good." Paxton pushed off from the wall.

"You?" Chris smiled at her.

"I swam in college. Well, for two years. I messed up my shoulder and couldn't compete anymore, but I still swim for fun whenever I can," Paxton replied. "What was your race?"

"Fifty, free."

"Speed demon, huh?" Paxton asked as she stood in the middle of the pool with the water coming up to just above her breasts. "I was the four hundred, free. But I did some short distance butterfly, too."

"How good were you?"

"State champ senior year. That's how I got my scholarship," Paxton replied.

"Of course, you were the state champ," Chris said and leaned forward in her chair.

"We should race sometime," Paxton suggested.

"I'd say we could do it now, but I'm not exactly dressed for it, and I didn't bring a suit."

"There's an extra in my car. That's where I got this one from. We're about the same size."

"You want to race me?" Chris asked with a lifted eyebrow.

"Why not?"

"All right, Champ. I'll grab the keys and change. Give me ten minutes."

"It's in the blue bag in the trunk. Side pocket."

Chris couldn't believe what she was doing. She grabbed Paxton's car keys from the table, went out to the parking lot, opened the trunk, and quickly found the one-piece suit. It was the same kind as the one Paxton had on, only a different color. She made her way back inside, found the restroom off the lobby, and changed into the suit. She slid her shorts over it but didn't bother putting on a shirt. When she got to the pool, Paxton was underwater, swimming to the end nearest to her. Chris stripped off the shorts, tossed all her things and Paxton's keys on the table, and dove into the side of the pool. When she broke the surface of the water, she opened her eyes and caught Paxton staring at her. She swam in her direction.

"You ready?" she asked.

"Let's do this," Paxton replied. "Pick your race. We'll do best two out of three."

"Then, it should be the fifty, because I'm already wiped from the day."

"Not exactly official size here. How about we just do one back and forth and call that a race?"

"Three of those? Best two out of three?"

"Let's get out and do it right, though. Dive in from the deep end." Paxton swam to the shallow end of the pool and walked out. Chris watched her for a moment until she did the same. They walked around to the other end of the pool where the water was at six feet. They lined up about five feet away from one another, since that was about all the space they could safely take. Chris looked over at Paxton and nodded at her. Then, Paxton said, "Three. Two. One. Go!"

Chris jumped into the water, instantly remembering her old training. The muscle memory launched her forward and then up in the water. She had no idea where Paxton was in relation to the lead. She knew she was close by the other woman but had no clue who was technically winning as they took the turn and headed back in the direction from which they'd come. When she tapped the wall under the water, she looked over and found Paxton was already well above the water.

"I guess you took the first one," Chris said through heavy breathing.

"Well, I was kind of warmed up already," Paxton replied. "Round two?"

Chris won the second race, but not by much. She also wasn't completely sure she'd won. It wasn't like anyone else had been standing above them to see who touched first. They didn't actually finish the third race. The pool didn't have ropes preventing them from running into one another. Neither knew who was actually at fault, but their legs ended up smacking into one another halfway through the final lap. They both popped up out of the water.

"Pax!" Chris half-yelled and gave Paxton's shoulder a shove.

"That was all you! I was in my lane, Chris."

"We have to start over," Chris suggested as she trod water.

"I think we should call it a night. Your leg is all muscle or something, because that actually hurt." Paxton reached down to her thigh.

"I hurt you?" Chris moved a little closer. "Where?"

"I'll be fine. But I should probably stop, since I'm driving tomorrow."

"I'm sorry."

"See? You're apologizing. That means it was your fault," Paxton argued.

"Bullshit, swim champ." Chris swam back toward the shallow end of the pool. "And for the record, you just forfeited. That means I'm the winner."

"If you're the type of person that likes to win because of a technicality," Paxton replied, following her out of the pool.

"I'll take any win I can get with you," Chris said.

CHAPTER 12

İT WAS THE STRANGEST THING TO Paxton. She'd spent the past three days and nights with Chris, and she hadn't felt truly alone the whole time they were together, even though they'd had their own rooms that last night. She'd just dropped Chris off at home, though, and within five minutes, she felt alone.

They'd taken a little longer to get back than she'd planned. They'd stayed at the hotel that morning, opening the door between their rooms, had room service brought up, and talked while they ate. Then, they checked out and took a scenic drive, as they'd done the previous day. They also took a look at another bed and breakfast and even stopped at a beautiful mountain overlook for a few moments so that Chris could take some pictures. They'd laughed some in the car. They'd talked about their swim race from the previous night as well as some of their good races from when they competed. Chris had begun to open up to her. After Paxton dropped Chris off, she went to her apartment to shower and change for bed. She smiled at the thought of Chris finally opening up to her as she checked the alarm on her phone to ensure it would wake her up on time the following morning. Then, she fell asleep.

***

"How'd your trip go?" Kinsley asked Paxton.

"Fine. We took the long way back. It was nice," she replied.

"We?" Kinsley asked.

"Oh, I took Chris with me. We made a business trip out of it."

"Where *is* Chris?" Kinsley asked as she looked around the mostly demolished property.

"She went to get us lunch. She should be back in a minute. I didn't know you were stopping by or I would have gotten you something," Paxton said.

"I was driving past this place on the way back from a showing, saw your car was here, and thought I'd check it out. It looks…" Kinsley glanced around, probably trying to figure out what to say next.

"Terrible?"

"Yes," Kinsley said through a laugh.

"I know. That's the idea. I want all this crap gone. Then, we'll make it look good."

"*We* again?"

"Yes, Chris and me. I mean, she's my only full-time employee. Wes helps on the weekends, and we had a crew in here this past weekend while we were gone, finishing the demo. I've got a contractor coming over tomorrow to check things out. We'll go from there."

"So, you're keeping the place?"

"I think so." Paxton smiled at her new friend. They were both sitting on the only remaining structure in the place, the front desk. "I have no idea how successful I'm going to be at owning or even running a hotel, but I'm going to try."

"I think I remember Kellan saying she knows someone who knows someone who runs hotels. Have you asked her about that?"

"No, I didn't know that," Paxton replied. Then, she saw Chris's car heading toward them and turning into the lot. She smiled. "I'll ask her about it, though."

"Hey, can I ask you something?"

"Sure." Paxton turned to Kinsley.

"What's going on with you two?"

"Who?"

"You and Chris," Kinsley replied.

"Oh, nothing. We're working together. Why?"

"I just saw you smile when she pulled in," Kinsley said.

"She's bringing food, Kinsley. I skipped breakfast this morning." Paxton climbed off the desk.

"She's single. You're single." Kinsley jumped down, too.

"So, because we're two single, gay ladies, we must be into one another?"

"Are you?" Kinsley asked with a lifted eyebrow.

"Hey. Oh, hey Kinsley," Chris said when she entered.

"Hi, Chris." Kinsley moved in Chris's direction. "I was just heading back to the office."

"Do you want to stay for lunch?" Chris asked as Kinsley walked past her.

"No, Riles and I are having lunch together today. Thanks, though. I'll see you guys later. Have fun."

Kinsley walked out. Moments later, Paxton saw her car leaving the lot. Chris approached the front desk and laid out their food.

"Everything okay?" she asked Paxton.

"Yeah. Why?"

"I don't know. Just thought something might be off or something," Chris said.

"What would be off?"

"I don't know, Pax. I was just asking a question," Chris replied. "God, just eat your damn lunch. I didn't get a lot of sleep last night, and I didn't have breakfast because I had to deal with a garbage disposal that Wes accidentally dropped a spoon into before flipping the switch."

"So, what you're saying is that you're hangry?" Paxton asked with a smile.

Chris laughed, despite her attempts to stop herself, and said, "Yes, that's what I'm saying."

***

It was a few days later, when Wes arrived to get started at work, Paxton realized that not only did she really like Wesley Florence, she also kind of missed his older sister. Chris worked with her Monday through Friday. Wes was there Saturday and Sunday. It was Sunday. The two of them were talking about Chris picking him up in a few minutes when her heart started to race at the thought of Chris being there. She actually looked down at her tattered jeans and dusty shirt and wished she'd thought to bring a change of clothes.

"Chris, what are we doing for dinner tonight?" Wes asked Chris almost as soon as she'd arrived.

"I don't know yet. Why?" Chris asked him, ruffling his hair. "Hey, Pax."

"Hi," Paxton offered with a wave from the front yard where she was loading up debris to take to the bin off to the side of the yard.

"Can Pax come over?"

"What?" Chris asked.

"She just told me she has nothing in her kitchen and was going to get fast food. I was thinking she could come over to our place instead. I could make burgers on the grill." He turned a little to Paxton. "My burgers are legendary."

Paxton laughed and stopped working.

"I bet they are," she replied.

"Paxton, do you want to come to our place for dinner?" Chris asked because she really had no choice.

"I don't want to intrude on your family night," Paxton replied because she also really had no choice.

"We don't have a family night," Wes said. "Come on. I'll make tater tots, too."

"Oh, well, if there are tater tots, I'm definitely in." Paxton laughed.

"Cool."

"Chris, is it really okay? You can say no," Paxton said

softly so only Chris could hear.

"It's fine. I'll run to the store to get everything. Can you give us, like, an hour?"

"I have to go home and change, so that's fine. What can I bring?" Paxton asked, rubbing her dirty hands over her jeans.

"Nothing," Chris replied. "Just you."

Paxton smiled at that. Then, she saw Chris smile, too.

"I'll see you soon then," she said.

An hour or so later, Paxton pulled into the driveway of Chris's house. She'd taken the extra time to stop for a bottle of wine, flowers for Chris, and grabbed a giant bag of candy for Wes, since she had no idea what teenage boys liked. She knocked but then heard Wes yelling at her to come around back. She walked around the side of the small house and saw Wes working an old charcoal grill. The backyard was small and butted up against another house's yard and chain link fence. In lieu of a patio, they had a slab of concrete on which rested a card table with three folding chairs.

"Hey, Pax," Wes greeted with a wave.

"Hey. I brought you this. I didn't know if you'd like it. It's a variety bag." She held up the huge bag of candy.

"Well, that'll get him through college," Chris replied as she made her way outside. "Hey."

"Hi," Paxton said.

It was as if something had changed between them without either of them knowing. There was a new kind of tension now that hadn't existed around them before.

"I got you this." Paxton held up the wine easily since Wes had taken the bag of candy. "And these, too."

"Flowers?" Chris asked with a smile. "I don't think I've ever been–"

"Chris, are the tots done?" Wes asked, covering the burgers.

"Yes, I just pulled them out. You want to go grab everything?" she asked him.

"You guys sit down. I've got this." He pulled out two chairs, one for the each of them, and went inside the sliding glass door.

"He really is a great kid," Paxton said.

"He is. I'm proud of him," Chris replied.

"You should be proud of yourself, too, Chris. You helped make him this way. He's respectful at work. He does everything I ask him, and sometimes before I ask him, too. He told me he's studying like crazy to get his grades up, and he's a great tennis player. Now, he's cooking us dinner. I don't know many seventeen-year-old boys that are like that. Give yourself some credit."

"I'll give myself credit when he graduates college with a degree in something he's passionate about," Chris replied, sitting in one of the folding chairs. "Should I open that? I don't even know if I have a corkscrew here." She pointed at the wine Paxton had placed on the table.

"Next time," Paxton replied. "We can open it next time. I'll buy a corkscrew for you."

"Next time?" Chris asked with a lifted eyebrow.

"Everything on your burger, Pax?" Wes peeked his head through the door.

"Everything's fine," Paxton replied.

"No onions for me," Chris added.

"Then, no onions for me," Paxton said with a glance in Chris's direction.

"I'll get it ready in there and then bring the plates out. We can add the burgers then." He disappeared inside again.

"And, yes, next time," Paxton said.

CHAPTER 13

THE WORK HAD OFFICIALLY begun on the remodel. Chris and Paxton had moved their stuff out back to the patio to work. They'd set a table with two chairs and worked most days side by side. They'd been doing so for a full week. Chris had noticed a difference in their ability to work together since they'd returned from Seattle. They'd been joking a lot more, exchanging glances they never had before, and Chris was happy. She smiled at the thought as Paxton walked away from their space to take a phone call from one of her employees back in Seattle.

"I have the samples you wanted." A man approached. "Should I wait for your…" He scratched the back of his head with his free hand. "Your partner?"

"Oh, this is Paxton's place." She looked up at him. This had happened twice before, with various members of the crew coming and going. One had even called Paxton her wife. "I work for her."

"She works *with* me," Paxton clarified, approaching the man from behind. "And are we talking tile samples or paint samples?"

"Paint today. Tile samples should be in tomorrow," he replied, placing a book of paint samples on the table.

"Okay. Thanks," Paxton replied, sitting down next to Chris.

He walked off. Paxton dove into the sample book. Chris moved in a little closer to take a look herself. When she did, though, she smelled Paxton's shampoo or lotion. It was fruity but mixed with sweat, that came from hard work, and the heat, from sitting outside. The breeze from the water was a Godsend. She glanced down at the samples Paxton was flipping through, and she had the strangest thought. What would it be like, doing this with Paxton for real? The hotel was real, obviously, but she was considering what it would be like to paint a house with Paxton or pick out tile for a bathroom they shared. She shook her head and turned out to the lake.

"Beautiful day, huh?" Chris said.

"It is." Paxton looked up at her. "Hey, Adler and Morgan are back tomorrow night. I was thinking about having a little thing for them at their place. Nothing big. Maybe just a dinner and some drinks. I'd do it at my apartment, but it's tiny, and I haven't unpacked."

"Sounds like fun," Chris replied, running her hand through her hair.

"I'm probably going to take off from here tomorrow, to pick up the stuff I need to cook. I have to be extra careful, since my sister thinks I'll burn the house down any time I cook." She laughed a little and looked back down at the swatches. "Do you want to maybe cut out of here with me and hit the grocery store?"

"You need me to supervise your grocery shopping?" she joked.

"No, I was thinking you could come to the dinner thing. I could bring you with me." Paxton looked up at her for a moment and then averted her eyes to the water. "We could cook together. I know Adler would feel safer if I had a chaperone in her kitchen."

"So, you need a cooking supervisor?" Chris asked with a smile.

Paxton met her eye again and replied, "Sure."

Then, she looked back at her samples. Chris knew something had happened there, though. Paxton's smile had disappeared with Chris's last couple of questions. She'd only been joking, but that hadn't come through to Paxton, apparently. Chris didn't know what to say now. She wasn't certain if she and Paxton were going to cook together tomorrow or not, after all. She looked over at the water again and wondered why it mattered so much.

***

"Morgan doesn't like tomatoes," Chris explained. "She eats tomato sauce, but not uncooked tomatoes."

"How do you know that?" Paxton asked her while she chopped the tomato on the cutting board in front of her.

"Hi, I'm Chris. I waited on Morgan at Donoto's for nearly a dozen years." She waved at Paxton and laughed at her own joke.

"I guess you would know, then. Do *you* like tomatoes?" Paxton asked.

"You can put them on my salad, yes."

"What about peppers? Onions?"

"Are you putting onions on the salads?" Chris asked.

"No, I just wanted to know."

Chris stood on one side of the kitchen island while Paxton stood on the other. Chris was getting the dishes out of the cabinets before taking them to the table where she'd set it for the surprise dinner to welcome back Adler and Morgan.

"I like onions okay; just not on burgers. And I'm not a fan of onion rings." Chris placed four plates around the table. "I can do without peppers, but I'll eat them."

"What about carrots?"

"Carrots are fine," Chris replied, placing the silverware next to the plates. "What about you?"

"I hate cooked carrots. Raw carrots are fine, though.

Peppers are good. Onions are okay."

"I already know you like asparagus, since I've seen you eating that. What about broccoli or cauliflower?"

Paxton placed tomatoes in three bowls of salad and replied, "Broccoli – yes. Cauliflower – no."

"Me too." Chris looked up at her and smiled.

Paxton smiled back and then returned to her chopping. Chris finished setting the table and moved back into the kitchen, standing next to Paxton, who was cleaning up the cutting board mess she'd made. Chris took a tomato from one of the salads and ate it. Paxton looked over at her and laughed.

"You couldn't wait, like, an hour?" Paxton asked.

"Nope. I didn't have lunch today because someone needed me to take a call with the contractor," Chris retorted.

"Because I was–" Paxton started and stopped. "Do you want a snack before dinner?" Paxton asked her. "They won't be home until, like, six-thirty."

"What can I have?" Chris asked.

"Cheese and crackers? I can open some now, and we can still have some later when they get here," Paxton suggested.

"I'll get the cheese. You get the crackers," Chris replied, moving to the refrigerator.

Paxton pulled out the box of crackers they'd bought and tore open a sleeve. Chris returned with the sharp cheddar. They sliced some while chatting. Then, Paxton pulled out the two bottles of the same red wine she'd bought, poured them into Adler's decanter that she'd gotten her for one of her birthdays, and poured the contents of both bottles into it, allowing the wine to breathe well in advance of dinner. Chris watched and ate as she worked. She smiled at Paxton occasionally but rescinded that smile when Paxton stole the last piece of cheese from the plate on the island.

"What? Did you want this?" Paxton asked, holding up the slice of cheese between two fingers. "I didn't know."

She smiled at Chris.

"You know how hangry I can get," Chris said. "Are you sure you want to take the last one?"

"Maybe I like you when you're hangry," Paxton replied with an ever-widening smile.

"You do, huh?" Chris took a step toward her. "Why is that?"

"It's funny."

"My hunger is funny to you?" Chris asked.

"Maybe," Paxton replied, laughing. "Do you want this, though? If you do, you'll have to come and get it."

Chris's phone rang in her pocket. She pulled it out and said, "It's Wes. Hold that thought." She put the phone to her ear. "Hey. What's up?"

"My car died again. I'm at the tennis courts. Can you come pick me up? There's no one here to jump it," he replied.

"It has a new battery."

"I know. I'm not even sure it is the battery. It just won't start."

Paxton placed her hand on Chris's stomach over her shirt as she leaned in a little, more likely, to make sure everything was okay with Wes. It was such a simple gesture, and in no way it meant anything, but that didn't stop Chris's body from reacting.

"I'll be there as soon as I can," she replied.

"What's wrong?" Paxton asked.

"His car won't start. He's over at the school." She covered the phone and met Paxton's eyes. "I need to pick him up. I can come back later."

Paxton picked up her phone and asked, "The high school, right?" She opened something on her phone.

"Yeah. Why?"

"Tell him I'm sending an Uber to him right now."

"Pax—"

Paxton took the phone from Chris, put it on speaker, and said, "Hey, Wes? I'm ordering you an Uber. It'll be there soon, okay?"

"Hey, Pax. Okay. That's cool."

"Is it cool if your sister has dinner with me and my sister tonight? And my sister's girlfriend?"

"Yeah, of course," he replied, appearing to be surprised she'd ask.

"I'll have her home before midnight," Paxton joked, smirking up at Chris.

"Wes, are you sure? I can come get you."

"No, I'm good. You have fun at dinner. I'll make a frozen pizza or something."

Paxton handed Chris back the phone. She said goodbye to her brother and disconnected.

"You didn't have to do that," Chris told her, placing the phone on the counter.

"I didn't want you to leave." Paxton looked up from her own phone. "The car is four minutes away. We can track him from the app if you're worried or something. Do you guys have triple A?"

"No," Chris replied.

"Okay. When we leave later, I'll call a tow truck to meet us out there. I'll have them take it to a shop, and they can figure out what's wrong with it."

"Paxton, you don't have to do that." Chris took a few steps away from her and ended up with her back against the pantry door. "We can't—"

Paxton took a few steps toward her and replied, "You don't like people taking care of you, do you?"

"I wouldn't really remember what that's like. Wes tries, but he's a kid," Chris said.

"He's a great kid that's about to be a great adult soon. He'll be in college or somewhere else, and you'll be on your own. Who's going to take care of you then?" Paxton asked with a smile.

"I like to think I can take care of myself, Paxton," Chris retorted.

"Sure. I know that. You've made it very clear how self-sufficient you are. To be honest, it's…"

"It's what?" Chris asked when Paxton faded and looked down at the floor.

"It's sexy." Paxton looked back up at her. "*You* are sexy."

"I am?" Chris asked, a little surprised.

Paxton nodded and said, "Yes." She paused. "And when I asked about someone taking care of you, I didn't mean it how you took it. I just meant that it's nice to have someone around to take care of you from time to time. Make dinner. Do the dishes."

"You just described a housekeeper," Chris replied. "Is that what you meant?" Paxton shook her head from side to side; her green eyes were now a little darker than they'd been a few minutes earlier. "Then, what did you mean?"

Paxton didn't reply again. She moved into Chris then. Her hands went to Chris's waist. Her green eyes remained on Chris's blue ones. Chris's heart pounded. This was not at all how she thought this night would go.

"Don't you want someone who's there with you through everything? Adler has Morgan. Kinsley has Riley. Reese has Kellan."

"Who do you have?" Chris asked.

"A few ex-girlfriends that never amounted to much," Paxton replied.

"Pax." Chris gave her a light show backward.

"What?" Paxton asked, taken aback a little.

"You were supposed to say something like, *'no one'* or, *'I don't know yet, but I want to see where this goes,'* or something better than referencing your ex-girlfriends while you were about to kiss me."

"Who said I was about to kiss you?" Paxton fired back.

"Your hands were on my hips, Pax. What else were you going to do?"

"Maybe I just thought you needed a hug," Paxton returned.

"Really? Really?" Chris moved around the open

doorway of the kitchen and into the foyer of the large house. "Bullshit, Pax."

Paxton pulled Chris's arm back and pressed the woman into the wall. The picture frames hanging from it shifted with the bump. Then, Paxton's lips were on Chris's. Chris's arms wasted no time. They moved around Paxton's shoulders, pulling her in closer, because this was it; this was what she wanted. She didn't know it, at first. Then, she thought she knew it. Now, she definitely knew it. Paxton Williams was a great kisser. Her lips were soft and hot. They moved against Chris's. Chris felt like saying 'finally' out loud, but that would break the kiss, which she did not want to do. Paxton's hands were on her hips again. Then, they were traveling up, under Chris's shirt. Chris thought about stopping this, but only for a moment. Paxton's lips were on her neck then. They were nipping and sucking at the same time her hands grasped both of Chris's breasts through her bra, and Chris moaned when Paxton squeezed them. She couldn't remember when she'd last done this. It had been so long ago. She tried to remember who it had been with, but as a few names swirled around in her brain, Paxton's lips met her own again, and all those names disappeared.

"Pax," she whispered.

Chris's hands moved to Paxton's jeans. She unbuckled the belt, then unbuttoned and unzipped the jeans to let Paxton know where her mind was heading. Chris knew what she wanted now. She wasn't waiting any longer. Paxton pulled back for only a second to pull the shirt over Chris's head. She glanced down at Chris's breasts, smirked a cocky smirk, and met her lips with Chris's again.

"Upstairs," Paxton said into Chris's mouth. "Guest room?"

"No, here." Chris maneuvered Paxton against the wall across from them. "Now." She slid her hand down into Paxton's underwear.

"Fuck," Paxton let out in a sexy husk.

Chris stroked Paxton hard, loving the wetness that

now coated her fingers. She pressed into Paxton, kissing her neck for a few moments while she sped up her strokes. Paxton reached for the hem of her own shirt, pulling it off her body and tossing it to the floor. Chris used her free hand to lift the cups of Paxton's bra, revealing the breasts beneath. She bent just enough to take a nipple into her mouth. Paxton's hips bucked when she nibbled on it. Then, Chris slid inside and stood up straight, watching Paxton's eyes close and open. She was inside Paxton. Her fingers were thrusting up and into her. Paxton was pulling down at her pants because she wanted more of Chris. Chris knew by Paxton's expression that she wanted Chris everywhere. Chris used her free hand to help Paxton lower her own jeans down past her knees.

Chris pumped inside her, curled her fingers, and used her thumb to play with the clit that had grown swollen and hard since she'd last touched it only moments before. She wanted to tell Paxton how sexy she was right now. She wanted to explain why she'd needed to just take her against this wall instead of going all the way upstairs to some guest room. She'd needed her after that initial kiss. She couldn't wait to go upstairs because her brain might try to talk her out of what they were currently doing. What they were currently doing felt so good, she couldn't imagine *not* doing it. She watched as Paxton tossed her own bra to the floor before reaching for Chris's. Then, Chris's was on the dark hardwood beneath their feet, too. She knew Paxton wanted to touch her. She could tell by the way Paxton was reaching for her jeans and unbuttoning them. Chris didn't want that, though, not yet.

"Pax, you first," Chris whispered into her ear. "Come for me."

"Oh my God," Paxton replied.

Chris thrust harder, stroked faster. Paxton's hips moved off the wall. Chris knew Paxton was close. She also knew she wanted to see her. Chris wanted to see all of her, touch all of her, taste all of her. She knelt in front of Paxton then, pulling on the light gray panties that were the only barrier to Paxton's sex. She pushed back inside Paxton, who was clearly ready to come if the way she gripped Chris's head and moved her mouth to her center was any indication.

"A little greedy, aren't you?" Chris joked.

"I'm so close, Chris," Paxton replied.

Chris couldn't wait any longer. She parted Paxton with her free hand and slid her tongue through her folds. She'd never understood how some women said women they'd slept with tasted good. She'd slept with a few women who had said that to her the first time they'd gone down on her, and she'd been convinced it was just their way of saying they liked doing that to her. In Paxton's case, though, Chris thought she did taste good. She wanted more of her. She pulled out of Paxton entirely and looked up at the woman's shocked expression as Paxton met her eyes. Chris slid both of her fingers coated in Paxton's desire into her own mouth, sucking on them until she was done. Paxton's jaw dropped slightly. Her eyes closed. Her head went back against the wall. Chris moved her fingers back inside and filled her. She sucked Paxton's clit into her mouth. Paxton's hand tightened in her hair. Then, she said Chris's name a few times, her hips bucked hard against Chris's face, and she came.

CHAPTER 14

"HOLY SHIT, CHRIS," Paxton said.

Chris was still kneeling between Paxton's legs; her tongue was sliding around Paxton's folds, her inner thighs, and her abdomen. Chris's lips kissed her hip bones. Then, she lowered again and kissed Paxton's still hard clit, staying there for a moment.

"Yeah," Chris replied. "Holy shit."

"I can't believe–"

"Neither can I."

Paxton rubbed the back of Chris's head to get the woman to look up at her, and then said, "I want to do that again."

"That can be arranged," Chris replied; her tongue slid between Paxton's lips.

"Not right now," Paxton said through laughter. "I'll fall over if you do that again."

Chris looked around and said, "I am kneeling on your sister's floor."

"You are. And I'm practically naked, leaning against the wall." Paxton laughed. "I am very, very content right now, so I do not care." Then, she looked down at Chris. "I'd like to make you very, very content right now. Can I?"

"You're asking permission?" Chris chuckled and moved to stand, but Paxton kicked off the rest of her clothes and surprised Chris by getting down on the floor with her. "What are–"

"You said here." Paxton pulled the woman in by the hips. "And you said now."

"Pax, what time will they be home?" Chris asked as Paxton kissed her neck.

"Not until six-thirty. We're fine," Paxton replied,

lowering Chris to the floor.

"So, that wasn't their car I just heard pulling up?" Chris asked. Paxton shot up and stared at the door. Chris burst into laughter. "I was kidding."

Paxton looked down at her and smiled. She reached for Chris's jeans and pulled them down as Chris watched. She lowered them along with the woman's underwear until Chris was nude and beneath her.

"You're annoying, but you're beautiful," Paxton told her.

Chris wrapped her arms around Paxton's neck. Paxton fell into her eyes then. They were so blue, so intense, so dark and yet so light at the same time. Paxton leaned down and pecked Chris's nose with her lips.

"Pax, maybe we should talk before…"

"I think it's a little late for before, Chris." Paxton laughed but grew serious when she realized Chris wasn't laughing. "What's wrong?" She sat up, straddling Chris.

"Nothing. Nothing's wrong. We just kind of started and we didn't talk about–"

"Shit. That *was* a car pulling up," Paxton said, climbing off Chris instantly.

They both rushed to their clothing. Then, they rushed in two different directions to dress. Paxton wasn't sure where Chris had ended up, but she had ended up in the dining room. She threw her jeans over her legs without the underwear, which she'd tucked into her back pocket. Her bra went on. Her shirt was pulled over it. She tried to straighten it, but she had no time. The front door opened. She hustled to the kitchen and went to the sink to wash her hands, but Chris had beaten her to it and was washing her own. Paxton just stood there with her hands pressed to the island as Adler and Morgan came into the kitchen.

"Hey, guys. I saw your car out there, Pax," Adler said. "Hey, Chris."

"Hi," Chris replied without looking at them.

"She's just cleaning up," Paxton said. "We were

making you guys dinner."

"You were?" Morgan asked as she approached from behind Adler. "That's awesome. Addie and I were just trying to figure out what we were going to have. Do I have time to change?"

"We haven't even started cooking yet," Paxton replied.

"I'll get everything out of the fridge," Chris added.

"I assume you'll be keeping an eye on my accident-prone sister?" Adler asked Chris.

"One time. It happened *one* time," Paxton replied with a smile in Adler's direction.

"You can go change, too. I'll keep an eye on her," Chris offered.

"Awesome. We'll be right back."

Adler and Morgan made their way up the stairs. Paxton turned around to see Chris staring at her. They didn't say anything for a moment. Paxton reached for Chris's hand and took it with her own.

"When we finish up here, we'll talk, okay?" Paxton said.

"It's fine, Pax." Chris turned around to face the sink, placing both hands on the edge.

Paxton turned back to make sure the coast was clear. Then, she turned to Chris, brushed the hair away from her neck, pressed her lips to the skin, and wrapped her arms around Chris's waist.

"Please don't pull away from me."

"I'm not." Chris sighed. "Your sister's home, Paxton."

"I don't care if she knows about us," Paxton said and kissed the spot again.

"What about us? We just had sex in her hallway. Are you going to tell her that?"

"I wasn't planning on it, no." Paxton pulled back, leaving a foot of space between them.

"Then, what would you even tell her, Paxton?" Chris moved to the refrigerator.

"I guess nothing," Paxton muttered to herself.

***

"I'll see you at work tomorrow," Paxton said.

Chris turned her head to Paxton, sighed, and looked away. Then, she got out of the car. Paxton watched her walk to her front door, open it, and close it behind her. Paxton stared at the house for a while, not knowing what else to do. They'd gone from flirting to kissing, from kissing to having sex, to then not speaking the rest of the night. Paxton had called the tow truck for Wes's car while Chris had been talking to Adler outside. They said they'd take care of it. Earlier that day, when Chis had dropped her car off at home after work and Paxton had driven them both to the grocery store and later to Morgan and Adler's, neither of them, it seemed, predicted the night would go like this and that a drive home would get awkward as a result.

Paxton put the car in reverse. She turned around to check behind her. Then, she looked ahead again, noticing the front door open. She watched Chris emerge. The woman stood there with her arms folded over her chest. Paxton stared at her, not knowing what to do. Then, Chris went back inside, leaving the front door open behind her. Paxton looked around, as if thinking her surroundings would provide the answer. Then, she turned off the car, climbed out, and went toward the house. She closed the door quietly behind her. Wes wasn't in the living room or kitchen, which meant he was likely in his bedroom. She wasn't sure if he was sleeping, but she was pretty sure Chris didn't want him to know what had happened between them.

Chris wasn't in any of the locations either, which meant she was in her own bedroom. Paxton had gotten the tour her first time there, so she walked down the short narrow hall past the closed door of Wes's bedroom and the bathroom the siblings shared. Chris's door was partially open. Paxton pushed it the rest of the way, praying she'd interpreted Chris's message correctly. Chris was standing in front of her bed. She was facing the window that was covered by curtains. Paxton closed the door behind her but didn't move into the room any farther.

"I'm sorry," Chris said.

"For what?" Paxton asked softly.

"I've never done that before, Pax." Chris turned to her.

"Sex?"

"What? No." Chris laughed softly. "I've had sex. I've had a lot of sex."

"Okay... TMI." Paxton held up one hand and made a disgusted face.

"I'm assuming you're no virgin, either," Chris replied, still laughing.

"No, I am not. I mean, I wasn't before you–" She didn't finish her sentence.

"Basically attacked you at your sister's house?" Chris sat on the bed.

"I wasn't complaining."

"I meant that I've never *just* had sex with someone."

"Who says it was just sex, Chris?" Paxton asked, taking a few steps into the room but not touching her.

"I've always been in a relationship, Paxton. That's what I mean. I've never just slept with someone without some kind of a commitment beforehand. I'm not a one-night stand kind of person, and I've never been one to sleep with someone on a first date."

"And we haven't even had a date?" Paxton asked her.

"Right."

"So, that's why you pulled away tonight?"

"I pulled away for that reason, but also because I have no idea what I'm doing with you," Chris said.

"You seemed to know what you were doing earlier," Paxton replied and smiled at her.

Chris looked up at her and smiled back.

"You know what I mean," Chris said.

Paxton knelt on the floor in front of her, pressing her own hands to Chris's knees.

"Let's go out."

"What?" Chris laughed.

"Let's go out, Chris. Christina Florence, will you go out with me?"

"We work together, Pax. You're my boss."

"Shit." Paxton pulled back at that. "Am I about to get sued for sexual harassment?"

"No," Chris replied, sliding her hand through Paxton's hair. "I'm the one that pushed you against that wall and shoved my hand down your pants."

"I'm the one that's wanted you to do that for a while now, though."

"Yeah?" Chris asked.

"Will you?"

"Go out with you?"

"That's what I'm asking you, yes."

Chris bit her lower lip and replied, "Do you want to stay?" She nodded toward the bed.

"Yes. But I won't if you're not ready." Paxton kissed Chris's knee through her jeans.

"Stay," Chris replied.

Paxton looked up at her and said, "Okay."

She stood. Chris followed her movements with her eyes. She reached forward and pulled on Paxton's silver belt buckle to get her to move closer. With Chris's legs spread, Paxton moved completely into her. Paxton's arms wrapped around Chris's neck. She watched Chris unbuckle her belt for the second time that day. Then, she watched Chris lift up her shirt and kiss her stomach. Paxton's skin registered the sensation and reacted with tingles all over it. She leaned down to lift Chris's shirt over her head. Chris let her and followed by unclasping her own bra. Paxton removed her bra next. Then, she slid out of her jeans. Chris looked at her. Her eyes roamed over Paxton's body. They stopped at Paxton's underwear. Chris leaned forward and kissed Paxton just above her center. That caused a rush of arousal and heat to flood Paxton's system, which made it harder to do what she was about to do. She pulled down her own underwear, reached for Chris's jeans, pushing Chris on the bed in the process, and tugged them off her body along with Chris's underwear. Once they were both naked, she climbed on top of Chris. They made their way to the top of the bed. Paxton hovered over Chris and kissed her lips gently. Then, she looked back down at her.

"What's wrong?" Chris asked.

"Nothing. Nothing's wrong. But you still haven't agreed to a first date." Paxton smiled at her.

"Pax—"

"No, now that I know the rules, I think we should follow them."

"That's easy for you to say. You're the one that had an orgasm earlier," Chris returned, wrapping her arms around Paxton's neck.

"You want one now?"

"Yes." Chris laughed. "But I also know what you're doing, and I appreciate it."

"Would you appreciate me holding you tonight?"

"Yes, I would."

"Then, that's what we'll do."

"Pax?"

"Yeah?" She kissed Chris's forehead.

"Am I being completely ridiculous?"

"No, you're not." Paxton kissed Chris's lips, rolled off her, and moved into the woman's side. "I kind of like the idea of just holding you tonight. I wanted to do that in the hotel that first night."

"You did?"

"Yes. And that night in my apartment, too."

Chris rolled onto her side to face Paxton and replied, "You did? After the bar?"

"Yes. Why?"

"Because I did, too," Chris said. "I thought we had a moment there, and then you just went to bed."

"You hadn't exactly given me any signals that this was

on the table, Chris. You hated me there for a while, remember?"

"You were kind of an asshole there for a while, remember?" Chris fired back.

"I was an accidental asshole."

"Still counts."

"Anyway, I thought we had a moment, too. I wasn't going to do anything about it, though, since it didn't appear you wanted the same thing."

"And the night at the hotel?"

"In the suite? You made some sounds when you were sleeping. At first, I thought you were awake, but you didn't move or get up. I don't know... I just thought it would be nice to hold you then."

"But you didn't?"

"I can only imagine what the police report would claim. You woke up in a hotel room, with your boss holding you from behind for no reason. I would be in jail, for sure."

Chris laughed softly and said, "I wouldn't have called the cops. I would've probably kicked your ass, though."

When Chris moved into her, Paxton moved to lie on her back, allowing the woman to wrap an arm over her waist and lay her head on her chest.

"I don't know... I seemed to kick *your* ass in swimming," Paxton replied.

"You cheated."

"I did not cheat."

"Please, you faked an injury." Chris's words were coming slower.

Paxton ran her fingers through Chris's hair and said, "I did not fake an injury. Your leg hit my leg."

"Liar."

Paxton smiled, kissed Chris's forehead, and looked up at the ceiling fan that was whirring around and around. A few moments later, Chris was asleep. Paxton followed behind, still with that smile on her face.

CHAPTER 15

CHRIS WOKE UP NAKED in her own bed. That hadn't happened in a very long time. She didn't sleep nude and typically put clothes on after sex before she went to sleep. She realized moments later that Paxton wasn't in bed with her and sat up quickly, hearing the shower running. There was only one bathroom. Wes was in the house. They had a morning routine when school was in session. She showered at night. He showered in the morning. She'd go in and brush her teeth if she was in a hurry. Wes knew this and usually left the door unlocked just in case. She hoped against hope that Paxton had already left.

"Hey," Paxton said from the kitchen table. "I made coffee. I hope that's okay." She stood, made her way over to Chris, and kissed her. "Also, Wes doesn't know I'm here. He went straight from his room to the bathroom. I heard the shower start, and then I made coffee. I was just going to come in and say good morning."

"Good morning," Chris replied. "No woman has ever been in my kitchen like this."

"Making you coffee?" Paxton asked, pouring a cup from Chris's old-fashioned coffee maker.

"No, Pax. I don't have sleepovers very often. When I do – usually, they leave before breakfast."

"Should I have left?" Paxton asked, passing her the cup.

"That's not what I'm saying." The shower turned off. "That's not what I'm saying, but it is what I'm saying. Wes is going to come out soon, and–"

"I get it," Paxton interrupted, leaned forward, and pecked her lips. "I'm gone. I'll see you at work."

"Weird."

"I'll choose to take that the right way," Paxton replied with a wink. "You look cute in the morning," she added.

"Shut up and go," Chris replied with a laugh.

Paxton smiled at her one more time, opened the front door, and left. Moments later, Chris heard her car start up at the same time Wes emerged from the bathroom.

"Morning," he said.

"Hey," Chris replied.

"I was asleep when you got home. Sorry."

"It's okay. I assume practice wore you out." She sat at the table and watched her baby brother pour himself a cup of coffee.

"That and the car thing. I tried to figure out the problem myself. I was wiped. Do you have time to run me to school?"

"Of course." She took a drink of her coffee.

"I guess I'll ask Michael if we can borrow his dad's truck to tow it. He's got a hitch that should work."

"Pax already towed it for you. It's at the shop now. They're going to take a look at it this morning. Hopefully, it won't cost an arm and a leg. I'll pick you up after tennis today."

"I'll just get a ride from Stephen. He made varsity with me. He lives, like, five minutes away and offered last night." Wes sat down. "And what do you mean Paxton towed it?"

"She called a truck last night."

"How much is that going to run us?" he asked.

"I don't know yet. She hasn't told me."

"And you just let her do that?" Wes took a drink. "That's unlike you."

"What do you mean?"

"You don't let people do stuff for you or pay for stuff, I guess."

"Yes, I do." Chris took another drink.

"No, you don't. You even hate it when I offer to pay for stuff."

"That's because you're in high school, Wes. You're supposed to be focusing on school and tennis."

"I'm paying for the tow, Chris." Wes took another drink of his coffee and leaned back in his chair. He looked like such a man in that moment that Chris had a hard time believing he was a teenager. He hadn't shaved recently. His hair was combed back, though still wet from the shower. His hands were on the coffee cup. He nodded and added, "I'll ask Pax to tell me how much it was, and I'll work more hours to pay her for it."

"You don't have to do that. I'll take care of it. Knowing Pax, she probably won't even tell me how much it costs; she'll just take care of it."

"Good."

"Good?" Chris asked.

"It's about time a woman tried that tactic with you."

"I'm sorry, what?" she asked, swallowing hard.

"She likes you, Chris." He shrugged a shoulder. "It's obvious. I could see it at dinner that night. You guys have a good time together. Don't think I didn't notice you offering to take me to the hotel or pick me up for no real reason just so you can see her."

"I do not do that. Your car sucks, Wes. I'm just trying to make sure you get to and from school and save you the gas money."

"That's bullshit." He laughed. "Were you saving her gas money last night when you asked her to stay over?"

"What?" Chris nearly choked on her coffee.

"Chris, I saw her car last night. It was, like, one in the morning. I went to the kitchen for water. I'm not an idiot." He smiled at her and then turned serious. "I'm also not a little kid anymore. You don't have to protect me. You're allowed to date."

"I know I'm allowed to date. I've dated."

"A little here and there, yeah, but nothing serious. You've never moved in with anyone, for example."

"I have you to think about."

"And I'm going to college in a year. What will be your excuse then?" Wes asked and stood. "I like Pax. She's cool. I just want you to know that I'm okay with it. So, if you decide not to do anything about it, that's on you."

***

"Sorry, I'm late. I had to drop Wes off at school," Chris greeted when she entered the hotel.

"It's okay. You're allowed to be late if you go out with the owner of this establishment." Paxton winked. "Okay... Now, I'm definitely getting sued for harassment."

Chris laughed silently. She found Paxton cute now. She used to find her annoying and rude. Last night, she thought Paxton was sexy as hell. This morning, the woman was kind when she made Chris coffee and left so Wes wouldn't notice her. Now, she was cute.

"I'll settle out of court for a small fee," Chris replied.

"What's the fee?" Paxton asked with a lifted eyebrow as Chris rounded the counter and came up next to her.

"You buy me dinner."

"I'm glad we were able to keep the lawyers out of this," Paxton replied. "When can I buy you this dinner?"

"I have to hang out with Wes tonight. We do this movie night thing every few weeks. I'm free tomorrow night, though."

"Tomorrow night it is," Paxton said. "Now, I'm going to put on my professional face for the rest of the day."

"Professional face?" Chris asked with a laugh. "What's that look like?" Paxton turned to her, gave her a serious expression, and Chris laughed harder. "That's just your regular face."

"I have this feeling you're going to want to separate whatever is going on between us from what happens here. Is that wrong?"

"You are, technically, my boss. I know you like to say I work with you, but the reality is that I work *for* you, Pax. This could get awkward really fast, and I do have Wes to think about. I can go back to Donoto's if I have to, but—"

"No way," Paxton objected. "If things get weird between us, we'll talk about it, okay? I don't want you thinking about some backup plan all the time, Chris."

"I have to think of a backup plan, Pax. You don't even know if you're keeping this place yet. You could decide to sell it at any time and move back to Seattle. Now, I don't just have a job to worry about; I might have my heart to worry about as well."

Paxton turned to her and said, "I'm removing my professional face for a minute, okay?"

Chris laughed softly and replied, "Okay."

"Tomorrow night, we'll go on a date, and we'll see where it goes. But I won't make any decision that impacts you without talking to you about it first."

"Okay. I appreciate that."

"I like South Lake, Chris. It's not just about you or this hotel. My sister's here. And she lives with her girlfriend, who I also really like. I'm pretty sure they're going to get married one day, and the idea of sticking around just to see that all unfold is pretty great to me. And, this place?" Paxton looked around the hotel that was still in shambles in the lobby, since that would be one of the last places they'd finish. "I've already put literal blood, sweat, and tears into it. I like thinking about being here in a year or two — or five, watching the different guests come and go, working with the staff, and sharing my life with someone while I do it."

She placed her hand on Chris's on the desk. "I have no idea if that someone is you yet, so don't freak out. I just know that I like you. I like what happened yesterday."

"Me too."

"And I can't wait for our date. Is that okay for now?"

"It's okay for now," Chris replied, leaned in, and kissed Paxton's cheek. Then, she pulled back. "Now, I'm putting my professional face on."

Paxton smiled and said, "It's a cute professional face." Chris glared back at her. "I mean – it's an appropriately professional face for the workplace environment."

"Oh, how much was the tow last night?"

"I don't know. Why?" Paxton asked back.

"Wes wants to pay you for it."

"Tell him not to worry about it," Paxton said and looked down at her laptop.

"Pax, he bought that car himself. He saved up from the time he turned twelve and started delivering newspapers. It's his baby. It's also a hunk of unsafe junk, but it's the best we can do right now. He wants to pay you for it. He said he'd work extra hours to make it up."

"Tell him it was, like, twenty bucks or something. He can buy me a couple of lunches to make it up to me," she said.

"Fine. But how much was it, really?" Chris pressed.

"It was a little over a hundred bucks, Chris. The repair estimate isn't in yet, but I'd like to take care of it for him."

"No, Pax. That's not how this works."

"Not how what works?" Paxton looked at her.

"You can't just pay for everything for us."

"I wasn't planning on it," Paxton replied. "Look, I get how important your independence is to you, Chris. I told you how sexy that is to me."

"Yet, you're trying to pay for his car?"

"No, I want to pay for the repair to make his car safer. If he wants to pay me back over time, that's fine, but it's also not necessary. Wes is a great worker. I've probably saved money because of how hard and how fast he worked. It would have taken a crew of three to do what he did in as many hours. I'd like to consider this a bonus for his hard work. But if you have a problem with it, I'll tell the shop to get you the estimate."

"A bonus?" Chris checked.

"It's not a handout. It's not charity."

"Okay. Just make sure to tell me how much it is."

"I will. Does he need a rental in the meantime?"

"No, I'll take him wherever or he'll get a ride from a friend," Chris said. "There's no way I'm letting you get him a rental car." Paxton rolled her eyes. Then, she returned them to her laptop screen. "Hey, Pax?"

"Yeah?"

"Thank you."

CHAPTER 16

"HEY, PAX."

"Hi, Wes. Are you here to see your sister? She's upstairs somewhere," Paxton replied.

It was a little after four in the afternoon. Paxton had been working outside using her phone as a hotspot. She'd been playing catch-up at her day job. She had payroll to do and some emails to send. Chris had been up in one of the guest rooms that had been completed by the crew. She'd been painting for the past hour or so. Paxton told her she didn't have to do that; the crew would take care of it. Chris had insisted. She'd been the one to pick out the colors for that room. She wanted to see it all through. Paxton had left her to it from there.

"I was actually wondering about my car," he said. "I got a ride here and figured Chris could just take me home when she's done."

"Your car has a few problems. The shop called me a couple of hours ago. They'll have it ready for you by the end of the week, though."

"Ready for me?"

"Yeah," she said.

"I came to find out how much the tow was so that I can pay you back. I don't know if I can pay for repairs, though. I thought they'd just do an estimate. Don't I have to approve it before they do anything?"

"The car is technically in your sister's name. She approved it. She and I talked about it this morning."

"About my car?"

106

Paxton walked around her makeshift worktable and nodded for him to follow her over to the railing overlooking the lake.

"Here's the thing, Wes. Your sister might get mad at me for telling you this, but sometimes, you need a little help to make something happen. You know I own my own real estate business."

"Yeah." Wesley matched her posture, leaning over the railing.

"I saved and saved and still needed help. I had to borrow money from my big sister to make it happen," she said.

"You did?"

"It wasn't much. And I've paid her back since then. It killed me, having to ask her, because I'd done everything else on my own. I had this dream, though, and I knew she could help me achieve it."

"So, you're helping with my car?"

"I figured we could make a deal that would appease you and your stubborn sister," Paxton said with a smile. "Do you have a summer job lined up yet?"

"I was planning to pick up hours at the bookstore."

"What if you worked here? I have no idea what shape this place will be in by May, but you can do odd jobs. Or, we can figure something else out. I'll pay your regular salary, but you work a few extra hours a week for me, and that'll take care of your car."

"That's it? A few extra hours a week?"

"Over the summer. While you're in school, you're focused on that." Paxton turned her head to him. "Deal?"

"Deal." He turned to her, putting out his hand for her to shake, which she did.

"Awesome," she said.

"Hey, Chris and I do this movie night thing every so often. It's usually when she doesn't have to work, or I don't have practice. We have one tonight. Do you want to come over?"

"I think that's your thing with your sister, Wes. But I appreciate you inviting me."

He squinted his eyes at her and asked, "You like my sister, don't you?"

Paxton turned back to the water and said, "Is it that obvious?"

"Not as obvious as your car in our driveway in the middle of the night," he replied.

"Shit…" She shook her head. "I should have parked on the street."

"Come over tonight, Pax. It'll be fun. I like when my sister is happy; and I haven't seen her happy a lot."

"And you think me being there tonight will make her happy?"

"I don't know. I won't know for sure unless you show up," Wes replied with a wink. "Seven. Bring Chinese food if you really want to win her over. Egg rolls from Sammy Chang's are her favorite. Make sure to get extra soy sauce and extra sweet and sour. She mixes them together. It's gross." He squished his face together in disgust.

"And what do you like?" Paxton asked.

He looked surprised at first and said, "The number four and number seven."

"Any sauce?"

"Nope. I'm a classic kind of guy."

She laughed at that.

***

Paxton sat in the driveway with Chinese food in the passenger's seat. She'd been out back working when Chris and Wes had left for the day. Chris had texted her goodnight and that she was excited about tomorrow. Paxton had yet to text back that she would see her later that night for two reasons. She thought Chris would tell her not to come, and she really wanted to go. She also wasn't sure, despite the fact that she wanted to, if she would actually go to this movie night. She'd gone to her apartment, showered, and changed. Then, she'd gone to the restaurant and ordered two of each – number four and number seven, three orders of egg rolls, a number sixteen with extra shrimp, a number twelve with extra chicken, and asked for enough soy sauce and sweet and sour sauce for an army. It was now all piled up in bags next to her. When she worked up the courage to grab the bags and head to the front door, she rang the bell and waited.

"Pax?" Chris asked when she opened the door.

"Hey," Paxton replied, holding up the bags. "I brought reinforcements."

"Hey, Pax." Wes waved at her from the couch.

"What are you doing here?"

"I invited her," Wes said, standing and making his way over to the door. "I got these." He took the bags from Paxton's outstretched hands. "We're watching The Matrix tonight."

"We're actually watching The Matrix for, like, the fifteenth time." Chris chuckled. "It's his favorite movie. I gave in easily tonight."

"He invited me. I wasn't sure if I should come or not," Paxton said just to Chris. "I can go."

Chris considered for a moment and said, "He's never invited anyone to these things before. I haven't, either."

"Right." Paxton looked down at the concrete under her feet and the linoleum under Chris's, along with the threshold separating them. "I should've gone with my gut and just declined. I'll see you at work tomorrow."

"Pax, come in." Chris tugged on her arm. "He invited you because he wants you here."

"But you don't?"

Chris put her hands on Paxton's hips and replied, "I'm a little surprised, but I'm glad you're here."

"Are you sure?"

"Oh, my God! Come in. The movie's about to start," Wes replied for Chris.

Chris laughed silently. Her eyes met Paxton's. Paxton wanted to kiss her then. She wanted to lean in and give Chris a soft kiss to get reacquainted with one another in that way after a long day at work where they both left this part of their new relationship behind. She wanted to, but she didn't. Wes was in the kitchen, pulling cartons out of bags. Instead, Paxton tried to express with only her eyes what she wanted. Chris smiled at her, leaned in, and did what Paxton hadn't done. She kissed her softly.

"Come in," Chris said.

"Gross," Wes replied. "And you got so much food."

Paxton laughed as she made her way into the small house and said, "I got what you told me to get."

"You told her what to get, Wes?" Chris pulled on Paxton's hand, and they made it over to the kitchen.

"I have my own Christina Florence cheat sheet," Paxton said.

"Then, I need to get closer to your sister so that I can have a cheat sheet of my own."

Paxton laughed at the thought of Chris using Adler to supply her with details about her. They doled out food onto paper plates. Paxton watched Chris mix soy sauce with sweet and sour. It did not look good, but Chris dipped an egg roll into it and smiled as she chewed. She passed Paxton the remainder of the egg roll after dipping it in the sauce for her and telling her to try it. Wes told her not to because it was disgusting. She did it anyway. Wes was right. Chris laughed. Wes laughed. Paxton nearly choked.

She'd seen the movie a few times herself. She didn't pay much attention to it until Wes started telling her little pieces of trivia about the movie. He explained that the numbers one and three were all over the place in the movie. Neo was an anagram for one. Then, there was a character named Trinity. The numbers spotted in the background of scenes also had the numbers one and three in them. While Paxton found this all very fascinating, what she liked more was the fact that she was sitting between Chris and Wes on their sofa, and Chris had been running her hand through Paxton's hair since they'd finished eating. Paxton had her arm over Chris's knee. It wasn't moving, but they were touching, and that was enough.

"I'm going to bed," Wes said as he stood.

"The movie's not even over yet," Chris replied, noting there was still about twenty minutes left in the sequel they'd put on after the first film ended. "You made me put this one on."

"I know. But I forgot how boring this one is. I'm about to pass out, and I have lifting tomorrow before class," Wes said. "And practice after," he added.

"Fine, quitter," Chris replied in jest. "I'll see you in the morning. Good night."

"Night. Good night, Pax."

"Good night," she told him.

"I'll see you in the morning?" Wes asked with a lifted eyebrow.

Paxton turned to Chris.

"Go to sleep," Chris said to her brother.

Wes waved at them both. Then, he departed for his bedroom.

"I'll stay and watch the rest with you if you want," Paxton said. "And then I'll go home."

"You can stay," Chris replied.

"No, I can't." Paxton shook her head at her. "You've been touching me in one way or another for the past couple of hours. Let's just say—"

"Oh," Chris interrupted. "You're turned on?"

Paxton looked over her shoulder to make sure Wes had closed his door.

"Yes," she whispered.

Chris looked over her shoulder, too. Then, she climbed into Paxton's lap, straddling her waist.

"Well, that's not helping."

"No?" Chris leaned down. Paxton held onto her hips as Chris's lips met her own. "This isn't helping?"

"No, it's not." Paxton leaned up to capture those lips again. "It's torture, really."

"We could go to my room." Chris moved Paxton's hair off her neck and kissed the skin there. "You were touching me, too, you know?"

"Barely."

"Do you want to do more?"

"Yes."

"Then, let's go to my room," Chris replied, sucking on Paxton's earlobe.

Paxton let out a few shallow breaths. Then, she lifted Chris's chin in order to look her in the eye.

"I would love nothing more than to go in that room, take your clothes off, and touch you everywhere."

"Then, let's go."

"This isn't a date, Chris. This was me spending time with you and Wes. Tomorrow night will be our first date."

"Pax, we've already been together. I appreciate you being noble right now, but we don't have to follow all the rules." Chris kissed her gently. "I want you to stay. Will you at least stay?"

Paxton couldn't resist the soft blue eyes and those somewhat pouty lips. She kissed them once more before she tapped Chris's hips with her thumbs, signaling that she should get up. They stood together. Chris loaded up all the leftovers into the refrigerator. Paxton took the trash out to the bins. She went back inside, finding Chris turning off the TV. Chris took her hand, kissing the top of it sweetly. Paxton smiled at her and followed her into the bedroom.

CHAPTER 17

CHRIS WOKE UP TO PAXTON holding her from behind. She smiled because they'd fallen asleep naked again. They hadn't done anything more than kissing. Then, they'd stripped off their clothing. Chris had gone to take her shower. Paxton had showered quickly after her. They hadn't bothered dressing before slipping beneath the sheets.

"I have to tell you something," Paxton had said.

"What?" Chris had turned in her arms, thinking this was a serious conversation.

"I just got off in your shower," Paxton had replied, following with an immediate laugh.

"You did what?" Chris had asked, laughing and rolling to face her. "You just masturbated in my shower?"

"Yes." Paxton had rolled onto her back. "But can you really blame me? You were touching me all night. Then, you got naked. And, your shower smelled like your shampoo. I couldn't help myself."

"You needed it that bad?" Chris had asked with a smile.

"Yes. I wanted to sleep tonight."

"Well, guess what, Champ."

"What?" Paxton had looked at her.

"I did the same thing." Chris had given Paxton her wide eyes. "Now, good night."

Paxton had laughed. Then, she'd held her all night. Chris knew when she woke that she could get used to this.

It worried her. It couldn't be this easy, could it? She couldn't have just met someone she could picture sharing her life with. It couldn't be Paxton Williams, could it?

"Hey," Paxton whispered in her sleepy voice and kissed Chris's shoulder.

Chris thought for a second that yes, it could be this easy.

"I should probably get going before Wes wakes up."

"Do you have to?" Chris asked, turning in Paxton's arms. "He knows about us."

"Knowing and seeing are two different things. I can stay, but are you sure?" Paxton asked.

Yeah, it could definitely be this easy.

"I'm sure. You're sweet for checking, though. If he were younger, I'd probably care more. But he's seventeen; he knows how this works," Chris replied and leaned up to kiss Paxton's lips. "Good morning."

"You know what's nice about working together?" Paxton asked, resting her elbow on the bed and her hand on her head, looking down at Chris.

"What?"

"We're each other's excuse for being late." Paxton rolled on top of her. "If you can spare a few minutes, I'd like to make out with you now."

"I think I can. But you should know that you're naked and on top of me. I might not be able to—"

There was a knock on the door, and then Wes said, "Hey, I'm not coming in there, for obvious reasons... Just wanted to tell you that Steve can't come to get me this morning after all. He just texted. Can you take me to the weight room, Chris?"

Chris sighed, met Paxton's eyes, and gave her an apologetic expression.

"I've got him." Paxton slid off her and stood. "You take your time this morning. Meet me at work whenever."

"You don't have to—"

"Wes, I'll take you," Paxton yelled through the door.

"Give me two minutes, okay? We'll stop for breakfast on the way."

"Pax," Chris stood and wrapped her arms around Paxton's waist, leaning in. "Thank you."

"Why don't you take the day off?" Paxton suggested.

"What?"

"When was the last time you had a day to yourself?" Paxton asked, kissed her, and then pulled away in order to get dressed.

"I don't know. Why?" Chris ran her hand through her hair.

"He's going off to school. I'm going off to work. You should stay here and relax. I'll pick you up for our date around six."

"I can't take the day off. I haven't even been working for you for—"

"*With* me." Paxton kissed her after donning her bra and shirt. "And that's an order."

"If I work *with* you, can you even give me orders?"

"I just did." Paxton buttoned and zipped her jeans. "Oh, can you stop by Morgan and Adler's store? Adler has something she keeps forgetting to give me. You should use it."

"What is it?"

"I'll let that be a surprise," Paxton replied with a smirk. "You'll like it, though. They can no longer use it for reasons they can disclose to you." She winked. "I'll pick Wes up after practice and bring him home, too. Then, we can go on our date."

"Pax, this is a lot. Are you sure? I still have to finish painting room nine."

"And that can wait until tomorrow. Plus, that's not actually your job. You're in charge of the restaurant, and there's nothing you need to do with that today. I'll see you tonight," Paxton said.

Just like that, she and Wes were gone, and Chris was left by herself in her own home. She felt strange. Having a day off was strange in and of itself. She ate cereal and drank coffee in silence. Then, she made her way over to McBride Outfitters, at Paxton's request; while the woman, herself, sent Chris a text message as a reminder to do so an hour after she'd left the house.

"Hey, what are you doing here?" Adler asked from behind the counter.

"Pax told me I needed to stop by here and get something from you for her," Chris replied.

"Something for her? Oh." Adler motioned for Chris to follow her behind the counter into one of the offices. "She had you come and get it? You're not running errands for her, are you?"

"No. She wants me to use whatever it is. She said you and Morgan couldn't."

Adler blushed. She reached for the top desk drawer and pulled it open.

"Do you remember when we told you we got kicked out of a certain day spa for…"

"Oh!"

"Yeah…" Adler said slowly. Then, she produced a gift card. "Morgan's parents have no idea, obviously. They got us an anniversary present. Wouldn't you know it's for the same day spa we can no longer return to, and they won't allow us to cash it out." The woman laughed a little. "Anyway, I told Pax she could have it. She got us a gift card for another one to replace it. I just keep forgetting to give this to her."

"I can't take this," Chris said, keeping her hand outstretched for Adler to take it back.

"If she wants you to have it, you should take it. It's a two-hundred-dollar gift card. You can get a lot of spa services with it."

"Then, she should use it."

"Paxton hates spas." Adler rolled her eyes.

"She does? Why?" Chris asked, thinking instantly of Adler being her Paxton cheat sheet.

"She said it's all too much. There's incense, and music. It's all too much for her. She told me that when she wants a massage, she just wants someone to get the tension out of her muscles. She doesn't need all that frilly stuff; her words." Adler paused. "Oh, and if she wants a face scrub, she can buy it at the store."

"She has some pretty strong opinions about spas." Chris laughed, sliding the card into her pocket when it became apparent that Adler wasn't taking it back.

"One of her girlfriends in college was a masseuse at a place like that. It didn't end well. I suspect it has something to do with that. Anyway, Morgan and I can't use it. She *won't* use it. You should totally go for it."

"It's a lot of money, Adler."

"My sister is a giving person. If you haven't figured that out already, you will." She smiled. "It's one of my favorite things about her. Case in point, that dinner you guys made for us the other night. She knew we'd get home late from our trip and wouldn't go shopping. She also knew we had to be at the Truckee McBride's the day after we got back. She just decided to surprise us with dinner. That's Pax."

"I'm starting to get that."

Adler squinted her eyes at her and replied, "You two have been spending a lot of time together, huh?"

"Adler..."

"What?" Adler sat in the chair behind the desk. "Is there something going on I should know about?"

"No," Chris said. "But only because I don't know what she wants you to know."

"So, there is something?"

"Talk to your sister."

"I would… But she's been busy recently. I think I'm figuring out why."

"I should go," Chris said. "Apparently, I'm supposed to go to a day spa."

"Have fun," Adler said with a chuckle.

***

Chris was certain she'd never been more relaxed than in this moment. There was a masseuse working the back of her thighs. She'd already worked the tension from her shoulders and lower back. Her calves were next and then, her feet. The tension in Chris's hands actually surprised her. She hadn't realized it was even there. The mud bath, the shower, and then the sauna was supposed to round out her experience, but an attendant had talked her into a facial as well. Chris had just enough to cover everything with the gift card. She tipped the masseuse and a couple of other staff members in cash. It was odd. She didn't exactly have money to throw around, but she was also making more working for Paxton and working fewer hours. She had a little more money to spend than usual. Tipping the people that had helped her relieve some of the tension that had built up over the past decade or so was completely worth it.

She'd finished her day lying in bed and drinking a lot of water because that was what the spa told her to do. She took a nap around four and woke at five, wanting to have plenty of time to get ready for her first official date with Paxton. She showered and looked into her small closet to find something to wear. As she'd told Paxton before, the only dress she owned was black and hanging in the back corner of the closet. Chris hadn't worn it in probably five years. She wasn't even sure it would fit. She also had a pair of black flats she hadn't had the occasion to wear in a long time that she thought would pair nicely. Having no idea where Paxton was taking her, Chris decided she'd prepare by dressing up.

She heard the front door open at just after six. Wes came inside and dropped his tennis bag near the front door. He went straight to the kitchen, not realizing she was sitting on the sofa, pulled open the refrigerator door, grabbed an energy drink, and downed the whole thing in seconds.

"Hey," Paxton said from the front door.

Chris had been distracted by her brother. She hadn't noticed that Paxton had crossed the threshold and closed the door behind her. She was wearing a pair of nice skinny jeans and a green and blue flannel shirt, with some gray in there, too. The green in the pattern really brought out her eyes. Her hair was down but back behind her ears. She looked casual and beautiful.

"I guess I overdressed," Chris said as she stood. "Just let me change."

"No way." Paxton walked toward her. "You look amazing."

"She's right, sis. You look good. I didn't even know you had a dress," Wes said.

"Thanks, Wes." Chris turned from her brother to Paxton, who was now standing in front of her. "I should change, though."

"Do not change out of this dress." Paxton shook her head. She looked her up and down and then met her eyes. "I like it."

"Okay. That's my cue," Wes said. "Have fun tonight. Feel free not to come home, Chris."

"Wesley!"

Paxton laughed until Wes closed his bedroom door. Then, she grew serious, pulled Chris into her, and kissed her.

"You look beautiful."

"You look casual." Chris looked down at the shirt. "You look good, though."

"I remembered how you were that night in Seattle… I thought I'd keep things casual tonight."

"Pax, let me change. It'll take a minute and then we can go," Chris replied.

"Can't. Time to go." Paxton pulled Chris's hand.

Paxton drove them for about fifteen minutes. She told Chris what she missed at work that day. One of the painters had kicked a can over and spent the rest of the morning cleaning up his mess. The restaurant's gutting had been officially completed, and it was now ready for the tile and brick work Paxton wanted done. When they parked, Chris knew exactly what Paxton was doing.

"Really, Pax?" She laughed.

"I would have grabbed it already, but I never did find out what sandwich you planned on getting that day." Paxton smiled. "We're not eating here, though."

"Really? We're not eating at the deli for our first date? Color me disappointed," she said sarcastically.

"Hey, do not doubt my first date planning ability. I have something planned for you, Christina Florence," Paxton replied. "Let's grab the food first."

Inside the deli, Paxton had her hand on the small of Chris's back as they ordered. It felt good, having someone standing next to her. It was something so simple, so trivial, that she doubted most people even thought about it. Chris had come to this place at least a hundred times. She'd never come with someone like this before, though. Paxton ordered their food and handed the guy her card to pay. Chris grabbed the bags when the sandwiches had been passed to her over the counter. Paxton grabbed two bottles of water and their chips. Then, they were off.

"Where are you taking me, Pax?" Chris asked.

"You'll see."

CHAPTER 18

PAXTON PULLED into the parking lot of the hotel she'd bought on a whim, if she was being honest, but had come to love every minute of owning. She turned off the car and then turned to Chris.

"You give me the day off and then take me to work on a date?" Chris asked, looking at the hotel through the windshield.

"Just… Come on," Paxton said.

They got out of the car, taking their food with them, and walked through the hotel and out onto the patio that overlooked beautiful Lake Tahoe.

"Paxton, it's beautiful."

"I may have skipped out on work a little myself to set this all up."

Paxton had left the hotel a little after lunch to run to the store. She'd needed white twinkle lights, poles, a few of those tiki torches to keep the bugs away, a couple of outdoor sleep mats that she'd bought at Adler and Morgan's store, and an overly large blanket that rested atop them. She'd also gotten a few throw pillows, some candles, and wine. She'd sat it all out, hung the lights, lit the torches, and then had gone home to shower and dress before she picked up Wes from tennis practice. It had been a lot of work, but judging by Chris's surprised expression, it had been worth it. She'd also hooked her old iPod up to a Bluetooth speaker.

Soft music played as they both looked at the setup and then the water.

"Paxton, I can't believe you did all this while I was in some spa."

"I'm glad you went." Paxton moved to Chris then. She dropped the bag of food she'd been holding on the blanket and pulled Chris into her, holding her from behind. "Did you relax?"

"I did, yes." Chris's arms went on top of Paxton's over her stomach. "But I feel pretty relaxed right now, too."

Paxton kissed her neck and said, "I thought we could have a nice, relaxing first date."

"I can't believe you did all this." Chris rested her head back on Paxton's shoulder.

"I wanted to."

"I've lived here for so long, but I so rarely actually look out at this thing." She pointed to the water.

"This thing?" Paxton chuckled against her skin.

"The lake; the reason most of us live here and so many visit." Chris turned in Paxton's arms, wrapping her own around Paxton's neck. "I've looked at it a lot since you got here, Pax."

"Well, we do work right next to it."

"That's not what I meant, smart-ass."

Paxton pressed her forehead to Chris's and kissed her gently. Then, she pulled back to look at the woman in front of her.

"Have dinner with me?"

"Later," Chris said. "You know what I love about this hotel?"

"What's that?"

"That it's secluded."

She kissed Paxton and walked them back toward the blanket Paxton had laid out earlier, not at all thinking this would happen. Chris knelt in front of Paxton on the blanket, unbuckled the woman's belt, unbuttoned and unzipped her jeans, and then pulled them down. Paxton unbuttoned her own shirt and tossed it aside. Chris's lips met Paxton's abdomen, her inner thighs, and then she kissed Paxton's sex through her underwear.

"This is not what I had planned," Paxton said. "Just for the record."

"Should I stop?"

"No. I mean, yes." Paxton tugged her underwear off her body along with her shoes and her jeans. Then, she fell to her knees, grasped Chris by the shoulders, and flipped them so that she was on top of Chris. "It's my turn."

Paxton was nude. Chris was still fully clothed, though she'd kicked off those adorable flats before Paxton had flipped them. Paxton kissed her. She kissed Chris's lips, her neck, her collarbone. Then, she reached to the woman's side and pulled down the zipper. That allowed her to free Chris's shoulder from one of the dress straps. She then freed Chris's breast from her black bra and pulled a nipple into her mouth. She'd longed to taste them. She took the other breast in her hand and squeezed.

"That's… good." Chris's hand went to the back of her head. Paxton couldn't see, but she could feel Chris lowering the other strap and pulling out her other breast. Paxton squeezed it and kneaded it outside of the bra for the first time. Then, she moved her lips to it. "Wow. Yes."

Paxton's hand slid down to Chris's thigh, which she pushed aside, giving Paxton the space she wanted to settle between Chris's legs. She lifted the dress and tugged at the panties beneath until they were down to Chris's knees. Then, she settled herself against Chris and rocked into her. Her teeth tugged at Chris's nipple. Chris's hand gripped her hair. It was all too much and yet not enough at the same time. Paxton could feel her own wetness mingling with Chris's as she moved against her. She opened her eyes and lifted up to look down at Chris, whose eyes were closed. Paxton watched her as she rocked her own hips. Chris spread her legs a little wider. Paxton heard Chris's underwear tear at the force of her knees moving apart. She closed her eyes at the sound, because that sound meant Chris needed her so much, she didn't care about anything else.

Paxton rocked into Chris harder then, bracketing her own arms on either side of Chris. She slid one hand between them, coaxing Chris's folds apart, and used two fingers to stroke her clit, then squeezing it between them. It was swollen. It was hard. It was ready to be touched, to be sucked, to be licked, and to be kissed. She moved down Chris's body, pulling the dress over her own head as she arrived at her destination. There was something sexy about doing this when the woman she was doing it to couldn't see her. She took Chris into her mouth. She flicked her tongue over her clit. She moved her tongue to Chris's lips, licking them up and down slowly before moving to the insides of the woman's thighs. Chris's sounds told Paxton she was doing something right. She could feel Chris's body tensing beneath her. Then, she felt Chris's legs on her back, gripping her tightly. She knew it was time.

She sucked Chris's clit hard into her mouth. The hips bucked up. Chris whispered Paxton's name. Paxton spread Chris's legs even further apart and slid her fingers inside, feeling the soft, wet skin she'd been craving. She sucked. She moved slowly inside, coaxing and coaxing until Chris bucked harder and faster. Then, Paxton thrust faster and sucked harder. Chris's body went limp. She let out a soft cry. Her hips fell to the ground. Her legs left Paxton's back. Paxton lifted the dress, wiped her mouth with a happy smirk, and looked up at Chris. The woman's eyes were closed. She was breathing hard. Her chest was rising and falling. Her breasts were still out of the cups of her bra. Her beautiful dress was unzipped, the straps were hanging off her shoulders. She looked sexy as hell.

"Gorgeous," Paxton whispered mostly to herself.

Chris opened her eyes and said, "That was…"

"What?" Paxton moved to hover over her.

"Wow."

Paxton smiled down at her then. She kissed Chris's lips, her jaw, her neck, and made her way back down to her breasts. Chris stayed there, still breathing hard, as Paxton sucked on her nipple again. When Paxton flicked it with the very tip of her tongue, Chris's hips shifted beneath her. As she slid her hand down between Chris's legs, she lifted the dress up in the process in order to see Chris. Her fingers disappeared into Chris's folds. She watched them move as if on their own, earning another orgasm from Chris. When Chris came back down, Paxton moved to kneel in front of her. She lifted Chris's hips enough to slide the dress the rest of the way off her body. Chris took care of her bra. Then, the woman was completely nude, lying before Paxton, who could only smile softly at the sight of her.

Chris watched Paxton watching her. She reached for Paxton with both hands, encouraging Paxton to straddle her. The woman obeyed wordlessly. Chris sat up and kissed her chest. She pulled a nipple between her teeth and tugged. Paxton gasped at both the pleasure and the pain of it, wanting more of her touch. Chris held onto one of Paxton's hips, her fingers digging into Paxton's skin. Her free hand slid between Paxton's legs, moving up to her clit first, stroking it. Paxton moaned. Chris moved her own lips up to Paxton's mouth and kissed her through her next moan, which came when Chris entered her.

"Ride me," Chris instructed.

"Yeah?"

"Come on my fingers. I want to taste you again," Chris said.

Paxton's hips rolled forward and back. Chris kissed her neck, holding onto her hip still, encouraging Paxton to move more. Chris's fingers were deep inside her, stroking while Paxton moved against them. Chris's thumb was on her clit, flicking left to right, then stopping to press hard, holding there. Paxton kissed her. She grabbed Chris's face, lifted it up, and kissed her. Her tongue slid inside Chris's mouth, meeting Chris's. She held onto Chris's head, keeping the woman there, kissing her. Then, she raised up and lowered herself down onto Chris's fingers. Chris gasped then. Paxton let go of her, grasped her own breast, and offered it to Chris, who immediately went to suck on the nipple. As Paxton started to lift herself up and lower down even harder and faster, playing with one of her own nipples, Chris continued to play with the other nipple.

She looked up at Paxton then. The woman had put her hand on the back of Chris's head and tilted it down. Chris watched her move up and down on her fingers. She smiled when she looked back up at Paxton. Paxton moved faster. Chris grasped her around the waist with her free arm. She lifted her own hips up and thrust her fingers inside.

"Yes!"

"So sexy, Pax." Chris kissed her neck, dragging her teeth along the heated skin.

Paxton rocked against Chris, holding onto her, and pressing Chris further into her own body. Her orgasm was building. When Chris connected their mouths and sucked on Paxton's tongue, Paxton came at the thought of what that mouth had felt like in the hallway the other night.

"Yes. I'm coming. I'm coming!" she let out.

Her body flailed against Chris's. Chris held onto her, moving inside and against her. The orgasm shot through Paxton like lightning, and without warning, she collapsed against Chris's body. Chris held onto her as they both went down to the blanket. Paxton's hips wouldn't stop moving. She hovered over Chris, taking the fingers into her body deeper, wanting to ride out her orgasm all the way. Chris watched her as she rode faster and harder. When Paxton came again, she sat up, slowing her pace, but moved with Chris's fingers still inside.

"You feel so good," Paxton said softly. "Like… Your fingers are supposed to be touching me like this."

"Maybe they are," Chris replied, keeping her fingers in place until Paxton stilled. Then, she removed them and put them to her lips. "I want to taste you now."

Paxton watched in awe as Chris slid her fingers inside her mouth, sucking on them and then removing them. Chris put them to Paxton's lips next. Paxton took them inside her mouth, sucked on them, and then let them slide out.

"You are so damn sexy," Paxton said as Chris put her fingers back into her own mouth.

"So are you." She kissed Paxton's neck where her sweat had begun to build. She licked Paxton's skin, nibbled at it, and then pulled back. "Lie down, Pax. I want to lie next to you."

Paxton rolled off of Chris. She pulled a pillow under her own head and moved one for Chris to lie on. Chris moved to lie next to her, but she rested her head on her elbow and stared down at Paxton.

"I thought you weren't the kind of girl that slept with someone on the first date," Paxton said.

"I've never had anyone take me on a date like this before. It doesn't feel like a first date with you, Paxton." She stroked Paxton's abdomen with her fingertips.

"It doesn't for me, either," Paxton replied.

Chris's fingers dipped into her wetness then. She stroked Paxton's clit softly, with barely-there touches that Paxton knew were designed to make her go crazy.

"I want you again," Chris said, staring down at her own hand working against Paxton's skin.

"I want you again, too," Paxton replied. "Kiss me."

CHAPTER 19

"I WANT TO FALL asleep next to you tonight," Paxton said hours later.

"You can come back to my place, or we could go to your apartment where we can actually be alone," Chris replied.

They remained on the blanket, lying next to one another, using Paxton's shirt and Chris's dress to cover them in an attempt to keep warm.

"I don't want to move, though," Paxton said.

"Neither do I. But we can't sleep out here, Pax. We'll freeze to death. Also, there's no bathroom, no kitchen, no heat or really anything else that works in there." Chris pointed at the unfinished hotel behind them. "Let's go to your apartment. It's kind of weird that I haven't seen it yet."

"Okay. But I have to warn you: it's full of boxes. I only have the essentials unpacked."

"Still?"

"Yes, still. I don't plan on staying there beyond my lease, so it didn't make sense unpacking things."

"Your lease is only six months, right?" Chris asked.

Paxton sat up, dropping the shirt and dress beside them. She then straddled Chris, running her own hands along the woman's stomach and over her breasts.

"Before you start worrying about me leaving… I'm talking to Kinsley tomorrow."

"Kinsley?" Chris reached for Paxton's hips.

"Yes. She's much more familiar with the area than I am, and I'm considering buying a place."

"You just did," Chris said, but her attention wasn't on Paxton's words as much as it was on Paxton's sex, which was moving ever so slowly against her own.

"This is a hotel; I don't plan to live here." Paxton looked down and caught Chris's eyes watching the movement. "Should I keep going?"

"Yes," Chris whispered.

Paxton smiled down at her. She reached between their bodies, slid into Chris's folds with two fingers, and started stroking her.

"You're still wet," she said.

"So, are you. I can feel you."

"We're both clearly turned on. What should we do about it?" Paxton asked with a lifted eyebrow.

"I think we should touch each other at the same time."

"You do?" Paxton asked as she rocked.

"Yes; with our mouths, Paxton."

Paxton's eyes got big, and she replied, "With our mouths, huh?"

Chris nodded.

"I would really, really like that," Paxton stated.

She lifted herself up, turned around, and straddled Chris again. She then rubbed her sex over Chris's stomach, causing the woman to gasp; first, at the heat of the touch, and then, the cool it left behind. Paxton slid closer to Chris's mouth and hovered her own center over Chris's face. Not wasting any time, Chris grasped Paxton's hips and lowered them down. Just as she tasted Paxton, soft lips engulfed her own clit, and Paxton sucked her hard.

***

Paxton had her pressed against the front door of her apartment. Her lips were on Chris's neck. Her hand was trying to work the key in the lock to get the door open. Her other hand was under Chris's dress.

"Pax, just unlock the door," Chris said with a laugh.

"I'm trying," Paxton said against her skin. "You're really distracting."

Chris pushed her back with a laugh, took the key, and put it in the lock. She turned it, unlocked the door, then pulled on Paxton's collar and pushed the woman inside her own apartment. She closed the door behind them, moved back against it, and dropped the keys to the floor.

"Now, continue," she said.

Paxton lifted an eyebrow at her. She was still very turned on. So was Chris. That last round on the blanket was enough for then, but it wasn't enough now. They'd dressed and packed everything away, stowing it in one of the guest rooms to deal with another day. Then, they'd taken the short drive to Paxton's apartment.

Paxton slid her hand under Chris's dress. Then, she was inside her again. Chris had thrown out her underwear. There was no point in keeping something she'd torn so much, it no longer even resembled underwear. Paxton kissed her neck, her lips, and her neck again. She pressed her thigh between Chris's legs.

Chris loved the pressure. She loved how Paxton took her, claimed her. She also loved how sweet Paxton was. In this moment, Chris wanted to be claimed. But she knew that if she asked Paxton to take her slowly, Paxton would walk her into her bedroom and make love to her all night long.

"There! There!" Chris thrust her hips into Paxton's hand and came. "Oh, yes!"

"I want you naked. And, in my bed," Paxton husked into her ear.

"And I'd like a shower," Chris replied.

"Even better."

Paxton unbuttoned her shirt, revealing the creamy skin beneath, and then unclasped her bra, letting it fall to the floor with her shirt. Chris watched Paxton's nipples harden in front of her eyes. She wanted Paxton now, but she'd wait for the shower. Then, she'd take her against the wall while the water cascaded over her skin. Paxton lowered her jeans to the floor, kicked them off, and they landed on a box in the living room behind them. They moved to the bathroom. Paxton started the water. They shared sweet kisses and light touches until the water was warm enough for them to get in. They washed each other first. Chris pinned Paxton to the wall, knelt down, and took her with her mouth.

***

"Hey, what's this?" Chris asked the following morning.

"What's what?" Paxton asked back.

"I thought you went to Washington," Chris said, looking down at the shirt she'd borrowed that had a University of Oregon logo on the front. "You had a shirt on the other day."

"Adler went to Washington. That's probably her shirt. I'm sure she has an Oregon one lying around her place."

"Oh," Chris said. She pulled on the borrowed jeans, sans underwear. "Why'd you go there?"

"Swimming scholarship, remember?"

"I guess I just thought you'd always lived in Seattle," Chris said.

"I have always lived there. I just went to Oregon for school and moved back."

"Right."

"Do you have something against the ducks?" Paxton lifted an eyebrow over her coffee mug.

"No, I'm sure it's a great school."

"It is," Paxton said. "Are you okay?"

"I'm good. Just tired. You kept me up most of the night." Chris looked down at her half-finished coffee. "I should go home. I need to change."

"Give me, like, ten minutes. Then, we can go."

"I'll just get an Uber. That way I can pick up my car at home. I'll meet you at work in an hour."

"Chris, I'll drive you to your place." Paxton placed her coffee cup in her kitchen sink.

Chris turned to find where she'd put her phone the night before. She located it on the coffee table that had a box on top of it that was open. Chris grabbed the phone and noticed boxing gloves in the box along with various other items.

"What are these for?" she asked.

"What are what for?"

"Boxing gloves."

"Oh, I kick-box sometimes. I haven't since I've been here, but I used to belong to a gym."

"You're a kick-boxer?"

"Not professionally." Paxton laughed.

"Okay. I should meet the car downstairs. I'll see you at the hotel."

"Chris, what's wrong?" Paxton made her way over to her.

"Nothing's wrong. I just ordered the car. It's only two minutes away."

"Chris, come on." Paxton placed her hands on Chris's waist. "Talk to me."

"Can we just talk later? I don't like making people wait, you know?" She kissed Paxton on the cheek.

"A cheek kiss? A night like that, and I get a cheek kiss the morning after?"

Chris kissed her on the lips quickly, gathered her stuff, and headed to the door.

"I'll see you later," she said, opening the door.

Then, Chris closed it behind her. She made it outside where she climbed into the car that had just pulled up. She took the short drive to her house, got out, and went inside. Wes was already gone. She went into her bedroom and flopped backward onto her unmade bed. She'd had a perfect date with Paxton. She couldn't imagine a better first date or any date, really. Paxton had planned everything so perfectly. They'd eaten their sandwiches and joked with one another about the day Paxton stole her parking spot. Then, they made love under the stars. Paxton had even asked her to dance. Their bodies were pressed together, no clothing separating them. They'd danced to a slow love song on a patio, overlooking the lake. It might have been the best night of Chris's life.

CHAPTER 20

"WHY ARE YOU here, Paxton?" Adler asked as she served Paxton her second cup of coffee that morning. "Shouldn't you be at the hotel?"

"Shouldn't you be at the store?"

"You're drinking my coffee there, Pax. You want to be a little nicer to your big sister?"

"Sorry. I had a weird morning."

"It's still morning," Adler said.

"It's been that weird."

"I assume you're here to talk about it." Adler sat next to Paxton at the kitchen table. "Does this have anything to do with Chris?"

"How'd you know?"

"Well, you did send her my way yesterday; to use your spa gift card."

"I don't like spas; you know that."

"I *do* know that. Now, would you like to stop deflecting and tell me why you're here?" she asked, taking a sip of her coffee.

"We've kind of been dating."

"You don't say." Adler feigned surprise.

"Do you want me to talk or not?"

"Go on." Adler laughed.

"It started when I got to town."

"You've been dating this whole time?"

"What? No. I just have to start at the beginning so that it all makes sense."

"Oh, okay. I was about to be really pissed that you didn't tell me."

Paxton told her about the first few days in Tahoe. Then, she talked about the trip she and Chris had taken together.

"You took her to the speakeasy?" Adler asked. "You wouldn't even tell *me* where that place was. And I'm your sister, Paxton."

"Oh, shit! I forgot you wanted to know all about that place when I told you. I totally planned on taking you one day. I was just postponing because it annoyed you." Paxton laughed.

"You really are an asshole." Adler glared at her.

"We had a moment there, Adler. We didn't do anything about it then, but it was there. When we got back, Wes invited me for dinner. Chris and I flirted a little. Then, we came here to make dinner for you and Morgan, and…" She looked down at her untouched coffee. "We maybe…"

"In my house, Paxton?!"

"In your foyer, technically." She blushed but looked up at Adler anyway. "I didn't plan it. Neither of us did. It just happened. Well, it happened to me. I mean, she…"

"I don't need the details, Pax."

"I just mean that she did stuff to me, and then you guys got home. But right before you did, she said she wanted to talk. It got weird through the dinner. I dropped her off at home. She invited me in and told me she doesn't sleep with women on the first date. She and I hadn't even had a date yet. Anyway, I stayed there, but we didn't do anything. Then, I went over to have a movie night with her and Wes. I stayed over again. Nothing happened, either. Last night, though, Adler, we had our first date."

"And something happened, I take it?"

"A lot happened. It was amazing. It was perfect, Adler."

"Yeah?" Adler asked and lifted the corner of her mouth into a small smile.

"Adler, it was the best sex I've ever had," Paxton whispered for no good reason. "Every time."

"How many times were there?"

"Many, many times. We went back to my apartment. She stayed over."

"It sounds like things are moving in a good direction for you two. What happened this morning then?"

"I don't know. She borrowed one of my Oregon shirts, made some comment about how she thought I went to U-Dub, and then she was surprised that I used to kick-box."

"Why would any of that be a problem? Is she a big Husky fan or something? I would understand that. Huskies over Ducks any day of the week."

"And the family feud continues… Back to me now, Adler." Paxton glared at her sister. "I don't know what happened, exactly. I just know she left the apartment acting strangely and gave me some awkward cheek kiss. When I called her on it, she kissed me on the lips, but it was like I had to convince her to do it."

"Did you ask her about all this?"

"No, she left. I got dressed and came here," Paxton answered. "I have to see her at work. I guess I'm delaying the inevitable."

"Just talk to her Pax. I'm sure it's something silly. You really like her, don't you?"

"Yes, Adler. I'm here dealing with an existential crisis because I really do like her. If I didn't really like her, I'd be at work right now, ignoring her."

"That's mature."

"Adler, I'm here because I *am* being mature. What the hell did I do? She wanted to have sex last night, even though it was our first date. I swear I didn't pressure her or make the night about that or–"

"Paxton, you'd never pressure a woman to have sex. I don't think that has anything to do with it."

"Then, what did I do?"

"Why are you assuming you did anything?"

"I don't know. She was fine; and then she wasn't."

"Maybe she's fine again. She could have just had a weird moment or something."

Paxton sighed, looked back down at her coffee, and asked, "So, I just have to talk to her."

"That's what a relationship is, little sis."

"Look who's an expert in relationships now." Paxton smiled up at her sister.

"Not an expert, but I am in a pretty good one, finally. The worst part of my relationship with Morgan came when we stopped talking. I hated it. I knew I needed to talk to her, to find out what was going on, but I was too stubborn. She was stubborn, too. We both had to work on our stuff, though. Then, we started talking again. Now, we're here."

"I get it." Paxton took a drink. "I just hope everything's okay. I want to stay here, Adler. I have a meeting with Kinsley this afternoon, to look at houses."

"Houses? You're renting an apartment."

"Not for long. I don't want to renew the lease. I want to move here permanently."

"Not because of Chris?"

"No. I like it here. I can see myself living here, running the hotel, being the maid of honor at your wedding. And yes, that's a hint." She winked at Adler, who smiled. "If you two decide to have kids, I'd be here to see them grow up. If I decide to have kids, you'd be here to watch mine grow up, and they could all play together."

"You planning on getting a wife before the kids?"

"Yes, that's the idea."

"And is Chris someone you might see filling that role one day?"

"We've had one official date, Adler." She pushed the coffee away. "If I'm being honest, though, I think I'm falling in love with her."

"Paxton, that's amazing. I'm happy for you."

"Don't be yet." She stood. "I still need to figure out if there's something wrong."

***

"You're later than usual," Chris said when Paxton made it up the stairs to the guest room Chris had been painting.

"Sorry, I stopped by Adler's place."

"You don't have to apologize." Chris flattened out the tarp that had been on the floor. "I got the crew started on the restaurant."

"Thank you," Paxton replied, watching her work. "Is this you putting on your professional face, or is something else going on, Chris?"

"I'm just working, Paxton," Chris replied too quickly.

"Here's the thing, Chris: I've done the whole dating a woman who does the hot and cold act. I've dated a woman who was crazy passive-aggressive. I'm not sure which one you are right now, or if you're a combination of the two, but I'd prefer to just talk this out. If I said or did something wrong, I want to know about it. I want to fix it, Chris."

Chris stood up straight, sighed, and replied, "You didn't do anything wrong, Paxton."

"You're using my full name; I think I probably did." Paxton leaned against the wall that was already dry.

"I got caught off guard this morning."

"With what?" Paxton asked, crossing her arms over her chest.

"I know so little about you, Pax."

Paxton softened as she replied, "Oh, babe… Is that all?"

"It's a lot."

"Okay. It is, but you can learn whatever you want by talking to me instead of fleeing my apartment and making me worry I'd done something wrong." Paxton uncrossed her arms. "Can you come here?"

"I've never been with someone like you, Paxton."

"Like what?"

"You're, like… You're everything." Chris softened

then. "I don't mean it like that. I don't know… Maybe I do. But that's too much for people who just started dating. I just mean that you've done so much more than I have. I haven't dated a passive-aggressive woman or one that goes hot and gold. My relationships were always pretty short-lived, but I knew them better than I know you by the time we took the steps you and I have already taken."

"We should have waited longer." Paxton sighed to herself.

"Pax, I wanted to do what we did every time we did it." Chris finally moved to Paxton. "I initiated it."

"Do you want to slow down? We can slow down."

"Paxton, I don't want to slow down. I guess I'm just having a hard time with us moving as quickly as we have. Wes really likes you, and he keeps asking if you're my girlfriend. You're my boss. If this goes sideways, I'm out of a job… I can't be out of a job right before Wes goes to college. It's just a—"

"Do you want to be my girlfriend?" Paxton interrupted.

"That's what you took from everything I just said?" Chris asked with a laugh.

"Chris, I'm happy." Paxton shrugged both shoulders and smiled. "I don't know what else to say except that I am happy. You're a part of that. I have this place that I'm hoping to turn into something. I have my sister back in my life, and all these new friends I really like. Plus, there's this girl I'm kind of crazy about. She called me an asshole once, and that was it for me."

"Because I called you an asshole?" Chris laughed.

Paxton moved into her, wrapped her arms around Chris's waist, and said, "Yes."

"I'm worried, Pax."

"Tell me why."

"What happens if this doesn't work?"

"Your job is safe, Chris. I'd never fire you if we broke up; you have to know that."

"It would be weird, though."

"We'd make it work."

"I'd have to go back to Donoto's."

"No, you wouldn't."

"I would do anything for that kid, Pax, but I don't want to wait tables again."

"Is that what you're worried about? Chris, you don't have to worry about that." Paxton hugged her then. She pulled Chris into herself, wrapped her arms around the woman, and hugged her hard. "Babe, you don't have to work at Donoto's. You'll run the restaurant here; or you can do something else, and I'll find someone to run that part if you don't want to work in food at all."

"I just don't want to wait tables. I like the idea of running the restaurant here," Chris mumbled against Paxton's neck.

"I like the idea of you running it." Paxton pulled out of the hug. "Listen, I'm meeting Kinsley in a couple of hours, to look at some properties she thinks I might like. Why don't you come with me?"

"You want me to look at houses with you?"

"Why not?"

"It's your house, Pax."

"And you're someone I would like to have over a lot." She kissed Chris's forehead. "Like, *a lot* a lot. I kind of want you to like the place."

"Paxton, I'll go with you, but it is your house… You should get whatever you want, no matter what I think. It's a big deal, buying a house. Take it from someone who's never had one and who wishes she could afford to buy something she and her baby brother could call home."

"I've never bought a house, either, Chris."

"What are you talking about? You're a realtor." Chris pulled back.

"I am. But I rented my apartment. I had never bought anything in the city."

"Why not?"

"I guess because I never thought I would stay forever. Now, I know it's because I was meant to be here.

"So, you're really staying?"

"Did you think I was lying to you about that?" Paxton checked.

"No, I didn't. I guess it's just kind of sinking in that you're staying." Chris smiled. "And, apparently, you like to call me *babe*. That's new."

"Is that bad?" Paxton laughed softly. "Do you prefer honey, or dear, or baby?"

"No, Champ. I think *babe* is fine. But *babe* is a term of endearment, typically reserved for someone with at least girlfriend status."

"Which you *don't* want? Sorry, you're very confusing today. I'm trying to figure out what you want."

Chris laughed at that, pulled Paxton in close, and whispered, "I'd love to be your girlfriend, Paxton Williams."

Paxton smiled, pulled back enough to look at Chris, and kissed her.

CHAPTER 21

CHRIS WAS EXCITED to spend some quality time with Wes. For the first time in a while, they both had a weekend afternoon free. Wes had worked that morning at the hotel. Chris, thankfully, no longer worked on the weekends. She had plans with Paxton that night, but her afternoon was reserved for Wes. They planned to grab a late lunch, go to a movie, and have ice cream afterward. Chris would then go home and get ready for the date she would have with Paxton later that night.

"Are you ready? If we're going to make the movie, we need to get to the restaurant, like, now, Wes," Chris said from the living room.

"I needed to shower, Chris. I'm almost ready," he replied from the bathroom.

"Who are you trying to look nice for? Is there some girl you're interested in seeing today?"

"What? No, I'm just combing my hair. Give me two minutes."

There was a knock at the door. Chris looked at it as if she could see through it to reveal who was there, but the solid wood made that difficult.

"Are you expecting someone?" she asked.

"No. You?" Wes asked back.

Chris stood, made her way over to the door, and looked through the peephole. It was an older woman. She might have been around seventy or seventy-five; Chris was guessing. She also guessed that the woman was either selling something or wanted her to accept Jesus Christ as her personal savior. Chris didn't need anything, nor was she interested in a lecture. She also knew the woman had likely heard her yelling at Wes and, therefore, knew they were at home. She opened the door a few inches and peeked out.

"Yes?"

"Are you Christina Florence?" the woman asked.

"Who are you?" Chris asked back.

"I'm your grandmother," the old woman said.

"I'm sorry?" Chris asked, opening the door a little further.

"I'm your grandmother, Christina."

"Chris," she corrected. "And my grandmother is dead."

"I'm your mother's mother," she replied with a small smile.

"My mother's mother was, or – I don't know – *is* involved in a group that doesn't allow them to leave their compound, somewhere in the Nevada desert," she argued, but at the same time, she knew the woman had her mother's eyes.

"My name is Lily Dakota."

"Is that supposed to mean something to me?"

"My birth name is Cheyanne Odell." The old woman paused. "Your mother was born Violet Dakota. But had I not been involved…" She looked down and back up at Chris. "She would have been born something else."

Chris stared at the woman for a moment and said, "You're my mom's mom; fine. What are you doing here?"

"I've left the church," she replied.

"You mean the cult?"

The woman gave a small nod, as if she was wrestling with that term, and said, "It didn't feel like that to us."

"My mom was going to be married off to some old man when she was fourteen. She had to run away from you to keep herself safe," Chris argued in response. "That's a cult, *Cheyanne*." She used the old woman's birth name in an act of defiance.

"Your grandfather – my husband – was a great man. He was our leader. I was one of the chosen."

"And I'm choosing to close the door on you, because you are not my grandmother," Chris replied.

"Christina, please." The woman held up her hands. "I just want to meet my granddaughter," she said. "I left the church several months ago. I researched my daughter on the internet. Some people at the library helped me locate her. That brought me to you. I found out she died some years ago. All I'm asking is that you give me a chance to explain."

"Chris, who–" Wesley stood next to her, looking confused.

"Is this your son?" the woman asked.

"Son? She's, like, fourteen years older than me. Gross," Wes replied.

"Where she's from, that's normal. Wesley, this is our grandmother."

"Grandmother? Grandma's dead." He looked at the woman. "Oh," he said softly when he understood. "Mom."

"Mom."

"You're Wesley?"

"Yes," he replied. "You're my mom's mom."

"I am." The woman smiled. "I was hoping I could come inside, and we could talk."

"We have a day planned, and I have a date tonight," Chris explained.

"I'd love to meet the man that–"

"How's your heart?" Chris asked her.

"I'm sorry?"

"Do you have any heart conditions or anything I should know about?"

"No, my heart is fine."

"Then, I'm gay. The *man* that's coming by later, to pick me up for a date, isn't a man. It's a *woman.* She's my girlfriend, and I'm a lesbian. I'm guessing they don't have those at the compound?" Chris knew she was being rude; she just didn't care.

"Chris…" Wes placed a hand on her shoulder. "Come in."

"Wes, we're going–"

"She's our grandmother, Chris."

Wesley – the younger sibling – was being the more mature sibling at the moment. Chris moved out of the way, letting the old woman walk into their house. Cheyanne stood there for a moment between the two of them until Wes moved into the living room and sat on the sofa. Cheyanne followed suit. Chris closed the door. She followed them but didn't sit. She stood with her arms crossed over her chest.

"What are you doing here, Cheyanne?" Chris asked her.

"As I explained, I've left the church. My husband – your grandfather – passed away several months ago. It's been almost a year, in fact."

"I'm sorry to hear that," Wes said.

"There's a new church leader. He's nothing like your grandfather. He's taking the church in a direction that many of its followers do not agree to."

"He wants to marry girls off at age twelve instead of fourteen?" Chris asked.

"Our faith teaches–"

"Save the faith talk; we're not interested," Chris interrupted. "You'll never convince me that what you've tried to do to our mother is okay."

"Your mother had left the church. She ran away. And I had no idea what happened to her."

"Because she feared for her life and for what would happen if you made her marry someone three times her age. How many wives did her future husband already have?"

"Chris!"

"No, Wes. You were young when they died. You didn't hear all the crap this woman put or tried to put our mom through. I've kept you from that because I don't want you to know."

"I'm staying in a little apartment not too far from here," Cheyanne said. "I wanted to find you because you're my blood. I also thought you would want to know that you have cousins. Fourteen of them have also left the church."

"I thought Mom was an only child," Wes said to Chris.

"It's true. I was only blessed with one daughter myself. But your grandfather had many wives. He had sixty-four children between all of us. Some wives were more blessed than others when it came to having children. I only had your mother, but many of his wives had at least four children. A couple had seven and eight."

"Jesus," Wes exclaimed.

"I've spoken with many of your cousins. A few of them have expressed an interest in meeting you, too. They've recently left the only home they've ever known. Like me, they want a fresh start and need some help."

"You need money," Chris stated. "That's what this is about."

"No, Christina. I'm not here for money," Cheyanne said.

"Good. We don't have any," Chris replied. "What are you here for?"

"To bridge the gap between you and your family. I'd like the chance to get to know you two while I still can. I'm hoping you can tell me about the daughter I never got to see grow up. In short, I'm just interested in getting to know my grandchildren."

"I can't tell you much about Mom. I was pretty little when she died," Wes said.

Cheyanne turned her head to Chris.

"I'm not interested in filling you in on something you should have experienced yourself," Chris added angrily.

"You *chose* to join a cult. You have to live with the consequences of not knowing your daughter or your grandchildren."

"Chris, come on."

"Wes, if you want to talk to her, I won't stop you. You're practically an adult; it's your decision. But I don't want any part of this." She held up both of her hands in supplication. "Mom showed me her brand, Cheyanne. Do you have one, too?"

"Brand?" Wes asked.

"They branded women in that cult. Once you hit thirteen and were of marrying age, they jabbed you with a white, hot poker. You were property."

"It was what the church taught, Christina."

"Chris. I've said it ten times now. Have you heard Wes call me Christina? No. Because I go by Chris. You'd know that if you were a normal grandmother, but you're not. You joined that cult willingly. I won't dignify it by calling it a 'church.' You were an adult. You made a choice. You married that man who had wives and children already. You didn't let Mom go to school because women weren't meant to be smart or do anything important. They were supposed to be slaves to their husbands." She sighed deeply. "Do you have any idea how hard it was for her after she left? Thank God she found our dad. I don't know what would have happened to her had she not found him."

"I can only apologize," Cheyanne said. "And hope that you can forgive me one day."

"I'm not in a very forgiving mood right now. I'm in a very irritated mood, if you can't tell," Chris replied.

"I understand." The woman nodded. "I caught you at a bad time as well. I should be going. Would it be all right if I arranged for us to spend some time together when you're both available?" She stood up from the couch.

"Wes, it's up to you," Chris told him.

Wesley looked at his sister. Then, he looked at his grandmother.

"I don't know," he said. "Do you have a phone number? I could text you."

Chris tried not to laugh out loud.

"I have a phone. I can give you the number. You can call me anytime."

"Okay," he replied.

"Do you have a piece of paper?" she asked.

"You can just put it in my phone. Here you go," he replied, unlocking his cell phone and offering it to her.

"I'm afraid I don't…"

"Oh, sorry." Wesley turned the phone back around. "What's the number?"

The woman gave it to him. He saved it in his contacts. Then, she moved toward Chris, took a moment to look at her, and moved past her to the front door.

CHAPTER 22

"YOU DIDN'T LIKE the first place, but there are other options," Kinsley said.

"I did like the first place. Well, it was okay. I wasn't ready to rule it out completely. But Chris didn't like it," Paxton replied.

"You two must be serious if she gets a say about the house you're going to buy," Kinsley suggested.

Paxton smiled and said, "It's pretty early, but it is serious. I'm happy with Chris. I'm not going to let her talk me out of the house of my dreams if I find it, though. I mean, we're not married or anything... I just want her to like where I live. I don't plan on asking her to move in anytime soon, but Wes is one year away from college. By that time, maybe we'll be ready to move in together. I don't want her to hate the house."

"A year from now, huh?" Kinsley asked with a smile and a lifted eyebrow.

"I hope so." Paxton shrugged. "I told my sister that I'm crazy about her. I sent Chris the listings you gave me, and there are two she really liked. I thought we could look at them tomorrow, if you're available. It's a Sunday, so I'd understand if you can't. I know better than anyone what it's like to work seven days a week. It can wait until Monday."

"Riley's out of town this weekend. She's working on a case in Las Vegas. I'm all by myself. I can talk to the sellers today and see if they're up for it. If so, I can swing by and pick you guys up."

"Great. Thanks. I'll talk to Chris about it tonight. We have a date, but we've spent every night together recently. I'm not sure if she'll want to stay in our own places tonight. It's strange. I've never dated someone with a kid before. Wes, obviously, isn't a child; and he's her brother, not her son. But, in a way, he is her kid. I don't know how it works, though. I want to respect their relationship and how important it is to her. I want her to know that it's okay if we have to spend the night apart so that she can have a night with her brother."

"But you also know you're going to miss sleeping next to her?" Kinsley asked.

"It's weird, right?" Paxton asked. "It's only been a few days. We went to Seattle together, but we weren't *together* then. I would say, we only started to flirt at the very end there. Now, we're a couple. I want to be with her every night already. I'm not codependent or anything, but I do know that I want her to stay with me or for me to stay with her as often as possible."

"My story is different than yours, but I know what you mean. I met Riley in college."

"I thought you two hadn't been together all that long," Paxton replied.

They were sitting in Kinsley's office. She'd called Paxton that morning to let her know that she had a few more listings for her to check out. Paxton had sent the links to Chris almost immediately. They'd texted about two in particular that they would want to see. It felt, oddly enough, completely normal that they would be looking for a house together, despite the fact that it was only Paxton who was actually looking to buy. Paxton had stopped by Kinsley's office after grabbing them both a coffee. Paxton, truthfully, was using Kinsley. She'd been bored. Chris had her lunch and movie date with Wes. Adler and Morgan were off doing some couple things. Reese and Kellan were in San Francisco for the weekend, visiting Kellan's friends. Kinsley said Riley was out and she was killing time at the office. Paxton had joined her.

"We haven't been," Kinsley confirmed. "But we met in college. Riley was a freshman. I was a senior. I liked her then, but she didn't like me."

"Really?" Paxton asked.

"Well, she didn't really like me or *not* like me. She was in her own little world back then. We would see each other every so often. I dated other people. She dated other people. She was actually in a long-term relationship when she moved back to Tahoe."

"Scandalous," Paxton said.

"She didn't cheat or anything." Kinsley laughed. "But I knew I wanted more than friendship. Eventually, she realized she did, too."

"And you've been together ever since," Paxton finished.

"And I hope we always will. I mean, we're getting married," Kinsley replied. "She's the one I'm supposed to be with. I guess I always knew that. I just thought it was a crush back then, when it was really much more."

"That's sweet."

"Did you feel that with Chris?" Kinsley leaned forward.

"I felt like she hated me," Paxton replied with a chuckle and took another drink of her cold coffee. "I think she thought I was stuck-up, or just an asshole. It *was* kind of hot, though, watching her freak out in that street when I accidentally stole her parking spot."

Kinsley laughed and asked, "It was hot watching her freak out?"

"Kind of. Okay, it was *definitely* hot. Her nostrils flared, and I may have thought about what would happen if…" Paxton widened her eyes.

"If they flared in a different situation? Got it." Kinsley nodded.

Paxton's phone rang. She pulled it out of her pocket, looked down at the screen, and caught Chris's name.

"Speaking of the devil," Paxton said. "I should take this."

"Tomorrow?" Kinsley asked as Paxton stood.

"I'll text you," Paxton replied. "I'm in. I just want to check with her."

"It's like you're already married," Kinsley joked.

"Maybe one day." Paxton waved at her, put her phone to her ear, and said, "Hey, babe."

"Hey. Can you come over?"

"Are you okay?" Paxton asked after closing the door behind her.

"No, something happened. Can you come over?" Chris sniffled.

"I'm on my way. Chris, what's wrong?"

"I'll tell you when you get here."

"But you're okay? I mean, physically? Wes?"

"I'm okay. He's okay. I just need you," Chris said, sniffling again.

"I'll be there in ten minutes," Paxton replied.

***

"Babe, what happened?" Paxton asked, walking straight into Chris's bedroom.

Wes had opened the front door. He hadn't said anything. He'd just looked upset. Paxton wasn't sure if it was angry-upset or sad-upset. He'd only opened the door to her. Then, he'd walked back into his bedroom and closed the door. She'd proceeded into Chris's room, wondering what the hell was going on.

"Where's Wes?" Chris asked, looking past her toward the open door of the bedroom.

"In his room."

"Can you close that?"

"Yeah. Chris, what's going on? You're kind of scaring

me," Paxton said as she closed the door and moved to the bed, where Chris was sitting back against the pillows. "What happened?"

"My grandmother stopped by today, out of the blue," she replied.

Paxton sat next to her and asked, "I thought your grandparents were—"

"Dead? Remember how I told you my mom was raised in a cult?"

"Oh, *those* grandparents. Her mom came here today?" Paxton asked.

"She did. I wasn't even sure she was still alive." Chris wiped her cheeks.

"What did she want?" Paxton reached for Chris's hand and took it in her own.

"She said she just wanted to get to know us. She left the cult, I guess."

"Wow. She left?"

"She said she left a few months ago."

"That's good, right?" Paxton asked; she had no idea what to say to someone in this situation. "She's safer now, probably."

"She was married to my grandfather, who was the leader of the stupid thing. She was always safe. She joined as an adult. She was twenty when she drove from Baltimore – where she'd been raised, out west – where she found the place she still lovingly refers to as a *church*. He swept her off her feet, I guess. She was wife number seven of thirteen."

"I can't imagine having thirteen wives… I can't imagine having more than one," Paxton said.

"But you do want one, right?" Chris asked, seemingly changing the subject along with her expression.

"What?"

"You want that, right? Marriage? One day?"

"Yes, Chris. I would like to get married one day. I'd just like the one wife, though." Paxton smiled lovingly at her. "Are you okay with her just coming here like this?"

"No," Chris replied. "I never thought about it as a possibility. My mom escaped for a reason. I never thought my grandmother would leave. I thought she'd die there. I knew I'd never go visit. I've kept Wes from most of this."

"He looked upset. Did something happen between the two of you?"

Chris rested her head on Paxton's shoulder. Paxton kissed the top of it, squeezed Chris's hand, and waited for her to say something.

"He's mad at me because I wasn't very nice or forgiving to her. I guess he wants to get to know her. I don't. He doesn't understand."

"You don't want to get to know her?" Paxton asked.

"No. Why would I?" Chris lifted her head and looked at Paxton. "She took part in teenage marriages, statutory rape, branding, and about a million other terrible things."

"I'm not saying you have to forgive her for any of that, or even excuse it. I'm just asking. She made mistakes; that's obvious. She's still your grandmother, though, Chris."

"So, I'm supposed to pretend like she didn't do those things?"

"No, I just mean…" Paxton sighed. "It's like when there's a killer that has kids. Sometimes, the kids have a hard time separating the killer from their father. They say that they still love him because he's their father, but they don't condone what he did. I'm not saying your grandmother is a murderer, obviously."

"She might be; I have no idea what they do there. They could be killing anyone that doesn't comply with their rules."

"What are you going to do about Wes?"

"I don't know…" Chris exhaled deeply. "He's seventeen. He was young when our parents died. Mom told me some of what happened there, but I know she left out a lot, and I was an adult. I've only told him some of what she told me. I didn't want him to know most of it until he was old enough. It hasn't even been something we've talked about in years. I was honestly hoping he'd never ask so that I'd never have to tell him."

"But he's asking now?"

"He put her phone number in his phone. After she left, he got angry with me for, as he called it, 'acting like a child.' He's not entirely wrong. I was mean. I knew it, and I did it anyway. I just didn't care. Wes yelled at me. He said we should get to know our only family member. I told him she's not family to us. He said she's blood, and that's all that matters. I said some more things. He said some things." Chris paused. "I don't know what to do. Those people are dangerous. *She's* dangerous."

"She's an old woman, and she's your grandmother. Is she really that dangerous?" Paxton asked.

"He's young," Chris argued. "What if she convinces him to go with her?"

"Chris, she left the cult."

"You don't ever really *leave* those places. My mom had *escaped*, but she never really left. She and my dad fought all the time about it, in the beginning. Her nightmares caused her to go to therapy for years. I think they almost got divorced once, because of it. Honestly, it was right around the time she got pregnant with Wes. I'm convinced, had she not gotten pregnant, they might have split up. And that was years later."

"Okay. But I can understand why he'd want to get to know his only family outside of you, Chris."

Chris stood and replied, "I'm not wrong about this, Pax. You don't know anything about it."

"I'm not saying I do," Paxton argued. "I'm just saying that I understand his desire to get to know his grandparent."

"And what if she's still involved in the cult? What if she takes him to lunch one day and decides to go on a drive to their compound? What if she keeps him there by force, or even just convinces him to stay?"

"Chris, you raised that boy. Do you really think he'd just leave you to join them?" Paxton asked and hung her legs over the side of the bed, facing her girlfriend.

"I never told him how bad it was there for our mom. He has no frame of reference. I've left him defenseless." Chris ran a hand through her hair.

"No, you haven't. You saved him from knowing terrible things your mom went through. You had no way of knowing this would happen, Chris. You just have to trust him. He's smart, and he's old enough to know–"

"My grandmother was old enough to know, too, Pax." Chris's voice grew louder. "You can't know what this is like; what's going through my head right now."

"I guess not," Paxton replied, defeated. "What do you want me to say, Chris? What can I do?"

"Just go," she said softly, motioning with her hand toward the door. "I need to think, and I can't do that with you here."

"You asked me to come over. Let's just keep talking, babe."

"No, Pax. I need you to go. I need some time alone. Then, I need to talk to my brother," Chris replied.

"Fine." Paxton stood after wiping her hands over non-existent wrinkles on her pants. "I'll leave you alone to take care of everything yourself; seems to be how you like things, anyway, Chris. Call me if you want to talk about any of this."

Paxton walked out of the bedroom past Wes's closed door. She made it to the front door, took the doorknob in her hand, waited a moment in hopes of Chris asking her to stay, after all, and opened the door. When it closed it behind her, she walked to her car slowly, still giving Chris time to catch up to her. When she started the car, she waited a few more seconds. Then, she backed out of the driveway and hit the road.

CHAPTER 23

CHRIS HAD KNOCKED on Wes's door once. She'd made them dinner. He didn't come out. She knocked on his door again later, but only heard his loud music blaring through the speakers. So, she left a plate in the microwave for him, thinking about the date she had missed with Paxton because of the events of the day. She knocked on the door one more time before she went into the bathroom to take a shower. She then went to bed, trying to figure out what she should have done differently that day, to at least make it so that her brother would talk to her. She tried to think about what she should do with the multitude of messes she'd created.

She'd had a night of restless sleep and finally gave up on it around eight in the morning. She'd made a pot of coffee and drunk about half of it. She'd try to talk some sense into her brother by being a little more open to his thoughts than she had been the day before. She'd sit him down, apologize for getting upset, listen to his opinions first, and then, state her own. Chris knew she didn't want him spending any time with their grandmother, but she also knew that, ultimately, it would be up to him to make that decision for himself. She knocked on his door around ten, deciding to let him sleep in a little.

"Wes, can we talk?" she asked calmly through the closed door. "I know I messed up yesterday. Can we just sit down and talk about it?"

He didn't respond. There was no sound coming through the room. She'd always done everything she could to respect his privacy. There was a lock on his bedroom door. Chris had never had a problem with him having the door closed or locked, knowing that teenage boys often did things in private that their adult sisters did not need to walk in on accidentally. Chris waited another few seconds. Then, she reached for the doorknob. She turned it, noting it was unlocked, and opened the door. Wes wasn't in his room. She headed out to the living room and peeked through the windows out into their small backyard. He wasn't there, either. Then, she went to the front of the house just as her phone chimed with a text. Chris had had it on do not disturb all night and often left it on do not disturb well into the morning on weekends. When she glanced out the window, Wes's car – recently repaired and returned from the shop – was not in the driveway. Chris swallowed at the thought that she had no idea where her little brother was. Then, she remembered the text message. Thinking it was from Wes, telling her where he'd run off to, Chris made her way back to her bedroom, picked the phone up off the bedside table, and checked the read out. She then exhaled deeply and dialed.

"Hey, there you are," Paxton said. "I've been calling and texting all morning."

"I had my phone on do not disturb. I was in the kitchen. It was in the bedroom. He's with you?"

"He came over to my apartment around seven and knocked on the door. I didn't know what to do. I fed him breakfast and tried to call you without him knowing, because he asked me not to."

"He's never done anything like this before," Chris replied.

"Has he ever had anyone to run off to before, though?" Paxton asked. "I guess his friends… But, I mean, an adult that he knows and trusts."

"I guess not," Chris said, sitting on the end of her bed.

"Should I come over and pick him up?"

"I think you should just give him the day, Chris. He doesn't seem angry anymore, but he is upset, and he's trying to think. He doesn't want to disappoint his big sister, but he's also looking for a way to connect with this person who knew his mother. I'm about to meet with Kinsley, to look at a couple of houses. I asked him if he wanted to come with me. He said yes."

"Houses?" Chris asked.

"I was going to invite you to come with me last night, but things didn't work out how I'd hoped," Paxton replied.

"Me neither." Chris sighed. "Listen, Pax. I'm–"

"He's coming out of the coffee shop. I sent him in there when I saw you were calling. I'm by Kinsley's office. I'll keep an eye on him today and try to convince him to check in with you, okay?"

"Oh, okay."

"Bye." Paxton disconnected the call.

Chris looked down at the phone, taken aback by the abrupt ending to their call as well as the fact that her brother had sought comfort from her girlfriend instead of from her. They'd always been each other's person. She trusted him. He trusted her. He had his friends from school and tennis, but Paxton was right: he didn't have any other adults he trusted. She was happy he'd found that in Paxton but also hurt that he needed to go to her for something like this at all.

***

"She's my girlfriend's sister, Chris. I can try to be objective, but it's hard."

"I know," she told Morgan. "I just needed to get out of the house. I saw your car outside the store and thought I'd stop in and unload my troubles on you."

"But they're troubles with Adler's sister. Paxton's basically my sister-in-law. She will be one day, when Adler and I get married. This kind of stuff should probably be brought up with Kinsley and Riley, or maybe Kellan and Reese."

"I don't know Kellan well enough to talk about this stuff with her. Plus, she and Reese are trying to get pregnant now. Kinsley is with my girlfriend right now, taking her on tours of homes. Riley's busy with work whenever she's not with Kinsley. I don't know her all that well, either, yet. You know I'm mainly a private person when it comes to family stuff. You know the most."

"If you want my honest opinion, I can give it to you. But you might not like it. Are you prepared for that?"

Morgan took a drink of her coffee from an oversized purple mug. They were sitting in the coffee shop by Kinsley's office. Chris was hoping she'd catch Kinsley, Paxton, and Wes heading back into Kinsley's building after they finished looking at houses. She faced the window. Morgan faced her.

"I need to hear it," Chris replied.

"Wes is seventeen. Your parents died when he was so young… He doesn't have the memories of your mother that you do. This is your mom's mother. She's someone that can tell him more about her."

"She'd only known her when our mom was a kid," Chris returned.

"I doubt that matters to Wes, though. Put yourself in his shoes for a moment: if you'd lost them when you were six years old, what would you even remember about them?"

"Not much," she replied. "I remember my dad would read to me at night. My mom made me breakfast; eggs and bacon on Sundays." Chris smiled. "She smelled like oranges on those days, since she used a juicer to make orange juice for me. In my mind, I see her wearing green a lot when I was that age. But I also know it was her favorite color because she told me later. I'm not sure if I'm making a connection when there's not one, or if she really did wear green that much when I was that young."

"And Wes doesn't have that because he didn't get later," Morgan suggested. "All his memories are from a time when he was so young, things were kind of blurry. He has you; and that's great... But you didn't know your mom as a kid. Her mother did, though. Maybe he just wants to have a conversation with her to learn more. Maybe he wants a relationship; I don't know. But it doesn't sound like you listened enough to know, either."

"I planned to make that up to him today. But when he woke up, he went to Paxton's instead."

"And that's the thing you're really upset about, isn't it?" Morgan asked, taking another sip of her coffee.

"I'm upset he ran off without telling me, yeah."

"No, I mean you're upset that he ran to Paxton."

"Why would I be upset about that?" Chris asked.

"Two reasons. One, because he didn't come to you; which hurts. Two, because you and Paxton just started this relationship. You're scared, Chris. What if he comes to rely on Paxton, and you and Pax don't work out?"

Chris swallowed hard and replied, "I don't like you all that much right now."

"I warned you," Morgan said with a chuckle. "You wouldn't like what I had to say about this."

"Pax is so much more than this place. Doesn't it feel like that sometimes?"

"What do you mean?" Morgan asked.

"Just that she grew up in this big city. Her apartment was amazing. She owns her own business. She's still running it from here, which is amazing. She just decided one day to buy an old hotel and rebuild it from scratch. She's buying a house here now, instead of just renting, because she can. She can do so much. She can pick up tomorrow and run off to Africa if she wanted. She could move to Brazil and sell houses there, or run a mountain town inn in Switzerland."

"Has she expressed an interest in doing any of those things?" Morgan asked with a smile. "Because the Pax I know wanted to live closer to the sister that she loves, build this hotel that for some reason she's really attached to, and fall in love with a woman she met in South Lake Tahoe." She paused. "Pax wants to settle down, Chris. She's not looking for adventures out there. She wants to have them here, with the people she loves."

"What if she changes her mind, though? A few months ago, she was happy in Seattle."

"Was she?" Morgan asked. "Have you actually asked her what were the reasons she was so fast in moving here?"

"No, but—"

"Chris, you're making a lot of assumptions about your girlfriend. You should probably talk to her, because I don't think that any of them are true."

"I've been afraid to," Chris admitted.

"Why, though?"

"Because what if they are, Morgan?" She paused on a sigh. "I could fall in love with this girl."

"Or, are you already?" Morgan asked thoughtfully.

Chris looked out the window. She caught sight of Kinsley's car pulling into a parking spot. Kinsley got out of the driver's side. Wes climbed out of the back seat. He was smiling and laughing at something someone had said, it appeared. Paxton got out of the passenger's side. When Wes walked over to her, she smiled at him. She then said something that caused his smile to disappear. He nodded. Then, Chris watched him pull something out of his pocket. Chris squinted to see it. A moment later, he put it away, and they all headed into the building. Her phone chimed. She glanced at it on the table. Wes had texted her that he was okay and would be home for dinner. Paxton had asked him to text her that he was all right. Wes had listened.

Chris texted him back that she'd make his favorite, macaroni and cheese. Then, she texted Paxton back a simple message of two words. Before locking her phone, though, she added something to her message of thank you to Paxton and sent another message to her. Then, she locked it and took a drink of her coffee. Her phone chimed moments later with Paxton's acceptance of Chris's dinner invitation.

"When are you going to tell her?" Morgan asked.

"Tell her what?"

"That you're in love with her and terrified that she might leave," Morgan replied.

"Oh, that." Chris laughed softly. "I'm not sure I will."

"Chris, you have to be honest with your girlfriend. I can tell you every day what I think about Paxton's plans, but she's *your* girlfriend. You need to ask those questions, talk about what the answers mean for the two of you, and decide if you're taking any of those steps together."

"I'm crazy about her." Chris smiled at Morgan. "She's the first girlfriend I've ever had that's understood my relationship with my brother and why it's so important to me."

"Then, you should tell her that, Chris."

CHAPTER 24

"Pax, what do I do?" Wes asked her.

They were sitting in his car. He'd driven them back to his and Chris's house. Paxton thought about driving herself, but Wes had asked to drive them. It meant that if she and Chris had another argument, she'd be calling a car to pick her up, but she wanted to give Wes what he wanted, given the difficult weekend he'd had.

"Wes, you're almost an adult. This isn't something I can tell you how to handle."

"She's your girlfriend," Wes replied, looking over at Paxton.

"And she's your sister. You've known her a lot longer than I have," she countered, punching him lightly on the shoulder. "Chris is important to me. You are important to me, too. I want both of you to be happy."

"I just feel like I should call her."

"Your grandma?"

"Yes."

"And you think Chris is going to be upset about that?"

"Yes." He nodded. "She doesn't want me to talk to her at all."

"This is going to get me in trouble later, I think, but it's your decision, Wes. She's your grandmother, too. Your relationship with her has nothing to do with Chris. If she doesn't want one, that's up to her. But you need to do what you feel is right for you."

Wes smiled softly at her and said, "Thanks. That can't have been easy."

"What?"

"Risking your life like that. If Chris hears you've given me that advice, she might try and kill you," he said with a laugh.

"The only thing she could do that would kill me, would be to break up with me."

"You really like her, don't you?"

"Wes, I'm going to tell you a secret. Not even Chris knows this yet, and I want to be the one to tell her. Can I trust you?"

"Of course."

"I'm in love with her," Paxton said. "When I asked you about a hundred times today if you thought she'd like the houses we looked at, it's because I want her to spend a lot of time there."

"You asked me if I liked them, too," he replied.

"Because I'd like you to spend time there, too. You are both important to me, okay?"

"Okay." He nodded. "I guess we should go in. Have you had her mac and cheese? It's ridiculous. She puts bacon in it. It's so good," he said.

As they climbed out of his car, Paxton laughed at how Wes could move so easily from such a heavy topic to the topic of macaroni and cheese. He opened the front door and held it for her. She walked in before him, saw Chris in the kitchen over the stove, got a flash of what that scene would have looked like in the two houses she'd toured today, and then smiled as Chris turned around.

"Hey," she said.

"Hi," Chris replied. "Hey, Wes."

"Hi," he said. "I'm going to wash up for dinner, okay?"

"Sure. It'll be ready in about ten minutes," Chris told him.

He nodded and moved in the direction of his bedroom. Paxton stood over by the now closed front door with her hands in the pockets of her jeans. Chris stood by the stove. They both looked at one another. Neither of them, apparently, knew what to do or say next. Paxton looked over at the living room and tilted her head in that direction. Chris nodded. They moved to the sofa just as Wes's bedroom door closed.

"I should start with an apology," Chris said. "I am sorry, Pax."

"Me too," Paxton replied.

"Why are *you* sorry? You didn't do anything wrong."

"I don't know… Maybe I should have just listened yesterday instead of offering my opinion," Paxton said.

"Pax, that's not how this works." Chris took Paxton's hand. "I messed up. You only tried to help. I guess I've had a lot rolling around in my mind lately, and I haven't exactly shared it with you."

Paxton gulped and asked, "Do you… Are you trying to break–"

"Pax, no." Chris smiled so softly at her, that Paxton knew in that moment that Chris wasn't leaving her. "I was worried you'd do that to me."

"What?"

"Not exactly that," Chris clarified. "I guess I've been worrying that you have led this amazing life. You still have things that could pull you back to Seattle at any time. You bought a hotel here on your first visit. What if you get through one hellish winter in this place and want nothing to do with it? What if you go on a trip somewhere else, love it more, and decide to stay there?"

"What? You're worried I might leave? Chris, I'm trying to buy a house here."

"But you could buy a house somewhere else, too. You're a realtor, Pax. You could sell any place you buy just-"

"Chris, I'm not going anywhere." Paxton touched Chris's cheek. "I never bought a place in Seattle, remember? There was a reason for that. I'm buying here because I want to make this my home. I told you that."

"I know. I just can't help but think you could change your mind."

"What do I need to do to get it through that thick head of yours?" Paxton asked with a smile.

"I don't know. I guess that's my fault, too. I'm not good at this."

"At what?"

"I've never been good at accepting help from others, Pax. When my parents died, it was just Wes and me. We've taken care of each other as he's gotten older. Then, you show up, and things change. I've been having a hard time dealing with it."

"I don't want to make you feel like I'm coming in and trying to take care of you guys. Chris, you've done so much already. You've supported yourself and your kid brother through all this with no one else to help you. I just want to be a part of your life."

"I know, Pax." Chris let go of Paxton's hand in order to place her own on Paxton's thigh. "I know this is new. We're still figuring things out between you and me."

"Chris, I'm staying here. I want to be with you. I'm looking for a house that you and Wes will both like, because I'm kind of hoping this thing continues for you and me. Maybe one day, you and Wes would live there with me."

"Move in with you?" Chris asked.

"Not tomorrow. I was thinking more about once Wes goes off to college." Paxton smiled at her. "If we get there sooner, that's fine, too. He could have his own room whenever he comes home on the weekend or for breaks. I want a future with you, Chris."

Wes emerged from the hallway and made his way into the kitchen. The rest of this conversation would have to be postponed, but the smile Chris was giving her told Paxton that there was hope Chris wanted the same things she did.

"Bacon, mac and cheese," Wes said.

"It's probably done. You can pull it out of the oven," Chris replied while still looking at Paxton. She then leaned forward and kissed her girlfriend's lips. "To be continued."

Paxton smiled at her. They stood together and made

their way into the kitchen, where they each prepared their own plate before sitting at the kitchen table. It was silent for a few moments as they all got settled, poured drinks, and Wes added hot sauce to his macaroni and cheese for some reason.

"Chris, can we talk about grandma?" Wes asked a few minutes later.

"Of course," Chris replied.

"Should I maybe…"

"No, Pax. It's cool. Stay," Wes said.

Paxton looked at Chris, who nodded and smiled softly in her direction.

"I'm sorry, Wes. I blew up yesterday. I shouldn't have done that. It wasn't fair to you."

"It was surprising for both of us. I get that." He moved his fork around on the plate, likely out of nervousness. "I want to respect that you don't want me to talk to her, but there's something in me that feels like I need to talk to her. Does that make sense?"

"Yes, it does. She's your grandmother, Wes."

"I was thinking I could call her first. Maybe she and I could just talk. I know you don't want me to talk to her. I don't want to upset you, Chris, but–"

"You won't." Chris took a drink of her water. "It's okay. You should talk to her. Just be careful, okay? That's all I'll say."

"And you won't be mad?"

"No, you're an adult. I need to treat you like one."

"Do you think you'll want to talk to her, too?" Wes asked.

"I don't know. Maybe someday. I know I'm not ready yet."

"She's old, Chris." He shrugged his shoulders. "You may not have all that much time left."

"That's a risk I'm willing to take, I guess. I don't want you to take it, though, if you feel like this is something important you need to do. If you want to learn more about

Mom, or what happened before or when she left, you should talk to her. She'd know."

"Maybe I could call her after dinner since I have school tomorrow?" he asked.

"You can call her from your room. I'll leave you alone," she replied.

"Pax, are you staying tonight?" he asked, turning to Paxton.

"We haven't talked about that yet," Paxton said, looking at Chris.

"Wes, finish eating. You can go call our grandmother from your room. I'll pack an overnight bag while you do. If everything goes okay with the call, I'll leave with Pax after, and we'll stay at her place tonight."

"Are you sure?" Paxton asked.

"I'm sure." Chris smiled at her.

***

An hour later, Wes was still in his room, talking to his grandmother. Chris had packed her overnight bag. Paxton had already loaded it into Chris's car. As they waited for Wes to come out of his room, Chris was lying on the sofa. Her head was in Paxton's lap. Paxton was running her fingers through Chris's hair while her other hand ran along the skin under Chris's t-shirt.

"Tell me about Oregon," Chris said.

"It's one of the fifty states," Paxton replied, looking down at her.

"Come on. I'm trying to get to know you better. Tell me about your time at Oregon," Chris said with a little laugh that Paxton found adorable.

"Oh, I was a business major. Finance, to be exact."

"Nerdy," Chris replied. "My girlfriend is a sexy nerd," she added.

"Is that a good thing?" Paxton laughed.

"Definitely a good thing."

"I graduated in three and a half years. Does that make me nerdier and, therefore, sexier?"

"Absolutely." Chris stared up at her.

"You're so beautiful," Paxton said.

"I'm already your girlfriend; you don't have to woo me anymore," Chris said.

"I'll woo you forever if you let me," Paxton replied.

Wes's door opened. He made his way down the hall. Chris sat up. The mood between them had instantly shifted. Now, they were concerned about Wes. A moment before, Paxton had been about to tell Chris she loved her for the first time.

"It's okay. I'm okay," Wes said as he sat next to Chris on the sofa. "We talked mostly about me. She asked about school. I told her about tennis. Pretty basic stuff."

"That's good," Chris replied.

"Yeah. I mean, I asked her about her stuff, too," he said.

Paxton watched Chris's expression change. She was suddenly more interested yet cautious at the same time.

"You did?"

"She didn't want to talk too much about everything. I guess I get it."

"Did she talk to you about Mom?" Chris asked.

"Only a little. We thought we could meet in person to talk more in-depth about that. She asked me to stop by her apartment next weekend if it's okay with you," he replied.

"She said that, or you added that part about it being okay with me?" Chris asked.

"I told her I'd have to check with you. She said she understood."

Chris resisted the impulse to roll her eyes, because, of course, their grandmother wouldn't suggest that. But Wes would. Instead, she sighed and nodded at him.

"I appreciate you checking with me, but it's entirely up to you," she replied.

CHAPTER 25

"I'M SORRY WE'RE such a mess," Chris said to her the moment they entered Paxton's apartment.

"Who's the they you're referring to?" Paxton asked, lifting her eyebrow as she tossed her keys on the table. "*We* are not a mess." She pointed between the two of them.

"I meant Wes and me," Chris replied.

Paxton turned to face her girlfriend. She noticed how tired Chris looked. It had been a long weekend for her and for Wes. She walked toward Chris, closed the front door of the apartment behind her, and reached for her hips.

"You guys are not a mess. Wes will decide what he wants to do about your grandmother, and so will you," she offered. "Just because someone comes swirling into your life asking you to change a part of yourself for them, doesn't make you a mess. I mean, I basically did that."

"You did not," Chris replied, staring at her with kind eyes. "Okay, you did. But that's the thing that happens when you're in a relationship with someone. I'm just stubborn."

Paxton smiled at her. She ran her hands through Chris's hair, leaned in, and gave her a quick kiss on the lips.

"Do you want to take a bath?"

"Are you joining me?" Chris asked.

"How about I run the water for you and get everything ready? You can just relax for a minute. Then, enjoy your moment of relaxation before we go to bed."

"Fine. I will accept your amazingly sweet suggestion." Chris sighed. "But if you would have added your naked body to the equation, I would have been eternally grateful."

Paxton chuckled at her. They headed toward the bedroom. She left Chris to sit on the bed and went into the bathroom. She started the water, located a towel, hung it on the rack next to the tub, turned off the lights, and lit a few candles. She rarely did this for herself, but every now and then, she found a candlelit bath relaxing. When the water had filled high enough, she turned it off and went back to the bedroom, where she found Chris lying on the bed, staring up at the ceiling. Paxton sat down next to her.

"You okay?" she asked, running her hand up under Chris's shirt to rest on her stomach.

"What if I meet with her and I like her?" Chris asked.

"You sound like you think that would be a bad thing," Paxton replied softly.

"She was in a cult voluntarily, Pax. What does that make me if I actually like the woman?" Chris turned her face to look up at Paxton's.

"It means she's your grandmother, Chris. You don't have to like everything about a person just to get along with them. I know you don't like when I leave my socks on the floor after kicking them off while I'm asleep." Paxton smiled at her. "It hasn't broken us up, though."

"What if it does, though?" Chris asked. "What if all my baggage ends up ending us?"

Paxton kissed her lips gently. Then, she stood and held out both of her hands. Chris took them, sitting up in the process.

"Take your bath. I'll be here when you're done. I'll be here as long as you want me to be, Chris." She kissed Chris's cheek. "By the way, Wes texted me. He asked if we were going to check out some more houses tomorrow and if he could join us if we were."

"He asked if *we* were checking them out?"

"He did. Why?" Paxton asked.

"I don't know." Chris shook her head. "I should go take that bath you just ran for me."

"Oh, okay." Paxton reached out again as if to escort her girlfriend to the bathroom.

"I know where it is, Pax." She laughed. "Unless you've changed your mind on joining me."

"No. I'll be out here when you're done, though." Paxton kissed Chris on the cheek. "Take your time."

Chris smiled, pecked Paxton's lips, and pressed her own forehead to Paxton's while closing her eyes. Paxton did the same. They remained that way for several moments before Chris pulled back, went into the bathroom, and slipped into the bathtub. Paxton could only hope it would help her girlfriend relax and assuage her worries.

***

As Chris bathed, Paxton readied herself for bed. She wondered about Chris's reaction to Wes asking about them looking for a house. She knew Chris was concerned by the word *we* in his sentence. Paxton was happy in Tahoe. She was happy with Chris. She wanted a life with her, but she was nowhere near ready to move in with her. She did want Chris to like whatever house she bought, though. That was important. Chris was renting. If she hated Paxton's new house, she wouldn't want to live there one day when they were ready. Paxton didn't want to find a great house just for now; she wanted to find something for her forever.

"That was just what I needed. Thank you," Chris said when she emerged from the bathroom completely nude.

"Oh, wow." Paxton turned to see her girlfriend standing in the doorway of the bathroom with the light from the room behind Chris, framing her body perfectly. Her hair was still wet. Her hands were at her sides. Her eyes looked tired but gorgeous. Chris was smiling. "You…"

"What?" Chris chuckled.

"You should get dressed for bed or…"

"Or what?" Chris teased. She stalked over to the bed, her hips swaying as she moved. "Is there a problem?" Her lips turned up into a sexy smirk.

"You're tired. We should–" Paxton was interrupted by Chris moving quickly to the bed and straddling her hips. Chris smiled down at her. "What happened to you? You went into that bathroom all doom and gloom, and now you're smiling."

"I wasn't *all* doom and gloom." She wrapped her arms around Paxton's neck. "Pax, thank you for not letting me ruin this."

"What?" Paxton asked, looking up at her girlfriend.

"I wasn't good to you. I nearly lost you because of that; because of something from my past that I still need to work out. You didn't leave. You could have… But you didn't."

"I couldn't have left, Chris," Paxton replied, sliding her arms around Chris's lower back. "I couldn't just leave you." She looked up into Chris's eyes. "I'm kind of crazy about you, Chris."

Chris leaned down and pressed her lips gently to Paxton's. Paxton's eyes closed at the gesture. She breathed Chris in and ran her hands up and down her back, reveling in the feel of the soft skin that was still warm from the bath.

Chris leaned into Paxton, pressing her lips to Paxton's ear, and said, "Pax, I love you."

Paxton's hands stopped moving against Chris's skin.

***

What had she just done? Chris could feel Paxton's heart pounding through the shirt as they were still pressed together. While she'd bathed, she'd thought about recent events. Her thoughts had turned from sad and angry with her grandmother and herself, to surprisingly happy and excited at the thought of Paxton waiting for her in the bedroom. Paxton was buying a house in South Lake. Paxton loved her brother. Of that, Chris was sure. Wes seemed to love Paxton. He was asking about the house she'd move into and wanted to be a part of the process. Chris knew they hadn't been together long enough for her to say those words. Had she ever even said those words to another woman before? If she had, she couldn't remember in that moment, because Paxton was staring up at her with an expression Chris couldn't read.

"Pax?" she asked softly.

"I had this plan, you know?" Paxton said, still looking up at her.

"Plan?"

"To say that to you," Paxton replied with a small smile, and Chris let out a sigh of relief. "I was planning on finding a house, telling you how important it is to me that you like it, and that one day I'd like you to live there with me, because I love you." Paxton's hands were on the move again. This time, they held onto Chris's hips. "I love you, too. I've never been particularly lucky in love, Chris. My past relationships were sometimes messy, and they never went anywhere; which is obvious, since I'm here with you right now. But, in this moment, with everything good I have in my life now, I wouldn't have had it any other way. Every stupid mistake I made and every good decision I made, they had all led me here, to you."

Chris smiled down at her girlfriend and said, "Damn, that's a good speech there, Champ."

"Oh, I was a state champion in speech giving, too. Did I not tell you that before?" Paxton asked with a smirk.

"No, you left that out. But I guess I should tell you now that I don't date nerds; I exclusively date swim champs."

"Good thing I was both, huh?" Paxton pressed her lips to Chris's neck. "I love you."

"I love you, too." Chris said, feeling the weight of those words as she did and realizing she was right in saying them.

Despite how they'd met, and how much Chris thought she had disliked Paxton Williams, she knew she loved this woman now. She kissed Paxton as Paxton's hands shifted Chris to lie underneath her. Paxton removed her own shirt while Chris watched. As Paxton stood, removing her shorts and baring herself to Chris, Chris knew she was lucky. She was very lucky. She had a job she liked that finally gave her enough money to support herself and her brother. She had a roof over her head, food to eat, a brother she loved that loved her back, and an amazing girlfriend that was currently settling on top of her.

As Paxton's lips pressed to her neck, Chris couldn't help but think about how different things could have been for her and for Wes. Had her mother not had the courage to leave when she was younger, she and Wes would have grown up in a cult. She'd be married off to a man probably twice her age. He'd have multiple wives, and she'd have at least six or seven kids by now. Just the thought of that made her cringe. She'd so often disliked the life she had after her parents died. She worried daily that she wasn't giving Wes what he needed, that they'd never have enough money, or running cars, or a house they could afford to live in. She also worried she'd never find someone to share her life with that could understand that Wes was a part of the deal; that also she had this baggage she'd likely never be able to get rid of.

Paxton kissed Chris's neck softly, as if this was their first time together, and moved slowly and carefully as she slid her hand down between them as her lips moved at the same pace to cover Chris's nipple. In that moment, Chris could only think that she'd almost lost all this, because she'd tried more than once to push this woman away. But as Paxton's fingers slid inside her, Chris thought of nothing else than the feeling of Paxton moving in and out of her with such gentleness and care. They hadn't made love all that much in the grand scheme of things. They hadn't been together that long. But every time they did this, Paxton knew just how to touch her. She knew where; but, more importantly, she knew how. Paxton knew to go fast or slow. She knew when Chris would want to see her face as Paxton made her come; when Chris wanted Paxton's face between her legs. Now, Paxton's eyes were on her. They were beautiful and kind. They were dark and filled with need at the same time.

When Chris came, it was with Paxton staring down at her with a near smile on her face. Chris's breathing slowed after several minutes. Paxton was still staring down at her with the same expression. Chris's eyes filled with happy tears, but those tears didn't fall. Paxton watched as Chris smiled up at her. She leaned down to kiss Chris. In response, Chris pulled Paxton closer to her own body as tightly as she could, never wanting to let her go.

CHAPTER 26

"PAX, YOU'RE SUCH an asshole sometimes," Chris exclaimed.

"What did I do?" Paxton asked.

"You picked this color," Chris replied, holding up a paintbrush.

"You agreed to it."

"No, I said, *'It's your hotel; do want you want.'* To which you replied, *'I'm going with this one.'* That is not the same thing," Chris said.

"It's not *that* dark," Paxton replied, using the roller on the wall to spread the color.

"It's navy-blue, Paxton. It's going to take, like, six coats to get this on right," Chris returned as she used the brush to go along the trim.

"I told you I'd hire painters."

"You could have just picked a lighter color," Chris returned.

"It's only an accent wall."

"That's your argument? The color is so dark, Pax."

"The wallpaper is ivory; it's going to work," Paxton replied.

"What are you two fighting about?" Wes asked when he entered the room, carrying a box of light bulbs.

"We're not fighting!" they both exclaimed at the same time.

"It sounds like fighting."

"We're arguing," Paxton said.

"How is that different?" he asked, placing the box on the floor.

"You'll understand when you–" Paxton stopped herself. "Get a girlfriend."

Chris looked over at her and then said, "And your girlfriend buys a hotel."

"Well, right. That, too." Paxton smiled over at her.

"I doubt that's anything I'll need to worry about," Wes replied, shaking his head at the two of them.

"You'll have to worry about it if you move in together one day and have to pick a color for the living room walls or something," Paxton replied, turning back to the wall to continue painting.

"That better be, like, ten years from now," Chris said to Wes.

"Right. Ten years," Paxton echoed.

"And when you do move in, don't let her pick the darkest color in the world to put on the walls. It'll take days to get the painting done," Chris said.

"And don't agree to the color and then take it back. Girls don't like that," Paxton added.

"And maybe, make sure you're really listening to your girlfriend when she doesn't agree. She just says that it's your hotel and you can do what you want," Chris fired back with a smile.

"And if you have that strong of an opinion about wall colors, maybe make it more well-known up front. That way you don't spend all this time painting a wall and then arguing about it," Paxton suggested.

"Maybe–"

"Okay… I get it," Wes interrupted with a chuckle. "Choose only light colors. Communicate clearly. Don't live with anyone for ten years. Did I miss anything?"

"Don't date a pain in the ass like your sister," Paxton said. "Or at least, if you do, make sure she knows you love her *in spite of* and, sometimes, *because* of it." Paxton winked at Chris.

"Don't judge a book by its cover," Chris replied, looking at Paxton. "I might never have given Pax a second glance, and she's definitely worth a second glance."

Paxton smiled at her and replied, "I'll finish up the wall. It's the least I could do."

"See? Compromise." Chris turned to Wes. "But I'll help, because it means I get to be in the same room with you."

"This just got weird," Wes interjected. "You two like each other too much now. Pax, I was going to install these in the rooms that are ready. Is that cool?" He motioned to the box of bulbs.

"Go for it. After that, you can take off for practice, though. I don't want you to be late."

"Thanks," he replied, picking up the box and carrying it out of the room with him.

"You know his practice schedule?" Chris asked, walking over to her.

"I had him put his schedule up on the wall in the soon-to-be back office. He has his school stuff on there, too. I want to make sure he's meeting his commitments and that I'm not working him too hard," Paxton replied, bending over to slide the roller into some more paint.

"You're an asshole sometimes, but you're also really sweet, Pax." Chris smiled.

"I hope you wouldn't date me if I was a complete asshole all the time," Paxton replied, standing up after leaving the roller in the tray.

"That hasn't stopped me in the past... Many of my dates have been complete assholes," Chris told her, placing the brush on the side of the tray, standing back up, and wrapping her arms around Paxton's neck. "I'm glad I found someone that only steals my parking space and doesn't try to steal my car."

"Wait… What?" Paxton asked, wrapping her arms around Chris's waist.

"Well, she didn't try to *steal* it, technically. She just borrowed it without asking one time, after she stayed over. I woke up, and it wasn't there. I texted, called; nothing. I almost reported it stolen. She returned it later that night, saying she had to run a few errands and that she thought we should break up. I'm pretty sure she used me for my car to do something illegal. But I never heard anything, so I left it at that."

"Like, she needed to bury the body of her ex-girlfriend or something?" Paxton asked.

"Yes." Chris leaned in, pressing her lips to Paxton's cheek. "So, you better behave, because I know where she took it, and there's plenty of room." She pulled back and winked at her.

Paxton smiled, laughed a little, and then turned them around, pressing Chris's back to the wall covered in fresh navy-blue paint.

"Oh, yeah?" she asked, placing her own hands flat against the wall, feeling the wet paint coat them. Then, she pressed them firmly over Chris's chest. "Now, what?"

"Pax!" Chris exclaimed, laughing wildly as she looked down at the palm prints on her breasts. She pulled herself off the wall, turned her head slightly to try to see the damage, and saw the wall instead. "Pax… We'll have to redo the whole thing." She laughed, pressed her own hands into the wall, and turned. But Paxton was already gone. "Paxton Williams! Get your ass back here so I can get paint all over it."

"Running away," Paxton yelled from somewhere in the hallway.

Chris followed her down the hall, laughing as she went, knowing she'd follow Paxton Williams anywhere.

***

"I only got paint all over you in order to get you in this shower with me," Paxton told Chris later that night.

They'd chased one another around the unfinished hotel, with some contractors giving them questioning glances as Chris tried to get her paint-covered hands anywhere on Paxton's body. She'd succeeded, but only because Paxton eventually gave into her laughter and couldn't breathe anymore. Chris had pressed her now nearly dry hands to Paxton's ass, cupping it as she did so, and leaving only small marks behind. Paxton had kissed her then. They'd been out on the deck; the place where they'd first made love. Everything – despite the sounds of construction going on behind them – had been perfect. Then, Wes had interrupted them, told them how gross it was, and left for his tennis practice.

They'd gone back to Chris's apartment, changed their clothes, and went to see a house together with Kinsley. It was a modest place. Four bedrooms, but one of them was on the small side and could have easily been called a walk-in closet more than a bedroom. It was a ranch-style, with a finished basement, which was where two of the bedrooms were located. Chris had smiled at Paxton when Paxton suggested Wes could have the finished basement basically to himself when he came home from college. It hadn't been an off-handed comment. Paxton had meant every word. She'd even tried to identify ways to give him as much privacy as possible by adding a separate entrance to the exposed back of the basement. The lot was smaller than some of the others Paxton had visited, but she didn't think that mattered. They wouldn't need a lot of yard space, anyway. Neither of them, apparently, liked mowing the lawn.

"You got paint all over me just so we'd shower together hours later, after we went to go see about a house?"

"Kinsley's my agent. It's not like I'm trying to impress her." Paxton ran her fingers along Chris's spine as she stood behind her, watching the water roll down her girlfriend's back. "Did you like it?" she asked softly; referring to the house, not the motion of her fingers.

Chris turned in her arms and replied, "Pax, I did like it. But it's more important that you like it. I know you want me to live there with you one day, but it's still your house. I don't know what's going to happen with us in the next few months." She wrapped her arms around Paxton's neck. "I know I love you. I know I want to be with you. I believe that one day we will get to the part where we live together. But I'd hate it if you bought a house that you only liked instead of loved because I liked it."

"But you liked it?" Paxton asked with a smirk.

"You're useless," Chris replied, kissing her lips and erasing the smirk.

When Chris deepened the kiss, Paxton knew they weren't leaving this shower until they'd both come at least once. The way Chris was kissing her neck, Paxton wondered if they'd maybe come at least two times before they left the shower. Chris touched her first. Her fingers grazed Paxton's sex; just gently touching the hairs there. Paxton spread her legs to allow Chris to press those same fingers to her clit. Chris moved into her more, pushing Paxton against the back wall. Paxton came the first time with Chris's soft and slow strokes. The second time was because of Chris's fast and deep trusts as Paxton's teeth practically dug into Chris's shoulder. She'd definitely have a mark there later. When she turned Chris around to take what she wanted, she knelt in front of her, and for a moment – just one moment, she wasn't thinking about sex. She thought about how she'd likely get down on one knee for this woman in the future. She'd be fully clothed, of course, and she'd be holding a ring.

"What's wrong?" Chris asked, obviously picking up on Paxton's wandering mind.

"Nothing. Absolutely nothing." Paxton smiled up at her, kissed Chris just below the belly button, and then went to work lower.

***

After leaving the shower, they climbed into bed together. Paxton pulled out her laptop, did some work, checked in via email with her team back in Seattle, and emailed Kinsley that she'd like to see the house again, along with a couple more. Chris pulled out a book and started to read until her phone rang.

"Hello?"

"Is this Christina Florence?"

"This is she. Who's this?"

"This is Lakeview Memorial. You're listed as the emergency contact for Wesley Florence."

Chris shot up in the bed and asked, "What happened? Is he okay?"

"Your brother's been in a car accident."

"What? Oh, my God." Chris flew out of the bed, dropping the book to the floor.

"Chris? What's wrong?" Paxton asked, moving the laptop off her body and leaning forward.

"Is he okay? Where are you, again?" Chris asked, ignoring Paxton's question.

"Lakeview Memorial. Your brother is stable. That's all I know. I'm the station nurse. You'll want to ask for his doctor when you get here. He's in room 411, on the fourth floor."

"I'm on my way," Chris replied, hanging up the phone at the same time she put her head on a swivel looking for her pants. "Where are my jeans? Where did I throw them?"

"Chris, talk to me. What's going on?" Paxton stood from the bed and walked over to her. "Is Wes okay?"

"He was in a car accident. He's in the hospital. I need my jeans, Paxton," Chris repeated as she continued to move around the room quickly, looking for her pants.

"Babe, they're in the laundry hamper. They had paint all over them. I was going to wash them for you," Paxton replied. "Wear something of mine. Second drawer; take whatever you want."

Chris heard her without really hearing her. Paxton moved to the dresser with her, pulled out a pair of pants for Chris, passed them to her, and then grabbed a pair for herself. She slid them over her legs as Chris did the same.

"What are you doing?" Chris asked after she slid on a borrowed shirt.

"Getting dressed," Paxton answered.

"You don't have–"

"You're my girlfriend. I'm going with you. In fact, I'm driving, because I don't think you can right now. Plus, I care about Wes. I want to make sure he's okay, Chris."

"Okay," Chris said softly. "Thank you."

"Don't thank me for this, Chris." Paxton moved into her, kissed her forehead, and looked into her watery eyes. "I love you. He's going to be okay."

"He's my baby brother, Pax. I can't–"

"You won't. Come on. Let's go see him," she said.

CHAPTER 27

"MY NAME IS Christina Florence. My brother is in room 411." Chris leaned over the first counter she saw the moment they entered the emergency room of the hospital.

"His name?" the woman behind the counter, who wore pink scrubs, asked.

"Wesley Florence," Chris replied, slightly annoyed.

The woman typed something into a computer without looking up and said, "Room 411."

"I know. I just said that," Chris argued. "I–"

"Where's the elevator?" Paxton interrupted, pressing her hand supportively to Chris's back.

"Down the hall to the right." The woman pointed.

"Thank you," Paxton replied, ushering Chris with that same hand in the direction of the woman's finger.

When they arrived on the fourth floor, Chris walked briskly as her eyes glued to the small plaques that indicated the room numbers. They made it about halfway down the hall before she spied 410 and then 411. She made her way through the open door, with Paxton hot on her heels. She passed the small bathroom on the right, and then the room opened up to reveal two hospital beds. A woman was sleeping in one. Wesley was in the other.

"Chris, hey," Wes greeted with a smile for a second before the smile disappeared and he held up his arm that already had a navy-blue cast on it.

"What happened?" Chris rushed to his side.

"I chose navy-blue for you, Pax. I thought it would be funny," he said.

"You're in a cast, Wes. Nothing about this is funny. What the hell happened? Did your car act up and cause you to lose control or something? What else is injured? Do you have any internal bleeding we need to watch out for? How long does the cast have to be on? Oh, God! You can't play tennis with a cast on. Why is there a tube coming out of your other arm?" Chris asked in rapid succession as her eyes flitted over every part of him she could see.

"Chris, calm down, okay?" he said and reached for his sister's hand. "I'm okay. I have a few cuts and bruises. I don't have any internal damage; they already checked. They said six to eight weeks for the cast. I only broke the arm in one place. No surgery is required."

Chris exhaled deeply and asked, "Wes, what happened?"

"I was driving home from practice, and grandma called me. She asked if I could pick her up and take her to the grocery store."

"She what?" Chris asked.

"She's old, Chris. Plus, she's still trying to get used to things out in the real world. She needed a few things and also wanted to see if I wanted to have dinner with her. I said yes. I picked her up. We went to dinner first. We just went to Donoto's. Then, I took her to the store. It took her, like, thirty minutes to find everything she wanted, even with my help. They had farms and stuff there, I guess. She didn't even realize how many different types of cereal there are now." He chuckled before stopping at her stern expression.

"Anyway… We were driving back to her apartment, and she kind of had an anxiety attack, I think. I don't know exactly what happened, but she grabbed her chest and told me it was hurting. I tried to pull over to help her. She accidentally leaned over, though, and kind of landed on my arm that was holding the wheel. I lost control for only a second. But the roads are so narrow here, it was too late. We went off to the side. I ran into a tree. I was only going about forty, though. I guess that was lucky."

"Lucky? Are you kidding me?" Chris asked.

"Wes, where's your grandma?" Paxton asked.

"I don't know," Wesley said. "I asked the nurse. She said she'd check for me but hasn't been back yet. I told her she's my grandmother."

"She's hardly your…" Chris stopped herself, squeezed his hand, and gave him a small smile. "I'll check with the nurse."

"I've got it. You stay with Wes," Paxton offered. She leaned over, kissed Chris's cheek, and added, "Love you."

"I love you, too," Chris whispered back.

Paxton winked at Wes. Then, she turned and left the room.

"Love, huh?" Wes questioned.

"Stop it," Chris said through a light laugh.

"I'm happy for you. Why can't I be happy for you? Pax is awesome, Chris," he said.

"She is. You, however, have a lot of explaining to do," she said.

"I do?" he asked.

"Wes, what about tennis?"

"I know…" He hung his head. "My season is over, but there's next year. That's senior year. That's when it really matters for scholarships. I don't know if Paxton has anything I can do one-handed for a while, but I'll still work."

"Wes, it's not about the money." Chris sat in the chair next to his bed. "You love tennis. I hate that you're going to miss it."

"Me too. But maybe I can still help the team out or something. I'll have to talk to coach tomorrow."

Of the two of them, Wes had always had the more positive outlook. Chris had, somehow, ended up with the pessimistic attitude while he'd gotten the optimism in the family.

"How's your car? *Where* is your car?" she asked.

"Still attached to the tree." Wes shrugged, winced, and grabbed his hip. "I have a bruise here, I think." He leaned back against his stacked pillows. "It's going to need some work. I'll use the money I've made so far from Pax to get it repaired. Hopefully, it won't take too long. I hate having to borrow your car all the time."

She watched as he closed his eyes and held onto his broken arm with his uninjured one. She wished more than anything in that moment that she had been better for him after the death of their parents. She had put her worries about money and the future on her kid brother, because she'd had no one else to put them on or talk to them about.

"Wes, I'm sorry," she said.

"For what?" he asked, opening his eyes and looking at her.

"I don't want you to worry about that stuff anymore, okay? We're not millionaires, but we're okay. I like my job with Pax. I thought it would be awkward, and it hasn't been. I want to remain on, like we've planned. And I think that will make us okay, Wes. I know you'll still need to get a scholarship or take out a loan – depending on what college you want to go to, but I don't want you to stress about that stuff anymore. I just want you to focus on being a high school student. Get good grades. Play tennis. That's it, okay?"

"And find the girlfriend we were talking about earlier, right?" Wes smiled at her.

"That can wait," Chris replied with a laugh.

***

"Hello?" Paxton said through the open door.

"Hello," a woman replied.

Paxton took a few steps into the room. She spotted two hospital beds. In one, there was an older man, who was watching the television hanging in the corner. Chris's grandmother was resting in the other bed. She had a bandage above her left eye, another one over most of her left arm, and her right arm was in a sling. She had bruises on her jaw, a cut on her bottom lip, and her right leg had an ice pack on top of it.

"I'm Paxton Williams. I don't know if you know who I am," she said after approaching the bed. "I'm a friend of Christina's and Wesley's."

"How is Wesley?" the woman asked immediately.

"He's okay." Paxton smiled. "He has some bumps and bruises, but he'll be fine. How are you?"

"I think my bumps and bruises take a lot longer to heal than his," she replied.

"Chris is in with Wes now. He asked about you. I told him I'd check to make sure you're okay," Paxton offered after a moment of awkward silence.

"Christina is in with him now? That's good," she said.

"I should get back to them. I just wanted to–"

"Can you ask her to come in here?" the woman asked hopefully.

"Sure. I can ask her." Paxton nodded. "I don't know if she will, though."

"You know about what…"

"I know." Paxton ran her hand through her hair. "I'll see if she can come in, okay?"

"Thank you. Paxton?"

"Yes?"

"This may be inappropriate, but Christina told me that she's…" The woman cleared her throat.

"Gay?" Paxton guessed. "Yes, I'm her girlfriend," she added.

"I see."

"I love her very much. She's an amazing woman that I hope to spend my life with. I don't know what you believe about all that, but–"

"I don't know what I believe anymore," the woman interjected.

Paxton didn't know what to say to that. She stood in silence instead.

"I'm an old woman, and I have no idea what I believe about most things in life."

"I guess the thing to remember is that you can always get to know yourself. It doesn't matter how old you are," Paxton offered.

"I guess so," she replied with a small smile so as not to open the cut on her lip.

***

"How is he?" Paxton asked when she caught Chris leaving Wes's room.

"He's okay. He's ready to be discharged. The doctor just stopped by to check on him. We can take him home," Chris said. "Well, back to my place. I need to stay with him tonight. I'm sorry," she added, wrapping her arms around Paxton's neck and pulling her in for a hug.

"I'll drop you guys off. I assume he has some prescriptions he needs to be picked up?"

"Just some pain meds, but they've got a pharmacy here. I'll run down and grab them before we leave," she replied, kissing Paxton's neck lightly. "Thank you, though. And Wes asked that you stay over tonight. Is that okay?"

"He did?"

"I think he feels bad about messing up our night. He also just really likes you." Chris smiled into Paxton's neck, loving the feel of the woman's arms around the small of her back, rubbing up and down.

"If you're okay with me staying over, I will."

"Stay over, Pax," Chris muttered against Paxton's skin.

191

"I need you there, too."

"Okay." Paxton squeezed her hard, offering even more support. "I visited Cheyanne," she added.

"Thank you for not calling her my grandma," Chris said.

"She asked to see you." Paxton pulled back to look at her girlfriend.

"I don't want to see her. She's the reason he's in that room."

"She's also all alone, Chris. I may have lied to the nurse that I ran into outside her room and told her I was family. I was told she'll be ready to be released tomorrow if her tests check out okay."

"And?" Chris asked with a lifted eyebrow.

"And my girlfriend isn't heartless." Paxton kissed her forehead. "I'll go help Wes get ready to go."

CHAPTER 28

CHRIS HAD A HARD TIME SLEEPING
that night. Even with Paxton's comforting and relaxed breathing to her right, Chris couldn't manage to calm her brain enough to sleep. She tossed and turned for a few hours before she gave up. She made her way to Wes's room first, where she checked to see that he was sound asleep. Then, she moved into the living room after pouring herself a glass of water. She stared at the TV she hadn't turned on for a while, trying to think about her parents and what they'd want from her right now.

It was a difficult thing to figure out. Her mother had never spoken of her grandmother as being a horrible person. She hadn't agreed with Cheyanne's choices, and she had left when she had been able to arrange it, but Chris didn't think her mother had hated the woman who had given birth to her. She probably still loved her, despite what Cheyanne had done. Chris's father hadn't ever had kind words to say about the woman, but they'd moved on in their lives by the time Chris was born. It was likely they never wanted to talk about it in order to put it all behind them and start over with their own lives and their children.

"Hey," Paxton whispered. "Chris."

Chris opened her eyes, immediately noticing that she'd fallen asleep on the couch. Paxton was sitting on the side of it, running her hand softly through Chris's messy hair while smiling down at her.

"I fell asleep, didn't I?" she asked.

"Yes, and not in bed with me." Paxton winked at her. "Are you okay? Should I have stayed at my place last night?"

"What? No." Chris sat up. "I couldn't sleep, and I didn't want to wake you. I didn't intend to fall asleep out here."

"I'm going to head over to the hotel to meet with the contractor. Why don't you stay home with Wes today, since he's not going to school? I can swing by here at lunch and bring you both something. I can work from here for the rest of the day. We can order in for dinner or something."

"You don't have to do all that, Pax." Chris kissed Paxton on the lips. "We'll be okay. You basically have two jobs already. You don't need the third one, taking care of us."

"I wouldn't mind it, though. I like taking care of you guys," Paxton said with a soft smile.

"Go to work, Champ." Chris gave her shoulder a light shove. "Come for lunch if you want. It's up to you." She stood as Paxton stood. "And if you want to work from here, that's fine, too. I wouldn't mind getting some work done today myself. We could go through the plans for the restaurant if you want."

"See? They think *I'm* the boss. But really, you're the one in charge."

"I'm glad you realize that, too." Chris wrapped her arms around Paxton's neck and smiled through the kiss she gave her.

"Have you given any thought to *you know what?*" Paxton asked.

"That would be the reason I couldn't sleep." Chris pulled away from Paxton and headed into the kitchen. "Do you want coffee before you go?"

"No, I'll get some on the way."

"Can we talk about the *you know what* you mentioned later?" Chris asked on a sigh.

"I guess so," Paxton agreed, clearly reluctantly. "I'll see you later?" she asked, losing the smile on her face.

"Lunch?"

"I'll be by around one," Paxton replied; although it was said without her usual enthusiasm, which was one of Chris's favorite things about her girlfriend.

"I'll see you later."

"Later, yeah." Paxton kissed her cheek, turned away, and headed out of the house.

Chris stood in her kitchen, knowing the cause of Paxton's unprecedented withdrawal. Her girlfriend had a big heart. That big heart was one of the reasons Chris had fallen for her in the first place. Paxton wanted her to talk to Cheyanne, and Chris knew that she hoped for some kind of reconciliation between the relatives. Chris had stared at the TV for a long time, trying to come to grips with the fact that the woman who had raised her mother in a cult was suddenly in her life, trying to get to know her and her younger brother.

"Hey, can I get you some breakfast?" Chris asked Wes, leaning against the doorframe of his bedroom.

"Maybe just one of the protein bars; it's in my gym bag. I'm not really all that hungry." He rolled onto his side to face her, clinching his cast.

"Are you in pain? Do you want one of the pills the doctor gave you?"

"I took one right before you came in. It just needs a few minutes to kick in. It'll make me sleepy, too, so if it's okay, I think I'll stay home from school today."

"Wes, of course, you're staying home," she replied, walking into the room. "If you feel up to it, you can go in tomorrow. But don't push it, okay? I've already called the school and your coach to let them know what happened."

"Thanks," he said and rolled onto his back. "Can I ask how she is? I mean, do you know?"

"I know what Paxton told us last night," Chris replied.

"That she's getting out of the hospital today?"

"If her tests came back okay, yes. I don't know if that's the case, though."

"Can we call the hospital? I can do it myself." Wes reached for the phone on his bedside table with his uninjured hand.

Chris let out a deep sigh and said, "I'll call them. I'll check on her."

"Are you sure?" he asked.

"Yeah, I'll take care of it. Get some rest." She moved to his gym bag on the floor, unzipped the side pocket, pulled out the protein bar, and tossed it onto his bed. "Eat this now. Pax is going to bring us lunch later, but let me know if you get hungry for something else."

"Thanks, Chris."

Chris closed the door behind her, went to the kitchen, picked her phone up off the table, and looked up the number to the hospital.

"Hello. I was wondering if you could tell me if a patient has been discharged. She's my grandmother," Chris said as she closed her eyes.

***

"You're all set," the nurse told Cheyanne after pushing the older woman's wheelchair through the outer doors of the hospital. "We've called you a taxi. I'll wait here and help you in when it arrives."

"Thank you," Cheyanne said.

"She doesn't need a cab," Chris said, witnessing the exchange from where she'd been waiting for the past ten minutes. She'd arrived at the hospital, parked her car, sat inside it for about five minutes before she'd walked to the hospital's door, and then, she'd just stood there. "I'll drive her home," she added, moving toward Cheyanne's chair. "I'm parked over there. I'll pull up."

She made her way back to the parking lot where she started the car and drove it to the door. Cheyanne hadn't said anything to Chris when she'd seen her, but she had smiled. Chris got out of the car and helped the nurse get

Cheyanne into the passenger seat. Then, without a word, she drove off to the address Wes had stored on his phone. She'd borrowed it after he'd fallen asleep, found Cheyanne's apartment address, and left Wes a note that she'd be right back if he woke up before she returned.

"If you give me your key, I'll go inside and pack a few things for you," Chris offered. "It'll be easier if you just wait here. Is there anything you need specifically, outside of clothing and the basics?"

"Pack for what?" Cheyanne asked, turning to her.

"You can stay with us while you heal. When I called the hospital earlier, they said you have a bruised knee that you need to stay off of, along with everything else. You can stay with us until the swelling goes down, and then you can be on your own," Chris said.

"You'd let me stay with you?"

"Just until you're better. And this doesn't mean I want to have a long talk with you or anything, okay?"

"I would be an imposition." Cheyanne shook her head from side to side.

"Grandmother or not, you're all alone. Wes cares about you, and my girlfriend… It's just easier this way. Can I borrow your key? Do you have any medication or anything up there?"

"No, I haven't been to a doctor or hospital since before…" The woman reached inside the small coin purse she had as her only possession and passed Chris the key. "There's a suitcase by the front door. It has everything in it that I'll need."

"Why–" Chris stopped herself, shaking her head. "I'll be right back."

She made her way up to Cheyanne's apartment, let herself inside with the key, and closed the door behind her. She looked around the incredibly small space and felt even worse about her action recently. It was a studio apartment, with a mattress on the floor. Cheyanne had a small table in a wide-open space that was to be a living area. The kitchen didn't look well stocked. Chris turned back to see a large roller suitcase a few feet away from the front door. She pulled it out the door, loaded it into the trunk, and climbed back into her car.

"You lied to us, didn't you?" she asked.

"What do you mean?" Cheyanne asked back.

"Before, you told us you didn't need money." Chris pulled the car out onto the street.

"I didn't want you to think I wanted to be in your life after all these years merely because I needed money. I can apply for benefits. I haven't yet, but I could. Your cousins, the ones I mentioned before, have helped some. I may not be rich, but I'm okay," Cheyanne told her.

"You're sleeping on a mattress on the floor."

"For now; it's only for now," Cheyanne said and then appeared to be completely exhausted from the conversation as she rested her head against the seat behind it.

CHAPTER 29

"HEY, WHAT ARE YOU DOING here?" Paxton asked when she saw Chris walk through the door of the hotel. "I thought I was bringing lunch to you."

"I thought I'd bring you lunch instead. I kind of have something I wanted to talk to you about, and I can't do it at my place," Chris said.

"Is everything okay with Wes? Did something happen?" Paxton closed her laptop immediately and stood up from behind the desk she'd haphazardly set up in the back office.

"Wes is fine. He's been asleep on and off all morning. I dropped his lunch off first and checked on him. There's just someone else at my house."

Paxton gave her a confused look for a moment before she smiled at her and said, "You did the right thing, Chris."

"It's just until she can be on her own. The doctor said about a week or so, until her knee is healed. She doesn't even have crutches." Chris sat down in the folding chair opposite the desk.

Paxton moved her chair over to join her and replied, "I'm proud of you for doing this. I know it's not easy." She placed her hand on Chris's thigh.

"No, it's not. Part of me thinks my mom is watching me and hates me for this," she said.

"Your mother could never hate you. No one could hate you, Chris." Paxton squeezed Chris's thigh with her hand. "I love you, remember?"

"I do, yes." Chris chuckled. "The house is going to be

199

a little crowded, though. It's probably not a good place to work from today. I've loaned Cheyanne my bedroom. I can't exactly kick Wes out of his. Besides, it pretty much always smells like gym socks and sweat."

Paxton laughed and asked, "Where will you be sleeping?"

"On the couch." Chris shrugged. "It's a pull-out. I'll be fine for a few nights. I'd stay at your place, but I can't leave Wes on his own with basically one arm and an invalid in my room."

"I understand. Why don't I give you guys your space this week?"

"This week?" Chris lifted her eyebrows. "I was thinking I'd stay on the couch myself tonight, but that maybe you could sleep on it with me tomorrow. No funny business, of course. It's not exactly private, but I don't want to be without you for a whole week, Pax."

"I was actually thinking about going back to Seattle to check in on the business for a few days. I was going to talk to you about it later, but maybe I could take care of that while you take care of your family. By the time I get back, Cheyanne should be back home."

"Oh. Is everything okay in Seattle?"

"It's fine. It's just hard to do both, you know? My heart isn't exactly in Seattle anymore." Paxton smiled. "On top of that, my brain has been pretty busy lately. It's not fair to the employees up there. I'm going to talk to my lawyer about planning for the future."

"You're thinking of closing up shop?"

"Not necessarily. I might sell… I don't know." Paxton shrugged. "It's just not what I want to do anymore."

"You want to be a hotel owner now."

"And a good sister, friend, and girlfriend. I want to be a good boss to everyone that works with me, and I don't think that's what I'm being to the team up there."

"When would you leave?" Chris asked softly, not wanting her to leave at all.

"I was thinking tomorrow if you're okay with it," Paxton replied. "And Chris?"

"Yeah?"

"This is a good thing," Paxton reminded her. "My business is the only thing still tying me to Seattle. I have family there we can go visit, but outside of that, everything I have is here. You were worried about me going back before, but I'm moving every piece of me to Lake Tahoe, because I love you. I love this place. It's my home now." Paxton placed both hands on Chris's face, cupping her cheeks. "Give me a few days, and I'll come home to you."

Chris smiled, leaned forward, and kissed her girlfriend. Paxton kissed her back. Chris felt Paxton shifting around in the chair, which caused her to laugh. She opened her eyes to witness Paxton's foot kick the door to the office until it closed.

"Pax, I have to get home," Chris said when Paxton stood, locked the door, and reached for Chris's hand. "We can't in here."

"Why not?" Paxton asked, pulling Chris into herself and backing up against the door. "We're in charge, and all the contractors are upstairs. I'm sleeping on my own for the next few nights, babe."

"And what? You're so hard up, you need it now? I didn't take care of you last night?" Chris asked with a lifted eyebrow.

"Oh, you took good care of me last night. I could use some of the same right now, though," Paxton said with a smirk.

"What's gotten into you?" Chris laughed at her.

"My hot girlfriend," Paxton replied, pulling Chris all the way against her.

"Your hot girlfriend is exhausted and has to get back home. But she promises she will take care of you the first chance she gets when you come home."

Paxton smiled, kissed Chris's lips, and said, "Fine. I guess I'll just have to take care of myself later."

"As long as no one else is doing the job, Champ, you and your hand can have all the fun you want."

"Please, it'll be me and my vibrator," Paxton returned.

***

"I thought Pax was coming for dinner tonight," Wes said as he, Cheyanne, and Chris sat around the table.

"She's packing and booking her flight for tomorrow. She's going back to Seattle for a few days," Chris explained. "She'll be back by the weekend, though."

"Seattle?" Cheyanne asked.

"Paxton's from there," Wes answered. "She moved here recently. Her sister lives here, too. She lives with one of Chris's friends."

"And that's how you two met?" Cheyanne asked Chris.

"Me and Pax? I guess so. When Morgan and Adler moved in together, Pax came for a visit and ended up staying. I guess we've been together pretty much ever since then."

"Morgan and Adler, those are both…"

"Women, yes. Morgan is a lesbian, and Adler loves Morgan." Chris took a drink of her water.

"I see."

"I'd imagine your old church has an issue with homosexuality?" Chris asked.

"Chris…"

"What?" Chris asked Wes.

"We don't talk about it as a good or a bad thing," Cheyanne said. "We just don't talk about it."

"I see." Chris picked up her fork.

"I'm not naïve, Christina. I am aware that women love women, and men love men. Do I understand it, no. But I'm not sure it's my place to try, either."

"It's not your place to try to understand how I could love Paxton in the same way that you could love your husband?" Chris asked.

"I only meant that I'm not sure it's my place to judge you for it."

"Oh, well, I guess that's good enough," Chris fired back. "Paxton is the reason you're here right now, by the way. You should thank her if you see her again. She encouraged me to make sure you were okay. I don't know if I would have picked you up today had she not."

"God, Chris! Stop acting like such an asshole," Wes said, dropping his fork abruptly on his plate. "You invited her here. If you're not at least going to be civil, just don't talk to her at all."

"Wes, I—"

"I think I'm finished," Cheyanne interrupted and lowered her head. "I'd help with the dishes, but…"

"I'll help you to your room," Wes offered and stood. "Chris can do the dishes tonight."

Wes stood, helping Cheyanne to do the same. He ushered her back to Chris's bedroom. Chris stood and began doing the dishes. A few minutes later, she heard the bedroom door close, and Wes came back into the kitchen.

"She okay?" Chris asked, drying a pan with a rag.

"She's fine. You're kind of an asshole, though." He crossed his uninjured arm over his injured one. "Why'd you even let her stay if you were going to be so rude to her?"

"Because of you and Pax, Wes. I'm trying here." Chris put the pan on the drying rack by the sink. "It's the best I can do."

"No, it's not. It's the best you're *choosing* to do. I'm going to bed. I'll see you in the morning."

"Are you going to school tomorrow?" she asked.

"Someone should be here to help grandma. Are you staying home from work?" he asked.

"I can't not work, Wes. You need to go back to school if you can handle it. I'll go in a little later tomorrow, make her breakfast before I leave, and I'll come back at lunch, okay? You'll be home after school, since you don't have practice. I'll bring dinner home for us around six."

"Fine," he said.

"Wes, what do you want from me?" she asked.

"I don't know." He shrugged, and for the first time, Chris noticed how similar his shrug was to her girlfriend's. It would have made her laugh if they weren't talking about something so serious. "You don't have to be nice to her. But maybe don't go out of your way to be mean to her. Is that too much to ask?"

"No, it's not." She sighed. "I'm sorry. I'm the adult here. I should be doing better with this."

"I know you had to hear more about what happened from Mom and Dad because I wasn't around yet. Maybe just consider for a moment that she *is* our grandmother. She's the only one we have, and the only one we can ever have. She's here, and the only thing she's asked us for is the chance to get to know us. We have cousins that left the cult too, Chris. They'd like to meet us. We could have a family."

"We *are* a family, Wes," Chris reminded him, trying to hold back the tears she thought might come.

"We are." He nodded. "I know we are. You and me – and now you and me and Pax are a family, Chris." Wes paused. Chris nearly let the tears fall at the mention of Paxton being a part of their family now. "There just could be more. We could have more, Chris."

"I'll talk to her, okay?" she offered. "I'll work on it, Wes."

"Okay. I'm going to my room to wrap my cast before taking a shower. I haven't showered in more than twenty-four hours; I think I'm starting to smell."

"Do you need any help?" she said through mild laughter.

"No, I'm okay."

Wes left the kitchen. Chris finished doing the dishes. She changed in the living room and went into the bathroom after Wes finished in there. Once she finished her nightly routine, she pulled out the sofa bed, made it, and climbed into it. She wished more than anything that she was falling asleep next to Paxton, but Pax had to get ready for her flight tomorrow and her trip. Instead, Chris opened the book she'd been reading last night before her world got rocked by a car accident. Then, her phone rang.

"Hey. I'm glad you called," she said with a smile.

"Yeah? What are you doing?" Paxton asked.

"Lying on this sofa bed, trying to read," Chris replied. "You?"

"Standing outside your house, hoping your brother and Cheyanne are already asleep so I can fall asleep next to you tonight," Paxton said.

"You're outside?" Chris turned immediately toward the front door.

"I'll leave before they wake up. My flight is at seven in the morning. I just want to sleep next to you. Is that okay?"

Chris stood, made her way over to the door, and opened it softly so as not to wake the other house occupants.

"Of course, it's okay. Get in here," she said.

CHAPTER 30

"How's your–" Adler thought otherwise and said, "How's Cheyanne? It's Cheyanne, right?"

"Cheyanne or Lily, depends on who you ask," Chris replied. "Thanks for helping out around here while Pax is away."

"Morgan is planning some surprise. She told me she wanted me out of the house today. I told her she's crazy. I came here to help with whatever you need."

"A surprise, huh?"

"I don't know… She does little things like that sometimes. I'll get home, and there are flowers on the counter. Or, she's planned a weekend away for us where we'll camp and get away from everything. She really is an amazing girlfriend. I'm so lucky I found her."

"I kind of feel the same way about your sister," Chris offered.

"Pax is amazing. I'm glad you two have each other. She's the most supportive person in the world. She's brilliant and could have done anything she wanted. Ever since she started her own business, she's been incredibly successful in her professional life. But in her personal life, she's just never been really all that settled. What I've seen since she met you, though, is the opposite of that. And I'm so glad. My parents are, too. Even though we've both now moved away from them, they love the fact that we're both finally settling down and that we're happy."

"They know about me?"

"Pax told them all about you. You didn't know that?" Adler asked as she finished cleaning the roller they'd used to finish painting one of the rooms.

"She mentioned it; she just didn't go into a lot of details."

"She does that." Adler laughed. "She told them all about you and Wes, though. We were on FaceTime with them. I could see how happy she was, and so could they. They'll start giving her a hard time about meeting you soon."

"I guess that's the next step for us, huh?"

"Meeting the parents? It happens when you know you've met someone worth introducing to them, yeah. I know she feels that way about you."

"I would have had her meet mine already, if that was an option," Chris replied, placing a few stray paint brushes into an empty can to store overnight.

"How are you dealing with Cheyanne being around?"

"It's been two days. I'm trying to be civil, for Wes. I know Paxton wants me to get to know her, too. I know they're right. She's an old woman, who's lost everything. But there's just something I can't seem to let go of."

"Is Pax pushing you to do this?"

"No." Chris folded her arms over her chest. "As much as I thought your sister was a complete and total stuck-up asshole when we first met, she's really the opposite of that. She's supportive, like you said. And she's so sweet sometimes. She doesn't push me to do something specific; she just pushes me to be a better person."

"I think that's one of the benefits of falling in love with someone. Morgan makes me better, too."

"I just don't know if I'm doing anything for Pax," Chris said.

"Are you kidding?" Adler chuckled. "Chris, you've changed her entire life, and it's for the better."

"I don't—"

"Chris, she hadn't felt at home in Seattle or at work for a while when she came here to visit." Adler sat in the white folding chair in front of the sink they'd been using.

Chris pulled a stray one from the other side of the room to sit next to her; proud of her decision to buy about six of the chairs so they'd have places to sit while the place was under construction.

"She liked you immediately; I could tell. You give her a run for her money." Adler laughed lightly. "You're no pushover, and that's what my baby sister needs. She's ready for you, Chris. It took forever, but she's finally ready for a real commitment. She adores you and Wes. She called me yesterday to tell me that Mom and Dad are thinking about coming here for Christmas this year, but all she could really talk about was you and Wes. She wanted to know if I thought you two would join us for Christmas dinner. She wanted to talk about having a New Year's Eve party. She even mentioned kissing you at midnight. She's crazy about you, and it's only made her a better person, Chris."

"Thanks for that," Chris replied, not knowing what else to say to Adler's admission. "I should probably wait for her to bring up the Christmas dinner thing, though, huh?"

"I wouldn't be surprised if she asks the moment she gets back. She's not hesitating at all with you, Chris. I love that."

"I love that, too. It's scary, but I do love that about her. I love her. She's intense, and she goes all-in on the things that she cares about. She gives, and gives, and doesn't take much, if anything, in return. She's buying a house here, and she wants to make sure I love it just as much as she does, because she hopes I live there with her someday."

"That's Pax." Adler smiled at her. "You know, you can tell her to cool it if she's going a little too far. She'll slow down for you."

"I don't know that I want her to," Chris replied. "It's a lot, but I think it's the kick in the ass I need to finally have what I want in my life. It wasn't all that long ago that I was waiting tables at the same place I've worked at since Wes and I moved here. We couldn't afford to fix Wes's car, and he was working way more than a teenager in high school should be so that we could make enough money to get by. I felt like I was always on the outside looking in with the friend group we share." She sighed. "I don't feel that way anymore. She's a big reason why."

"Have you told her that?" Adler asked with a smile. "I know Morgan always likes when I tell her how amazing she is," she added with a small laugh. "I mean, who wouldn't?"

"Paxton's ego's so big, I don't think she needs anyone else expanding that head of hers."

"Pax hides in that ego. You know that," Adler replied as she stood. "I'm sure she could use a little reminder that you're all-in on this thing you two have started."

"Did she tell you that?" Chris asked with concerned eyebrows.

"No, she hasn't said anything specifically. I think she's just stressed right now and trying to cover it up because she knows you're stressed. She started her own business from scratch in Seattle and made it a successful one. Selling it is a big deal for her. If she decides to keep it, even if she passes over the reins of the everyday stuff to someone else, it's still a big change. She's trying to manage finding a new home, having a new relationship, building a new hotel, and dealing with her business back in Seattle. It would be a lot for anyone, don't you think?"

***

"My knee is feeling a lot better. I think I'll be able to head back to my own apartment tomorrow. Would you be able to give me a ride?" Cheyanne asked from her seat next to Chris on the sofa. "If not, I'm sure I can call a taxi or…"

"I'll take you back to your apartment if you think you're ready to be on your own," Chris replied. "You can stay here if you need help, though. Things aren't exactly great between us – I know, but I'm not kicking you out, Cheyanne."

"Wes is back at school. You have a full-time job. You shouldn't be sleeping on your sofa bed because of me."

"It's fine. My back is getting used to it. It's started to just reshape itself to fit the springs," Chris replied.

"But Paxton is coming back soon. You don't need your grandmother in your way," Cheyanne said.

Paxton was supposed to return the previous night, but after a few meetings with her lawyers and a competitor real estate agency, she'd decided to stay for another two nights to try to get as much wrapped up as possible. They'd spoken every day, but the distance between them was starting to get to Chris. Paxton seemed overwhelmed. She was struggling with the weight of her decision. She had staff that was depending on her there to make a decision that would affect them. It wasn't just about her and the changes she was making in her own life. Chris tried to be supportive, but over the phone, it was difficult. It hadn't helped that she had to hang up on Paxton a couple of times to help Cheyanne and Wes with things they couldn't take care of themselves.

"She'll be back tomorrow, yes. But she understands the situation. Wes will be in that cast for at least another four weeks. You're out of the sling – which is good, but you need help changing the dressings on your arm. It's not just about your knee. Do you have anyone else that can help?" Chris asked, noting the eyes that looked so much like her mother's staring back at her.

"Your cousins have offered to help. I called one of them this morning. She's going to pick me up at my apartment tomorrow and take me back to her house in Nevada for a week or so. I should be fine by then," the woman said.

There was something in the way she said it, though, that had Chris wondering if something else was going on here.

"Why can't she just pick you up here?" Chris asked.

"I didn't think you'd want to meet her."

"I'm not really sure I do, but it doesn't make sense to drop you off there only for her to pick you up later," Chris replied.

"I have a few more things at my apartment I need to pick up before I go with her," Cheyanne said.

"I can grab them for you tonight if you want. Wes is over at a friend's house. I haven't made dinner yet. I can grab something for us on the way back."

"That's not necessary. The arrangements with her have already been made. You've done so much. I'm grateful for it, but I think it's time I move on." She stood up shakily from the sofa. "I'll be ready early tomorrow so that you won't be late for work if you can still give me a ride."

"Sure."

Chris couldn't shake the feeling that something else was going on. Normally, she would talk to Wes about these kinds of things, but he was at his friend's house, and this was their grandmother. He was trying to find something that Chris didn't quite understand but she had to respect. She could talk to Paxton about it, but with everything Paxton had going on and the stress Chris had heard in her voice the previous night, made that an impossibility. She wouldn't add to Paxton's problems to solve.

Instead, Chris fell asleep after they had a five-minute goodnight phone call. She woke a little earlier than usual, dressed and readied for work, helped Cheyanne into the car and drove her back to her apartment. She helped her into the room and to the bed, which couldn't really be called a bed. She made sure the woman had her pills and some water, and when she went to help further by offering to add the items she needed from the apartment to the suitcase, Cheyanne told her that she'd take care of it herself later because Chris needed to get to work. Chris said goodbye to her with the same feeling that she couldn't shake: something was off with this woman.

She left the apartment, climbed back into her car,

started it, and then she sat there. The cousin Cheyanne had mentioned was supposed to be by to pick her up in less than an hour. Chris didn't have a meeting until after ten. Paxton would be heading to the airport for her return flight soon. Chris had the time. She sat in the car, scrolling through emails and messages on her phone until she heard another car pull into the small parking lot. It wasn't a regular car, though. It was a white van with no windows in the back. Chris watched as two men climbed out of the front. They were wearing odd clothing that flowed from their bodies and were also all white. They moved toward the apartment building. Chris leaned over the steering wheel to get a better look, noticing the license plate was covered by a thick layer of mud, making it impossible to read the numbers.

She knew then who these men were. Her heart started to pound. She had a choice to make. She could let them take Cheyanne back to the cult she'd escaped from months prior, or she could call the cops and have them arrested for attempted kidnapping. The cousin Cheyanne had trusted must have turned her in. That was the only explanation for why these men would come today, of all days, to take her back to their sick cult. She reached again for her phone, tapped the emergency button to call 911, and just as the call connected, she saw Cheyanne being helped out of the building by one of the men while the other carried her suitcase. She wasn't smiling exactly, but she didn't appear to be upset in any way. She even laughed at something the younger man that was helping her walk said. The other man loaded her suitcase in the back while the first one assisted her into the front seat. Then, he took his own place in the back of the van just as the older man started the engine.

"911. What's the nature of your emergency?" the dispatcher asked.

"What?" Chris said. "Oh, I don't know," she added. "I thought—" She hung up the phone, not worrying about the consequences.

She climbed quickly out of her car, rushed toward the

van that was just about to pull out of the parking lot but had to stop at the stop sign before it could enter the street, and banged on the passenger's side window.

"Christina?" Cheyanne mouthed through the glass. She rolled the window down just enough so she could speak to Chris. "What are you doing here?"

"Who are they? Where are you going?"

"We are taking our sister home," the driver said.

"Bullshit, you are. I'm calling the cops," Chris said, reaching for her phone again.

"Chris, it's okay. This is my choice," Cheyanne said.

"What do you mean this is your choice? You left," Chris argued.

"Those who leave our flock are always welcomed back by our—"

"You better shut the hell up, preacher. I'm one tap away from having you locked up for kidnapping," Chris interrupted him.

"What's the problem?" the man, who had apparently opened the back door, climbed out, and walked over toward Chris, said. "Why are we stopped?" he asked as he looked her up and down.

"This is my grandmother." Chris pointed at Cheyanne. "And she's not going anywhere with you two."

CHAPTER 31

"WHAT IS GOING ON?" CHRIS asked
Cheyanne the moment the apartment door closed behind
them, leaving the two men outside the building still waiting
on Cheyanne, or Lily as they had called her.

"I have nothing. I have no one!" Cheyanne exclaimed
as she leaned against the kitchen counter in the open space
of the small apartment. "I have nothing, Christina. I am
alone. I am all alone. I wanted to go home."

"What are you talking about?"

"I called the church. I told them I was ready to come
home. They've not only accepted me back, they offered to
drive me home. I didn't tell you because I knew you
wouldn't approve and that you'd try to stop me."

"These men control women. They marry young girls
off to older men; men who already have wives and children.
They branded you, and you want to go back?" Chris could
not believe what she was hearing. "You left. You got out.
Why would you want to go back?"

"How can I stay?!" she yelled. "I have no job. I have
no money. Those cousins I mentioned to you, they want
nothing to do with me, Christina. They see me as the old
woman who kept them there. They see me as an old woman
who believes in the church's teachings still to this day."

"Maybe because you still call it a *church* instead of what it really is," Chris said loudly.

"Because it was my church!" Her eyes teared up. "It was my church. It saved me all those years ago. My husband saved me. I was happy until your mother left."

"Until she *escaped*," Chris reminded. "Because you were trying to—"

"And you hate me for that. You hate me. Wesley is trying his hardest to get to know me. But he will never fully let me in because you hate me, and he loves you."

"Wes has his own mind."

"But you hate me."

Chris sighed and said, "I don't know."

Cheyanne wiped a tear from her cheek with a shaky hand and said, "I thought I could leave. I thought I could come here and learn about my daughter and her family. I knew it would take time. I thought we could try, though. I thought I'd have a family again. You have pity on me now, but the moment I'm healed, I'll never hear from you again. Wesley will go to college soon. He'll want nothing to do with me. I can only afford this apartment for another month. I will be on the street. They will take me back to the church where I'll have shelter and food."

"And indoctrination," Chris reminded. "What they do there is illegal; you know that."

"It's not to them," Cheyanne argued.

"Is it to you?" Chris asked with tears in her own eyes now. "Is what they did to your daughter okay, Cheyanne? Is what they would have done to me okay? Would they have allowed me to marry another woman? Would they have forced me to marry a man I could never love? Would they have forced Wes to marry multiple women and have children with them even if he didn't want that for himself?" Chris's tears streamed down her face. "You had a choice. You joined them. You took my mother's choice away from her. She had to flee to survive. You show up on my doorstep one day and just expect me to have no problem with you

215

being a part of my life? Are you kidding?! You thought it would take a couple of months, and I'd be okay with you cooking us dinner or talking about your life there? Cheyanne, I'm not even sure if that's possible. But I know it's not possible in the amount of time you gave me before you called them." She pointed toward the closed door.

"What am I supposed to do, Christina? I have nothing here."

"You have a choice," Chris replied, wiping the tears away. "You have the choice that you never gave her."

"I have no choice. I have no money. I'll have no home soon. I—"

"She had no money. She had no home. She made the choice to leave because she was brave. She tried, Cheyanne. She tried until she wasn't trying anymore. She was living the life she wanted. You could have that."

"How?" Cheyanne asked softly through tears.

"I don't know. But I think you owe it to yourself to at least try to figure it out. Hell, you owe it to Wes, who actually seems to like you," Chris said. "He wants to get to know you, Cheyanne. If you leave, he won't get the chance. You'll find a job somewhere. You might not be able to live here, but you'll find a place. You'll do it because you have to do it. Trust me, I know all about that. It's hard out there, but at least it'll be your choice and your life. You won't just be going back to a place you left because you're scared. You said it yourself: you don't like the direction they've taken the cult. It's gotten worse since your husband died. I can't even imagine what that means, but if that's true, you can't go back there."

"They'd leave me in peace. I'd be respected as a wife of the former prophet," Cheyanne replied.

"You'd still be alone." Chris shrugged. "At least if you're here, you'd have Wes. You'd have a chance at, maybe, having some kind of a relationship with me and those cousins you keep mentioning someday."

"Someday?"

"I won't promise you anything." Chris gulped. "But if you, I don't know, come by once a month for dinner or something, I'd be civil. That's what I can offer you right now."

"And with Wes?"

"I won't stop you from being in his life. It's his life; he can make his own choices. If you do anything to hurt him though, I–"

"I wouldn't."

"We'll see," Chris said. "Listen, you still need help at least for another few days. Those dressings need changing every day, and your knee isn't 100% yet. Just come back to the house for the next few days. Wes can maybe help you with the job search. He's not playing tennis right now."

"Because of me," Cheyanne said. "I am very sorry about that."

"The doctor told me it was an anxiety attack," Chris replied. "I guess I can't exactly blame you for that now, given everything you've been worrying about lately." She paused. "He's got some time on his hands, and I know he'd like to help."

"I can't ask that of you."

"You didn't. I offered. I'm also offering to get rid of the two guys out there, but you have to do something for me; for her."

"What?"

"What they're doing is wrong, Cheyanne. It may have been a church to you, but it's a cult. They brainwash people, they abuse them, they detain them, and it's all wrong."

"You want me to do something about it? What could I even do?"

"You can talk to the police. Mom never could because you were there. She loved you in spite of everything. You can tell them what happens, what you've seen, and who's involved. They can decide what to do from there."

"That place was my home for–"

"There are two men standing right outside this door,

217

who are more than willing to take you back." Chris hooked her thumb back at the door. "Like I said, you have a choice."

***

"I am so glad you're home," Chris said, wrapping her arms around Paxton's neck.

"Me too." Paxton kissed her the moment they pulled back enough for their lips to connect. "I thought I'd come by your place, though."

"Wes and Cheyanne are having a movie night tonight. I have the night off caretaker duty," Chris explained with a wide smile.

"Really? You have the whole night off? You can stay over?"

"I am staying over, yes." Chris kissed her again. "And I want to hear all about your trip and the decision about the office. I'm making you dinner, too."

"You are?" Paxton pulled back to give her a once-over. "What's gotten into you? You seem different."

"I'm happy, Pax. You make me happy."

"I'm glad. You make me happy, too. But Adler and Morgan invited us over to dinner tonight. I got the text on the way here from the airport. I accepted on our behalf. Should I tell them no now, because I make you so happy, you want to cook me dinner?" Paxton teased. "And what happened with Cheyanne? Is everything okay there? You've hardly mentioned her the whole time I was away."

"It can wait," Chris replied. "This can't." She leaned back into Paxton, wrapping her arms around her girlfriend's waist. "I love you."

"I love you, too," Paxton said back with a slight confusion in her tone.

"What time do we have to be there?" Chris asked.

"For dinner? They said drinks are at seven. It's only five now, so I think we have some…" Paxton trailed off.

Chris had pulled back the moment Paxton had started

speaking. She'd removed her own shirt, unbuttoned and unzipped her jeans, and revealed a black lacy bra and panty set that Paxton had never seen her wear. Her nipples were visible, and they were hard. Paxton lowered her eyes to look through the see-through panties before she lifted her eyes back to meet Chris's. She gulped audibly at the look of desire in her girlfriend's eyes.

"I believe I promised you I'd take care of you when you got back," Chris said, reaching for Paxton's button-down.

"Well, this is a very nice homecoming," Paxton replied as Chris unbuttoned her shirt. "I missed you. I'm so happy to be home."

Chris smiled. Paxton knew why. Every time Paxton used the word *home*, referring to South Lake Tahoe, it made Chris believe that she was staying just a little more. Chris removed Paxton's shirt, dropping it to the floor of Paxton's living room. Then, she kissed Paxton's neck and shoulders, removing her girlfriend's bra, and dropping it to the floor, too. Paxton smiled when Chris fumbled with the zipper at the back of her pencil skirt. She'd had one final meeting with her attorney before she had to catch the flight. She hadn't bothered changing. Now, Chris was watching the skirt as it fell to the floor. Paxton was watching her. Chris moved her in the direction of the bedroom. Paxton was happy then that she'd given Chris a key to the place, because Chris had dimmed the lights, lit some candles, and pulled back the comforter and sheets before Paxton had gotten home.

"Chris, this…"

"Just lie down, okay?" Chris asked softly.

"I will do whatever you want me to do right now." Paxton lied down on the bed and watched as Chris removed her own bra, leaving those sexy panties on, and climbed on top of her. "Not taking those off?"

Chris only smirked in response as she pressed her center into Paxton, who still had her own underwear on, though a much less sexy pair. Paxton spread her legs to allow Chris to rock slowly against her. The feel of the lace against her body turned her on like crazy. Chris must have realized that. She lifted up, pulled at Paxton's underwear, and tossed them onto the floor beside the bed. Then, she climbed back on top of her and repeated her ministrations. She rolled slowly, pressing the lace against Paxton's center. Paxton gasped. Her breathing picked up in pace. Her hands went to Chris's ass and cupped it. Chris reached behind her to take one of Paxton's hands. She moved it between their legs and slid it inside her own panties. Paxton cupped her sex immediately. Chris bucked into Paxton's center at the touch. They'd been without one another this way for too long.

Paxton slid her fingers into Chris's wetness, moving them slowly up and down as Chris continued to rock her hips into Paxton's wetness. She moved her own finger just enough so that with each movement of Chris's hips, Paxton's finger would press down into her own clit. Paxton watched Chris's breasts as she moved against her. She thought she'd come from the sight of them until Chris moved her hand between their legs and stroked Paxton.

"Jesus!"

"I missed you," Chris whispered against Paxton's lips before kissing her.

Paxton felt Chris drift lower before she entered her. Paxton definitely missed Chris, too. She stroked Chris with the tips of her fingers at the same time Chris thrust slowly inside her. Paxton came when Chris's hips started moving too erratically for her to keep stroking the spot she knew Chris liked. It didn't seem to matter, though, because Chris came right after her.

"That was..." Paxton couldn't finish the sentence because Chris kissed her long and slow at the same time she pulled out of her.

Then, Chris lowered herself and rested against Paxton's thigh as she used fingers to spread Paxton. She moved her mouth to Paxton's sex and sucked her girlfriend's clit fully into her own mouth.

"Wow. I need to go on business trips more often."

"Pax?" Chris stopped and looked up at her.

"Why'd you stop?" Paxton ran her hand through Chris's hair.

"All your business is here," she said. "I want you here."

"I am here, Chris. I was only kidding."

"I mean, I want you here forever." She kissed Paxton just below her belly button, lifting herself up slightly to do so before lowering herself back down to lick Paxton from her entrance to the very tip of her clit. "I want what you want, Pax."

"Another orgasm?" Paxton lifted an eyebrow.

"A lifetime together."

CHAPTER 32

"YOU SAID DRINKS WERE AT seven," Paxton said to Adler a few minutes after they arrived. "We're only five minutes late. Who starts drinks that late, anyway? I mean, it's not like we're all in our twenties here. I'd like to be back in my own bed with my girlfriend by nine."

"I'm so sorry to inconvenience you." Adler chuckled at her sister as she pulled back from the hug they'd just shared. "And please tell me you showered after Chris gave you that hickey on your neck that your sweater doesn't quite cover all the way up."

"I did, yes." Paxton smiled at her. "Well, *we* did. That's actually where she gave it to me."

Adler laughed and pulled on Paxton's hand to take her into the kitchen where Morgan, Chris, Kinsley, Riley, Reese, and Kellan were all in conversation and in various stages of drink-pouring. Kinsley passed Riley a glass of red wine and then picked up her own to take a sip. Reese and Kellan were laughing with Morgan about something. Morgan had one hand on her wine glass and the other wrapped around

Adler's waist when Adler moved in next to her. When Paxton approached Chris's side, she snaked an arm around her waist and pulled her closer. Chris passed her a glass of wine but took a sip from it herself first. Paxton smiled as she looked around the room. She had this amazing group of friends and an even more amazing girlfriend, who'd just told her she wanted to share her life with Paxton. It really couldn't get any better than this in her mind.

"So, Pax, how's the business?" Kinsley asked her.

"Not mine anymore," Paxton replied. "It belongs to someone else now."

Chris kissed her cheek and whispered, "Are you okay?"

Paxton winked at her and turned back to the others to say, "It was the right call. I can't give it the focus it needs. The business needs someone in charge of it full-time, and my heart is here now. It's in good hands, though, and I'm ready to focus on the hotel and living in South Lake."

"That's great news, Pax." Riley smiled at her. "Now, will one of you tell us why we had to drop everything with no notice and join you for dinner?" She glanced in Adler and Morgan's direction.

"Oh, no reason." Morgan shrugged both shoulders.

"No reason? Really?" Adler's eyes were huge as they stared at Morgan. "We're only getting married."

Morgan smiled a huge smile at Adler before both women lifted their left hands into the air to show off their shiny and new engagement rings. Paxton met Adler's eyes and gave her the biggest smile. For so long, Adler had struggled to find the balance between work and love. She'd dated man after man; none of them were good enough for her or understood her drive. Morgan did, though. Morgan loved Adler more than anything. And Adler loved her back. Paxton moved around the kitchen island to hug her sister again. She hugged Morgan after, and welcomed her into the family. Then, she made her way back to Chris while everyone else gave the happy couple their well wishes and embraces. Paxton pulled Chris into herself and kissed her neck.

"I love you," she said into Chris's ear.

"I know you do." Chris kissed Paxton on the lips. "Let's celebrate with our friends now. Later, we can celebrate us, though."

"Us, huh?"

"Yes, we have lots to celebrate, Champ." Chris kissed her again.

"We do?"

"The love of my life is home." Chris gave Paxton another kiss. "And she makes me so happy. She's incredibly selfless, though, which means so many of our conversations and the things we do have been about me lately. I want to show her that, as giving as she is sometimes, it's okay to take a little, too." She kissed Paxton on the cheek and pulled her in for a hug.

They all sat at the big dining room table. Adler and Morgan sat at each end and could hardly keep their eyes off of each other. It would have been something Paxton would have mocked them for before; but now, she had Christina Florence sitting next to her. Paxton had a hard time keeping her hands off the woman's thigh, knowing that Chris had on nothing beneath those black jeans she'd donned at Paxton's place when they'd been running late for dinner. Riley and Kinsley were happy and in love, and they would also be getting married soon. Reese and Kellan would likely bring a kid into the world in the coming months or years. Adler and Morgan would be getting married. She'd be her sister's maid of honor. She wasn't worried about being too much for Chris anymore. Chris wanted all the same things she did. They'd have them together.

***

"Tell me about Cheyanne. I know something had happened. Wes texted me, like, three times today alone."

"Pax, tonight is about you. Will you calm the hell down and just let me give you a damn back massage?" Chris chuckled from her position, straddling Paxton.

"Is everything okay, though?"

"Yes. You are a good person, and you got through to me. Cheyanne is staying with us until she's fully healed, okay? We can talk about it this weekend if you want, while we go house-hunting. There's this one Kinsley showed me on her phone tonight that I think we should check out. It has four bedrooms, and a basement with a fifth one in it that I think would be great for Wes. It's on a bigger lot, too, and already has one of those swing sets on it that the owners left behind."

Paxton smiled from her position on her stomach as Chris ran her hands up and down her back.

"Swing set?"

"I'd say, we could use it one day for the kids, but you basically are a kid. My guess is you'll take it for a spin this weekend, and then find some way to update the damn thing so that adults can use it."

"Adults can't use it now?" Paxton asked through the soft laughter.

"I knew it!"

"Hey, can I ask you something?"

"It better not be about my grandmother while I'm straddling you naked and applying massage oil to your skin, Pax."

Paxton laughed again, deciding that now wasn't the time to bring up the fact that Chris had just called Cheyanne her grandmother.

"My parents want to come here for Christmas this year. The hotel should be finished by then, and I'm hoping to be in a house and out of this place."

"What's the question, Champ?" Chris stopped the massage.

"Will you join us and meet my parents? Bring Wes, too. It'll be Adler and Morgan, and the three of us."

225

"A family," Chris said so softly, Paxton almost didn't hear her.

Paxton rolled over onto her back and gave Chris a moment to resettle on top of her.

"Yes, a family. I thought it would be a nice start for all of us." She ran her hands up and down Chris's back.

"What are they going to think of your less than successful, former waitress of a girlfriend?" Chris asked.

"You always act like waiting tables is somehow beneath me; beneath all of us. It's not, Chris. It's a job, and it's a damn hard one, sometimes. You put food on the table for you and your kid brother when no one else could or would. You put a roof over his head, got him a car, made sure he earned good grades and got to participate in a sport that, I know, isn't cheap. You've done all that on your own, babe. So, when my parents asked about you when I saw them the other day, that's what I told them. I told them you're the hardest worker I know; that you inspired me to build this hotel and start a new life here, where I'm incredibly happy; that you gave me a relationship with a kick-ass kid in Wes; and that you love me, even though I stole your parking spot and ditched you that night at Donoto's."

"I do love you," Chris said through a watery set of beautiful blue eyes.

"That's all they need to know," Paxton replied. "Oh, and they'll want to know the wedding date and when the kids are coming… But we've got some time for that stuff, now that Adler and Morgan are engaged."

Chris laughed and said, "Yeah, we've got some time, huh?"

"Let them take the heat for a while. You and I can focus on us," Paxton replied. "And, right now, I would like us to focus on sleep. It's been a long and very eventful day. And tomorrow, we're finishing up the last touches on your new restaurant. We need to be well-rested."

"Pax?"

"Yeah?"

"I'm finishing this damn massage I started. I went to the store on the way here to buy this calming oil crap. You're going to lie here, get a rub down, and relax. Then, we can go to sleep." Chris smiled down at her with a lifted eyebrow that told Paxton she meant business.

"Whatever you want, babe." Paxton held up her hands in defense.

"Now, roll over, and at least pretend like you're not thinking about the million things you have to do tomorrow."

"Chris, whenever we're like this, I'm only ever thinking about you." Paxton smiled up at her, ran her own hand along Chris's cheek, and added, "Well, you and the million things I have to do tomorrow." She smiled before letting out a laugh at her own joke.

EPILOGUE

"CHRISTMAS WAS A DISASTER. This party better be good," Chris said.

"Christmas was *not* a disaster. My parents loved you. They asked how many grandkids we were going to give them, since Adler and Morgan said they're going to give it a few years before trying," Paxton replied, pouring Chris a glass of white wine. "This party is already good, babe. Everyone is out there smiling and laughing."

"I just don't want to run out of food," Chris said. "My biggest concern is that we're going to run out of food."

"Why?" Paxton laughed at her. "The caterers brought enough for an army. Currently, we only have about half an army in our living room and dining room. The patio with the heaters is a big help; makes it less crowded inside. That was a great idea you had, to steal those from the hotel deck for tonight."

"I've never hosted a party like this before, Pax. I don't exactly know what I'm doing. I mean, I've made the rounds. I greeted everyone. I made sure they all have drinks and know where the bathrooms and food are. I took their coats and put them on the bed in the guest room. What else am I supposed to do?"

"Relax and enjoy our party." Paxton left the wine bottle and glass on the counter and wrapped her arms around Chris, pulling her girlfriend into her body.

"I threw out the bone from the ham at Christmas. I thought your mom was going to kill me." Chris pressed her face to Paxton's chest. "How was I supposed to know she'd want it for a soup later?"

"That was a delicious soup."

"You are not helping," Chris muttered against Paxton's chest.

"Babe, my mom loves you. My dad loves you. My sister loves you. Her soon-to-be-wife loves you. Everyone loves you. Is that better?"

"Yes, that's better," Chris muttered again.

"It's New Year's Eve, Chris. It's already close to midnight. A few of our friends have already gone home because they want to watch the ball drop from the comfort of their own beds. We're going to go out there and just enjoy being with our friends, celebrating the new year and our new life together."

The hotel would open in two weeks. It was done. Technically, they could have opened earlier, but Paxton had insisted they have the holidays with their friends and families and take a little staycation. It had been a great suggestion. Paxton had closed on the house at the end of November. It was the one Chris had found for them. Even though Paxton was the one to sign on all the important lines, they'd treated it as their home from the beginning. Chris still had the house she rented. She spent some nights there and some nights at Paxton's place. Wes had already begun working on the basement apartment he claimed the moment he laid eyes on it.

Chris and Cheyanne weren't exactly close, but Wes had enjoyed getting to know his grandmother more and more. Chris was slow to embrace her, but she had allowed Cheyanne to remain at the house even after she'd fully healed from the car accident. Paxton knew one of the reasons Chris had softened a little where her grandmother was concerned was because Cheyanne had actually gone to the police to tell them what she knew about the cult. The

FBI had already been investigating the compound for the past five years, along with the ATF. Cheyanne could potentially help them bring an end to what had been going on there for decades. Chris had smiled when Cheyanne had told her that at dinner, and Paxton had smiled at Chris because she knew Chris was thinking about her mother and how happy it would have made her to know that others wouldn't go through what she'd gone through as a child.

"Where have you two been?" Morgan asked when they made their way out to the patio at the back of the house.

"We were in the kitchen. I got my girlfriend another glass of wine. Is that okay with you, Burns?" Paxton fired back with a light laugh. "Why are you guys even hanging out back here? It's gotten colder."

"We just turned those heater things up. It's not too bad now," Morgan replied. "Where's Addie?"

"She's yours to keep track of now." Paxton shrugged.

"So, I'm yours to keep track of, then?" Chris asked her.

"No, I think we both know you're the one that's going to be keeping track of me in this relationship." Paxton kissed her girlfriend's temple. "I've been whipped for a while now."

"Sounds about right, Champ."

"I was actually thinking about that the other day," Paxton said.

"Thinking about what?" Adler asked when she made her way out the sliding glass door to join them.

"A pool."

"A pool?" Chris asked.

"Yes. I seem to remember a certain race one night, in a hotel," Paxton said.

"Never tell me," Adler replied, shaking her head from side to side while moving in front of Morgan and taking Morgan's arms to wrap around her own waist.

"We were in a swimming pool, and we were fully clothed," Paxton explained.

"Bathing suits," Chris corrected. "But we just swam.

Champ, over here, had just regaled me with stories of her many swimming victories."

"She wasn't *that* good," Adler teased.

"Sometimes, it sucks spending this much time with your older sister," Paxton fired back.

"No one made you move here," Adler said, winking at her.

"You made me visit."

"Visit isn't the same thing as moving, Pax."

"She's right," Morgan added.

"It's not like I could leave," Paxton said.

"Why not?" Adler laughed.

"You know why, Adler."

"The hotel?"

"I met her." Paxton nodded in Chris's direction.

Chris looked over at Paxton and realized that her girlfriend had gone shy all of a sudden. She wrapped her arm around Paxton's waist and pulled her into her own side.

"I am very awesome," Chris said to try to take the focus off her blushing girlfriend.

"That's true. You are pretty awesome," Morgan replied.

"I'm going back inside. It's almost midnight. Come inside and kiss me?" Adler asked, turning her head slightly back to Morgan.

"Sorry, ladies. Duty calls." Morgan followed Adler back inside the house.

"Hey, why'd you get all reserved just now?" Chris asked, turning to stand in front of Paxton.

"I didn't."

"Pax…"

"Adler made fun of me a little bit when I first got here. I never told you about it, but she picked on me for meeting a girl and moving where she lived immediately."

"Didn't she do the same thing?" Chris asked.

"Not exactly. It took a while for Adler to move here. I moved here practically the day you and I met."

"Because you loved Tahoe, and because you wanted to buy the hotel," Chris said.

"And because I loved you." Paxton shrugged again.

"Hey, guys… The ball's about to drop," Wes said through the sliding glass door. "Grandma said she's going to leave after that. She's pretty tired."

"Tell Cheyanne you two can stay here tonight so you don't have to drive home in the snow," Paxton told him.

"Cool. Thanks, Pax. Can I sleep downstairs in my room?"

"Wes, we talked about this. It's not your–"

"Yes, you can sleep in your room," Paxton interrupted Chris.

Wes smiled and closed the door, leaving them alone on the patio outside.

"It *is* his room, Chris. He knows it, and we know it. I know we're not *technically* living together yet, but it's his room as much as this is his home and your home. I mean, we picked out the bed for the master bedroom together. I even let you pick the painting that hangs over it."

"Let me?" Chris asked.

"I wanted the other one, with the trees and the little rowboat. You wanted this one."

"So, you let me have it?"

"Yes, because I want the flat screen."

"I already said you could have the flat screen; you just want a huge one."

"It's not huge. I just want to be able to see what's on the screen all the way from my bed. Chris, our bedroom is huge." Paxton laughed.

"Ten!"

"Nine!"

"It is huge, but that doesn't mean the TV has to be."

"Then, I want the rocking chairs my parents gave us for Christmas in there."

"Those are oak; the furniture in the bedroom is cherry. I thought we could put those in the living room."

"Six!"

"Five!"

"Fine. But you're explaining to my mom and dad why they're in the living room when they come to visit. My mom said she specifically got them because we have the bay window in the bedroom."

"Three!"

"Two!

"Why is everyone yelling in the–" Chris stopped herself when she saw the TV through the glass. "Oh."

"One!"

Paxton pulled Chris into her body then. She smiled at her girlfriend as the people inside their house celebrated.

"Happy New Year, babe," Paxton said.

"I've never actually had a midnight kiss," Chris confessed.

"You can have one every year for the rest of our lives." Paxton leaned in, pressed their lips together, and reveled in the warmth of the touch against the cold of the winter outside.

"Pax?"

"Yeah?"

"I think we kind of just decided that this is my house, too."

"It's cute that you think it wasn't already." Paxton kissed her again. "Welcome home, Christina Florence."

Chris kissed Paxton once more before she pulled her in for a hug. Through the window, she could see Wes sitting next to Cheyanne on the sofa. Adler and Morgan exchanging light kisses in the corner of the room. Riley was sitting on Kinsley's lap in the chair. Reese and Kellan were coming out of the kitchen, laughing about something. A few of the people they'd hired for the hotel were talking to one another in the open dining room. The snow started to fall around them, making it a little colder, but the warmth from the heaters and – more importantly – from Paxton, kept Chris from wanting to rush inside. She finally had a home.

She finally had a family. She finally had the love she'd seen so many others find.

"Never call me Christina," she whispered in Paxton's ear.

"Fine. But I'm getting the painting with the damn rowboat and putting it in the living room."

Paxton let go of Chris quickly, moved to the door, slid it open, and went inside. Chris shook her head and laughed. She'd get her back later for that one. If she gave Paxton the boat picture, she could pick out the paint for the bedroom. Chris was thinking navy-blue. She was thinking Paxton would do all the work. As she watched Paxton wink at her through the closed glass door, and then slide it open for her, she was thinking about how she'd finally made the life she'd always wanted for herself.

Manufactured by Amazon.ca
Bolton, ON

11112281R00141